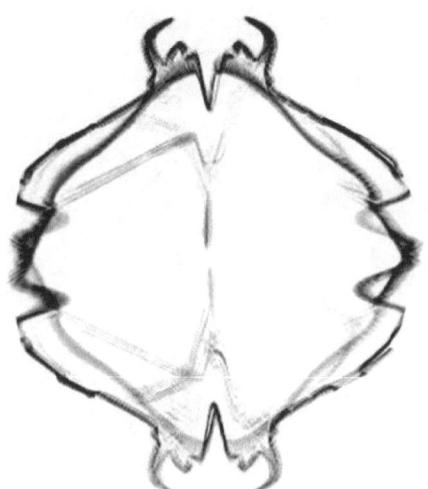

The Phantom Paradigm

M. J. Waters

An Intellect Publishing Book

ISBN: 978-1-945190-056

Cover design and artwork by
www.cyber-theorist.com

Proofreader
Ellie Lockett

First Edition: 2016
V11PDF

Visit the website: **www.ThePhantomParadigm.com**
Comments? Suggestions?
Email: comments@ThePhantomParadigm.com

Intellect Publishing, LLC
6581 County Road 32, Suite 1744
Point Clear, AL 36564
www.IntellectPublishing.com
Inquiries: info@IntellectPublishing.com

Dedication

To Syra & Ivy, may your phantoms be honorable.

The Phantom Paradigm

Chapter One
The Lower String

I guess if you wanted, things could be traced back to a stupid infatuation.

It was an infatuation with a vapid, self-interested bore of a girl that had me chasing her all the way to Australia and ultimately led me here. Well, chased is a bit of a strong, stalker-like interpretation of things. It was more of a casual pursuit, at least from my and my dick's perspectives. She reeled me in without ever knowing her role. It's almost a certainty that she was manipulated herself in so many ways into eventually being in a position to manipulate me.

I mean, she really had no business being in college let alone trying to earn a degree in biology. I never got to see the source of her influence but my guess is it wasn't an honorable one. Then again, maybe it was. I haven't yet reached the place where I can start getting those kinds of answers.

It's a bit hard though to jump right in and explain what that means. It might make more sense if I started a bit further back in my timeline. A point when I was just another asshole college student.

Two semesters ago, I walked into my first class, Plant Systematics. A Bachelor of Science in biology was the collegiate path I was on, so there I was that day about to dive into the origins and diversifications of plants. Why biology? As I look back, it probably wasn't my idea. I originally had planned on a business degree, but through my first two years of general education I had countless encounters with other students who were also planning on pursuing business degrees.

All these encounters were unpleasant and all those particular students were douches. I had classes with them. I had study groups with them. I ended up at parties with them. The more time I was around them, the more the idea of pursuing a degree in business soured for me. I didn't want to spend the next couple of years of my life in classes surrounded by these douches. I never could concentrate well while in the company of douches and would have been destined to fail if I were to continue in business.

So there I was, majoring in biology, surrounded by people who for the most part I was indifferent about, studying a subject I actually did have some interest in. And when I say my first two years of general education, I mean my first four years of general education. Two years' worth of credit. Four years to accumulate those two years' worth of credit. The real plan was to stretch out college for as long as possible because the real world looked to be saturated with douches.

On day one of Plant Systematics, I was sitting in my usual spot at the back of the class so as to avoid any possible recognition or interaction with the teacher. Class was about to begin when in she walked. Ariel.

She was more of a crafted beauty than a natural beauty. She was the type of girl you knew had at least a ninety-minute regimen each morning getting herself ready. Moisturizing, plucking, brushing, curling and freshening up her lady-pipes with some kind of fruit spray.

Her body was finely tuned as well and she had no reservations about showing it off. The clothes she wore all seemed a size or two too small for her. She appeared to be a dedicated student when it came to classes like Pilates and spin. Biology classes, not so much. She had a highly manufactured presence but her craft was honed. Every time I saw her walk into class, the little monkey working the buttons and levers to my libido started break dancing.

Class began and there she sat, four seats diagonally ahead and to the right of me, giving me a side profile to stare at for fifty minutes, twice a week. It was a welcome visual treat to be able to stare unnoticed at an attractive girl for an extended amount of time without having to throw dollar bills at her onto a slime and depression laced stage.

That whole semester I was entranced with her side profile. I'd find myself in that back row creating fantasy scenarios in my head of me saving her in the campus parking lot from a would-be carjacking or something of that sort. After I would vanquish her make-believe accoster, she would then throw herself into my arms while whispering in my ear that she was a virgin nymphomaniac incapable of getting pregnant. She'd been waiting for the right person to surrender her sexual desires to and that was me. She also had a roommate who was a barren, virgin nymphomaniac with whom she'd like to share me if I was into that kind of thing.

That was just one of the many fantasy scenarios that were a constant throughout that semester.

There were many days she didn't even bother showing up for class and I'd actually succumb to a mild depression when that happened. I ended up getting a subpar grade in Plant Systematics. My retention for the class lectures was hindered by my continual staring problem and fantasizing. Not once all semester did I attempt to talk to her.

The following semester I thought I had hit the jackpot. She was in three of my five classes. Two of those classes were in cavernous lecture halls with over a hundred students in each. For classes that big, the seating was up for grabs each day. I'd tried coming in as close to starting time as possible and checking to see where she was sitting so I could maybe find a seat next to her, but it never really worked out. She was continually late or didn't show up at all sometimes, so trying to arrange a seat next to her was futile.

The third class we had together was different though. This class was a lab that only had about thirty students in it. In this class we worked in teams of four on weekly experiments and projects. So by chance, quite possibly not by chance as I think about it, through a random draw by the professor, there I was in a group of four with her.

When we first got assigned to our groups, we all introduced ourselves to each other. Her name was Ariel. Her voice wasn't what I expected, as this was the first time I'd actually heard her speak. Up until that point, I had always imagined her to have one of those melodic princess voices you'd hear in an animated movie that attracted songbirds and other affable wildlife. No, her voice had an off-putting affectation to it. It was kind of like a Valley-girl but a lot shittier. She also had these juvenile inflections that you might hear being used by children in kindergarten but she managed to carry them all the way to young adulthood with her.

Didn't matter much to me though as my penis only had one eye and no ears and couldn't hear her shitty voice.

After she introduced herself, I mumbled out my name to our lab group of four. Rounding out our quartet was pudgy Brenda and Asian-guy. Asian-guy's name was Leaf or Lice or some kind of L-name I wasn't paying attention to. I looked right past him and pudgy Brenda as I was beaming with being so close to Ariel after all of the fantasizing I had done last semester.

I was thinking this was inevitable now. She was here, two feet away, confined to this small group. She was in a position where she'd have to interact with me on a weekly basis. We'd get to know each other. We'd do study groups on the weekends. I'd eventually ask her out for a drink. This was it, or so I thought.

Day one though, Ariel suggested that our group of four should split into two groups of two. She and Asian-guy would do one-half of the work and I and pudgy Brenda would do the other half. For some reason, nobody argued.

It became apparent pretty quickly that Ariel had been tricked into thinking her biology major was the pathway to becoming a floral decorator for celebrity weddings or something. She showed no interest in the subject material or contributing to our lab group. Asian-guy had to do all the work on their side of things. On the days she actually showed up to class, Ariel would pour all of her focus into texting on her pink, fuzzy-cased phone.

I knew then that she was a bit of a moron. A beautiful moron with a shitty voice. There was no denying it though; I was still attracted to her. Over that entire semester I made zero headway in capturing Ariel's attention.

There were only two occasions when she talked directly to me. Both interactions were her asking me if I could take notes for her because Asian-guy was out sick with bird flu or whatever the fuck makes Asian-guy miss a class. She said she had to leave early, most likely for a trip to the mall or to go look at herself in a mirror for a couple of hours. *Of course, I will take notes for you Ariel. Does taking notes for you mean we are closer to having sex?*

I somehow continued to ignore her unwavering dismissiveness towards me. My attraction to her only intensified. I knew that I had little or no chance of ever capturing her affections, yet the dick wants what the dick wants.

It was the last day of the semester and of that lab class. I had convinced myself that today would be the day. I was going to work up the nerve to talk to her. As the class ended, I walked out with her and asked if she was taking any summer classes. Then it happened. She completed her main directive. She revealed the twisted path I was supposed to follow her down.

She said, "I'm going on that Australian rainforest thingy with the Biology Club. It was the only way I could get my dad to send me on a vacation, seeing I'm on academic probation. He's such an asshole sometimes. I just told him the trip counted for two credits towards me graduating."

I said (actually my dick said), "I guess I'll see you there. I signed up for it, too." Note to self: run to the Biology Club and sign up for the Australian rainforest thingy, whatever the fuck that is.

She said, "That's cool. I hear they have some hot nightclubs in Australia. I hope the rainforest is close enough to the night life there." Her phone then beeped and she started texting and, without any kind of goodbye, walked away from me in a different direction.

What a fucking idiot this girl was. I think I love her.

As I stood there and watched her walk away, another one of our biology lab quartet had worked up some last-day nerves. Pudgy Brenda tapped me on my shoulder and asked me what I was doing later.

Chapter Two
Bad Decisions

I was having a dream where my head was stuck between two thick prison-like bars. Someone kept squeezing them, then releasing them, squeezing them, then releasing them, causing a rhythmic agony to my skull. Each time they were tightened, they made a strange sound like a grizzly bear gargling the blood and bones of a small forest animal. It was some kind of sadistic dream accordion.

My eyes slowly opened and I was staring up at a ceiling fan I didn't recognize. Where the hell was I? I knew I was awake but I was still hearing the intermittent grizzly bear gargling noises from my dream. The intensity of my hangover was monumental as it was hard to move my head even the slightest of degrees. Random images from last night started skittering through my memory. Where were they leading to? Oh wait, no. Shit! I turned my head and realized I was lying next to a passed-out and naked pudgy Brenda. Damn!

The escape alarms sounded off in my head as if I were in a burning building. I braced myself for the pain of moving then oozed myself off her futon as stealthily as possible to prevent the waking of the slumbering beast. She thankfully continued snoring like fucking Chewbacca.

I located and collected my clothes, then tip-toed to her front door. Luckily, it appeared there were no roommates or anyone else around. I got dressed, then quietly unlocked her front door and slowly pulled it open. When there was a big enough space for me to slip through, I eased outside and closed the door behind me as gently as I could manage. I looked around and didn't see anyone, so I walked a couple of paces then leaned over and barfed in some bushes next to the walkway by her door. The acid that flushed through my mouth and into my nasal passageways tasted of tequila, carne asada burrito and shame. I wiped my mouth with the sleeve of my jacket then peeked at my phone to see it was 9:36 am.

I walked towards campus and stopped at the little market at the gas station to get some water and some gum to cover up my acidic shame-breath. The throbbing in my skull was almost blinding. Drinking is fun. I really hope I wore a condom.

Ten minutes later, I made it to campus where I stopped in a restroom to relieve myself and to wash the weird glaze that was on my face. It felt like I had eaten a bunch of jelly donuts last night and never wiped the sticky sugar residue from my mouth and cheeks. Fuck, what was I doing last night? I washed my face a couple of times then made my way over to the Biology Club office.

There was one girl in the office, working behind a desk. She looked like she could have been pudgy Brenda's sister. I approached her and asked her about the Australian rainforest thingy. She handed me a flyer. It read, "Join the Biology Club on a ten-day trek through the Daintree, one of the oldest tropical rainforests on earth." Sorry Ariel, no mention of nightclubs.

THREE GRAND!

Three thousand dollars, fuck a rainforest. I'm not this dumb am I? There was no way I would spend that kind of money in hopes of somehow falling into a cross-continental romance with this awful girl.

"How do I go about signing up for this?" I asked pudgy Brenda's possible sister behind the desk.

10

So after I placed three thousand dollars across three credit cards, I walked in the direction of my apartment, stopping briefly by some new bushes upon which I barfed. That one tasted like tequila, carne asada burrito, shame, gum and buyer's remorse.

As I slogged my way home, my alcohol-soaked brain reshaped my remorse into optimism. I figured the Biology Club would purchase all the plane tickets at the same time, therefore the seat assignments would be grouped. There were eighteen people total who signed up for this trip, so with a little luck from almighty Zeus, Ariel would be seated next to me on the flight to Australia. What's that, like a thirty-five hour flight? Without her being able to use her phone, she'll be lost and vulnerable. I'll study up on celebrity gossip and horrible top-twenty pop music so we'll have something to talk about. A few complimentary international-flight cocktails later, I might just take her hand and ask her where she goes to get her beautiful manicure.

Then again, even if we didn't sit together on the plane, we still had ten days of isolation in a rainforest where I'd have my advantages. I couldn't imagine any other guy in the group was going to be as non-geek as I was. Ariel would naturally have to gravitate towards me because hollow pretty girls require attention and my somewhat non-geek attention would hold more value than the regular Biology Club geek attention.

I would lend a sympathetic ear to her plight of boredom at one of the earth's most rare and beautiful evolutionary playgrounds. I'd say things like, "I didn't know you needed an international calling plan to be able to text when on a different continent." Or, "They should have mentioned it in the Biology Club flyer that all we'd be doing on a biology trip would be biology-related activities and not night-clubbing or shopping."

Over the following two weeks, my anticipation steadily grew, ready to climax as our departure date approached. I studied up on my Hollywood gossip. I bought some stupidly expensive jeans that I read some current, desirable Hollywood actor was wearing around town. I figured what's $239 for a pair of jeans with some fruity embroidery on it when I already invested three grand and fifty IQ points in this foolish quest for this awful girl.

The night before the trip, I went out with some friends to a couple of bars around the college area. Just my luck. Who grabbed my arm out of the crowd and pulled me towards her? There she was in all her drunken glory, with her clammy hand clenching my wrist and her untamed fingernails cutting into my skin. Pudgy Brenda was smashed. Within three expletive-filled and slurred sentences, she went from calling me a fucking dick to then trying to get me to go home with her.

I asked her, "What are you doing tomorrow?" and held my breath. I thought the odds were long, but I didn't know for sure. What if pudgy Brenda was one of the eighteen people going to Australia tomorrow? She'd be a salt-laced tsunami laying to waste my planned courtship/fingership/sodomyship of Ariel.

Pudgy Brenda looked at me with drunken conviction and said, "Tomorrow you are making me breakfast in bed, asshole."

So I followed up bluntly by asking, "So after breakfast did you have any afternoon plans, say around 1:20 pm?" 1:20 pm, of course, was the flight time tomorrow; so if this specific time didn't strike any kind of chord in her sloppy mind, then I was safe. An awful scenario quickly flashed in my head of me in the window seat, Ariel in the aisle seat and pudgy Brenda in the middle seat raising her armrest between us so she could be closer to me and my onboard snacks.

So the question of 1:20 pm tomorrow hung in the air between us like a vampire bat with HIV. She looked at me with a dizzy confusion, then refocused. Then, with a fairly impressive spray of beer-spit lacing each word and sprinkling my face, she said, "1:20 pm? What is that, some kind of asshole code for something? 1:20 pm tomorrow, you'll be making me lunch in bed, jackass."

What's with this girl and eating in bed? And technically, I'd be serving her breakfast and lunch in a stained-futon, not bed. Regardless, I exhaled with relief, pried off her clam-hand grip from my wrist, wiped her beer-spit off my face, then walked backwards away from her and towards the exit. What was I doing out drinking anyway? Tomorrow starts the beginning of my planned two-and-a-half-month relationship with Ariel. I figured after two and a half months, my tolerance for her horrible personality and repugnant voice would diminish and it would no longer be worth the enjoyment of sexual relations with one so attractive.

So out the door I went, not saying goodbye to pudgy Brenda or the friends I came with. My focus was on getting back to my apartment without further incident. I needed to get my shit in order. Lock the doors and sleep twelve hours. I needed to look refreshed and be sharp. I even recently started my own kind of morning regimen over the last two weeks. Scented body-wash, facial scrub, aloe-heavy moisturizer for out-of-bath application and some eucalyptus hair gel.

I was becoming everything I hated for a chance at some human junk-food, delicious but vacant of any and all nutritional value.

M. J. WATERS

Chapter Three
P Lament

I took a taxi that smelled like a hobo's couch to the airport. The whole ride I was worrying the hobo-couch stench of this taxi was permeating and embedding itself in my clothes and skin. I did have a small bottle of body spray in my luggage but there are certain odors so funky in this world that they can't be masked. I feared this was one of those types of funky odors.

I arrived at the airport three hours early to be safe. I was worried about the additional red-tape involved with international travel. This was on top of the usual airport time-suck concerns of long lines and security ineptitude. This particular day though turned out to be one of those rare airport anomalies. I made my way to the counter of my airline and the area was pretty much deserted. Within ten minutes my bag was checked and I had my boarding pass in hand. I then headed over to security and the lines were minimal and all moved quickly. I was done with all the airport work and still had over two and a half hours to spare. It was comforting at first but slowly gave way to the oncoming shadow of tedium. I was about to be on the longest flight of my life. I really didn't need an additional two and a half hours of sitting around to prepare for it.

I did a quick walk-by of my flight's gate. It was still way early but I did see a few people from my biology classes gathering in one area of the gate seating. I didn't see Ariel yet and I wasn't in the mood for socializing so I made my way to the small bar in that terminal and settled in for a couple of rounds of tedium drowning.

I managed to put down three pints of some mediocre local beer they had on tap while waiting for our flight to arrive. My buzz was strong but steady. I was primed and ready for Ariel.

Off in the distance I saw our gate had begun boarding and I decided to wait until everyone boarded before I went. I never understood the mad rush to get on a plane with assigned seating. Mob mentality usually doesn't fall on the side of reason. I felt aglow as I pushed back from the bar and walked towards the gate. I got my boarding pass scanned then made my way down the jet bridge to our plane. Come on Zeus, give me that seat assignment I prayed to you for or I'll start worshipping the Kraken. Seat me next to Ariel and I'll spread the word of your greatness and unparalleled skills with lightning.

I ducked under the top of the hatch and stepped onto the plane. It was a big fucker. It had three seats per row on each side next to the windows with an eight-seat row down the middle. I quickly realized from the seat number on my boarding pass that I would be in the far back of the plane. I looked around the front of the plane and I didn't see any familiar faces. This was good, our seat assignments would be grouped, I thought.

The middle of the plane was the same, with no familiar faces. I then made my way into the last partition of the plane where I started recognizing some people. I quickly put my head down and studied the seat number on my boarding pass. I made a concerted effort not to look at any more faces until I had arrived at my assigned row and seat. It was a stupid game I was playing with myself trying to build the suspense. With each step and each new row, my anticipation heightened.

There was a frenetic excitement inside me that peaked when I finally arrived at my row. I slowly looked up to see if I was truly in Zeus' favor. And there I was, face to face with fucking Asian-guy. Damn. I nodded my head towards Leaf or Lice or whatever Asian-guy's name was and took my seat.

I took a quick glance around but couldn't see where Ariel was sitting. I was in one of the smaller three-seated rows by the windows. There was still an empty seat between me and Asian-guy. I was pretty sure I was the last person boarding the plane but I still held out a little hope for the empty seat next to me. If Ariel was her usual late self, then there was still a chance she'd be seated next to me if she hadn't boarded already. That scenario in my mind was shut down within five minutes when the captain's voice could be heard over the intercom telling the crew to prepare the cabin.

The flight crew did their cabin check; then, after a fifteen-minute taxi, we were cleared for departure and off towards Australia. Thirty minutes into the flight, we reached our cruising altitude and I had the green-light to unbuckle and take a much-needed three-pint-beer piss. I decided to use the bathroom that was in the middle of the plane, even though I was a couple of rows away from the one in the back. On the walk to and from the bathroom, I scouted the entire back of the plane, row by row, and didn't see Ariel anywhere. What the fuck? Was she in first class? She was definitely the type of girl who could whine her father into upgrading her ticket.

I returned to my seat and started to get a bit anxious. What if she didn't make the flight? Will she be on the next one? Will she be able to reconnect with the Biology Club group if she's on a different flight and we've already left for the rainforest? I looked over at Asian-guy next to me who was completely immersed in a video game on his tablet. I tapped him on his arm to get his attention then asked, "You know that girl, Ariel, who was in our group in lab class? Have you seen her today? I thought she was supposed to be on this trip."

Asian-guy said, "She's in Paris." Fuck you, too, Zeus!

"Paris? How do you know she's in Paris?" I tried to come across as nonchalant as possible but my words were glistening with panic and despair. Asian-guy then proceeded to throw a shuriken into my entire Australian-Ariel fantasy, leaving it bloody and lifeless on the filthy blue carpeting by our feet.

He said, "My sister is a travel agent. She was able to exchange Ariel's ticket to Australia for two tickets to Paris. Ariel's boyfriend has some relatives that have an apartment in Le Marais."

A chorus of hysterical cackling trumpeted through my mind like a million tortured hyenas. I had an overwhelming urge to open the emergency exit door and throw Asian-guy out of the plane and off plummeting to his death. The voices in my head then went silent and I was comatose, staring at the back of the seat in front of me for what felt like an eternity. It was just this epic, disastrous, well-deserved failure. It was as if I had trained for months, bought all the high-tech gear, traveled the great distance and tried to climb Mt. Everest and then ten feet from the summit, bitch goes to France.

My penis shed a single yellow tear.

Chapter Four
Reboot

After about twenty minutes or so of being lost in my head, I noticed my feelings of dismay began dissipating rather quickly. I wondered why for a bit, then it became obvious. Granted, I'd been pining over this girl for what seemed like a lifetime. I even went so far as to chase her to Australia to fulfill some fantasy scenario of romancing her in a rainforest. But there I sat in my ridiculous two-hundred-dollar jeans, plans and hopes smoldering in a fiery shit-pile, and yet I was feeling better by the minute. I finally was allowing the truth to wash away the selective blindness caused by my shallow desires.

Every conversation she had was substance-free. Every action from her was self-serving. She was conceited, immature and a bore. This wasn't a heart crush. A heart crush requires weeks of grief before starting the slow and painful return to normality. Within the abyss of a heart crush, food becomes inedible and the pain and loneliness are palpable and all consuming. No, this wasn't a heart crush at all. This was just a penis crush.

My complete remedy came when Asian-guy and I got our first round of complimentary international cocktails. I said, "Cheers!" and we clicked our plastic cups together. "I know we were in that lab class together for months, but I completely forgot your name and never bothered to find out."

"That's fine," he said. "I forgot your name, too. I was kind of distracted when I was paired up with that imbecile for the semester. My name is Wynn."

Wynn? Where the fuck did I get Leaf or Lice from? Most likely I got it from my complete apathy for learning the names of Asian guys. "What's up Wynn? I'm Serin."

"Sarin, as in the chemical weapon?" he asked me.

"It's spelled differently but yes, basically the same phonetic pronunciation as the nerve gas used to murder millions of human beings in a horrifying manner."

"Any particular reason why your parents picked that name for you?" he asked.

"My mother thought she was being sentimental and clever. Her two grandfathers were named Sean and Erin. She decided to mash their names together and came up with Serin. She either never made the connection or didn't think anything of it because my name was spelled differently. I never really bothered to have that conversation with her. So here I am, with a first name homophone for one of the most evil things ever created by the human race. I'm fine with it though. Could always be worse right? She could have named me Christian or Keith."

I pounded the rest of my cocktail then peeked down the aisle, trying to locate the air attendant with the booze cart. "So what's with the disdain for Ariel?"

"She just grates on my nerves. Have you ever tried talking to her? She's basically a cyborg but a really dumb one. An idiot infused with simple technology. I would attempt to talk to her and could only get her attention for five-second bursts. Her eyes would almost instantly drift back to her stupid pink phone as soon as I started trying to explain something to her. She never once even pretended to help with any of the lab work. The only thing she produced was a never-ending stream of irritating clicks from all of her texting. The days she actually decided to show up to class, I would feel this underlying nausea being around her. Then on the last day of class, she started asking me about Australia. When she told me she was going on this trip, I almost lost it. But then she mentioned the reason she was going, because it was the only trip her father would send her on. When she told me that, I instantly went to work on salvaging this trip for myself.

"I met with my sister later that day to see what she could do, then I called and told Ariel I could get her ticket changed if she wanted. She was thrilled and so was I. There should have been an IQ prerequisite to go on this trip in the first place. We are going to one of the most biologically incredible places on the planet and she had seriously asked me if I knew how the nightlife was. She didn't deserve to go where we are going. It'd of been a waste, like explaining quantum theory to a pigeon."

With those words, Wynn cured any lingering sadness in any and all of my body parts. Hearing him say what I already knew was exactly what I needed to break her spell on me. I had reached my lounging altitude and was now free to get drunk about the cabin. I waved down the beverage cart lady and got me and Wynn a couple more drinks.

"I must admit," I said, "I kind of had a thing for Ariel even though I already knew basically everything you just mentioned about her and her utter lack of character."

"Wait, did you come on this trip solely because you found out she was supposed to be on this trip also?"

There was no way to spin that question. It was pathetic.

"What, you don't like girls or something?"

"Going through all this trouble for that dunce of a girl? Kind of speaks volumes about you and your own character, now doesn't it?"

"My being attracted to a half-witted college chick shouldn't reflect on my character at all. If I slipped her some Rohypnol and violated her unconscious body, then hell you

21

win and I lack character. But for me to overlook a wall of stupid to admire the flesh that rests behind it, I don't see an issue with that."

"I guess I can grant you that point, seeing you just got me another drink. But her so-called wall of stupid offset her flesh by miles."

"Really, you didn't find her that attractive?" I asked.

"I've never really been attracted to Caucasian girls. Compound that with my first-hand experience with her moronic personality, I'd say she was about as attractive to me as you are."

"To each his own, I guess. I thought she was hot. I had a laundry list of things I had planned on doing to her this trip."

"What were you planning on doing to her? Teach her how to speak using full sentences? I swear, she'd use texting acronyms in regular conversation. *ILU for finishing our lab work.* So much good could have been done with the wasted tuition spent on her non-education."

"So what are you saying, Wynn, you like her or do you like-like her?"

"What I'm actually saying is that Paris is about to get a fresh injection of stupid American, thanks to me and my sister."

I felt an instant kinship with Asian-guy, thanks to Ariel. That flight proved to be cleansing. We drank and talked and Ariel became a remnant of an afterthought in my memory. Wynn actually came on this Biology Club trip for the sake of biology. He was well-read on the Daintree. He clued me into all the biological phenomena we'd be seeing. One hundred and sixty-nine million years of biodiversity and evolution all in one place. He showed me images on his tablet of ancient plants and rare animal species we'd more than likely be encountering. I was almost excited. By the time we landed, I was drunk.

Chapter Five
Hourglass Running Out of Sand

We touched down in the land of kangaroos at noon local time. My internal clock was somewhere in yesterday. We got off our plane and went through immigration and got our passports checked. We then grabbed our bags and went through customs, where they decided to take me for a secondary inspection. I guess I fit the profile for young dumb American carrying a bag full of drugs. I knew I had nothing in my luggage worth worrying about but it still made me nervous. I'd seen too many movies where the kilo of heroin mysteriously showed up in somebody's luggage and the unknowing drug mule gets sent to the third-world prison to break rocks and fend off rape for twenty years. After the guy tore through my luggage, I was left with a disheveled pile of clothes. He then looked at me like I was the asshole and said, "You can collect your belongings now."

By the time I repacked my bags and made it out of the secondary inspection area, our group had reassembled outside at the passenger loading zone. The Biology Club had arranged two vans for transport. It was a ninety-minute drive from the airport to the outskirts of the Daintree. I ended up passing out almost instantly when we got on the road and would have kept sleeping if it weren't for an aggressive elbow from Wynn. We'd arrived at our lodging for the night, which was a cheap-looking motel. Everyone had this day to shake off their jet lag and relax in a normal bed. Tomorrow we'd move to our campground area within the rainforest.

Wynn and I ended up sharing a room. With all the travel and drinking we did on the plane, neither of us had any trouble passing out for five hours. At around 7:00 pm, we cleaned ourselves up, then walked across the street for a little Bio Club mixer at a restaurant/bar called Wooly's. Turns out the Bio Club people weren't so bad. They were a homely, nerdy bunch for the most part, but they were also smart, interesting and capable of having a good time.

The organizer of this entire Biology Club trip was a guy named Orif. He had a bit of an accent that I'd place from some obscure country that had a lot of consonants strung together in its name. He gave us a run-down of our itinerary over the next ten days. Or were we already down to nine days? Or was it now eleven days because of intercontinental time-travel? Anyways, he explained that we'd be setting up a base camp. Everyone would get their own tent. There would be daily excursions to different points of interest in the rainforest. Everyone's meals were included in the supply chests but we'd also be stopping at a market tomorrow morning if anyone needed or wanted something additional to the food that was provided for us. Yes. A healthy supply of booze would be purchased.

There were eight girls in our group of eighteen. Granted, I did call the group homely as a whole, but there were one or two ladies in our group who could merit my attention given the isolated circumstances and the right amount of Australian liquor. Actually, after waking up next to pudgy Brenda the other morning, any of these girls would have been a platinum upgrade.

We all ate dinner together at three adjoining tables. We took turns going around introducing ourselves to the group. After dinner, we all moved over to the bar area and continued drinking and getting to know each other a bit. It wasn't the best recipe for overcoming jet lag but fuck it. We were on vacation. We stayed until our bloodshot eyes threatened to ignite. Right before we called it a night, Orif had a waiter take a group photo of all of us. At the time of that photo, with my left arm around Wynn and a Bundy n' Coke held up high in my right hand, I was oblivious to how good things really were.

In a photo album somewhere in my mom's house, there is a picture of me at an amusement park when I was five years old. I always liked that five-year-old version of myself with what little I knew at that moment in time. I'd yet to be poisoned by any of the conventional toxins of the human race. I had no clue that the people at the amusement park operating the rides were all miserable, trying to live on their shit wages. I just thought they were part of some magical world and were so lucky to work in such a wonderful place. That five-year-old version of me didn't understand politics, bigotry, violence or unfulfilled lust. I was swimming in a contentment of childhood ignorance.

The picture the waiter took of all of us that night at Wooly's had a parallel significance to the one of me at the amusement park. I was content but didn't know it. I was content swimming in a much more substantial ignorance that was soon to be ripped to pieces.

Chapter Six
First Day - Last Day

Jet lag, Australian rum and a 7:00 am wakeup call equated to a mass bodily exodus in the bathroom that then required a thorough shower followed by a fistful of antacids and aspirin. By 7:45 am we were all packed into our vans and en route to our campground. We made one pit-stop at a market for any additional supplies anyone wanted. I grabbed bottles of rum, vodka and whiskey in addition to some mixers. I was glad to see other members of our group were stocking up on adult beverages also. Wynn had grabbed a healthy supply of local beer and we agreed to share each other's stashes.

Once everyone finished shopping, we piled back into our vans then got back on the road. The ride was mostly silent as I think everyone aboard felt the same as I did after last night, hung and lagged. The ride didn't really require idle chatter anyway. The scenery was unreal. The deeper we got into the rainforest, the more the surroundings looked like computer-generated graphics implemented into our reality by some cosmic nerd at his laptop.

After about an hour, we arrived at the campground that was on the sand at a place called Noah Beach. We all pitched in unloading all the gear and supplies. Once unpacked, the van drivers headed back to civilization, leaving us to the wilderness.

Orif was somewhat militant in directing us on how everything should be laid out. He placed down markers for the tents that would be set up in six rows of three. It would be a grid leaving eight feet in between each tent for a generous walking path between all rows.

I quickly claimed a marker as close to the center as there was, third row and middle spot. My theory was that if some ancient fucking Velociraptor crept out of the jungle or water to feed on some human flesh, the screams of its first victim would be on the perimeter of our campsite giving me time to flee in the opposite direction before it got to my tent.

After a couple of hours of bustling around, we had our base camp set up. It was a small city of tents with the beach and water on one side and the forest on the other. On the water side of our tent city, there was a circle of beach chairs surrounding a seven foot fire-pit Orif and two other guys constructed. Open fires weren't allowed at our location but Orif managed to pull some strings through the University for a special permit. He had to pass a four-hour fire safety course before he could even apply for the permit. I didn't like him but I gave him points for dedication and preparation. Some people had gotten the fire going and were boiling water so we could heat up our premade lunches.

Orif and another guy were occupied with some peculiar looking equipment. There was a triangular device covered in metal mesh that Orif secured on a high branch of a tree. The device had lengths of wire running down from it that latched into a small control box. The control box seemed to be wired to something that looked like a half-sized car battery. They secured everything with zip ties then flipped a switch on the control panel. They then produced a bag full of small black devices. They started playing with those for a bit then the other guy went around to all the tents and summoned everyone to the fire-pit area. Once everyone was together, Orif addressed the group.

"Alex here will be handing each of you a locator clip. The engineering department at our school was generous enough to allocate these for our trip. If you are leaving the campsite for any reason, please be sure to have your locator clip on your person. Up there on the tree is a homing beacon. It's sending out a recurring ping that these locator clips can interpret. The clips will tell you the distance from and direction towards the beacon and our campsite. So in case any of you gets lost, just hit the red button on your clip and the LCD screen will show an arrow in the direction of the beacon and the exact distance in kilometers to our camp."

Alex walked around with the plastic bag, handing everyone their own locator clip. They looked like old-school beepers you'd see in drug dealer movies before the dawn of the cell phone. They supposedly had a fifteen-mile radius so if one of us got lost, we could find our way back to camp. It only worked from the locator clip to the beacon, though, so if one of us was abducted and gang-raped by some spider monkeys, nobody would be able to find our defiled corpse via our locator clip. It was a one-way insurance policy, which would soon merit its setup.

As the afternoon shifted to evening, everyone was winding down for an early night as they were still beat up from the jet lag and previous night's activities at Wooly's. We ate dinner around the fire-pit and Orif laid out the next day's itinerary. There would be a six-mile hike at 8:00 am that would mostly follow a popular trail through the rainforest. The hike would include a two-mile side excursion to a less ventured part of the Daintree. This hike was optional for everyone. Basically, every planned excursion this entire trip was optional. At that moment, I had pretty much optioned out of the hike and optioned into sipping rum in the shadows of a tree on the beach all day.

As the night set in, people started retiring to their tents to get some rest for the hike the following morning. Soon there were just seven of us left around the fire-pit. Wynn and I were talking to two of the girls in our group who Wynn knew from a different lab class. I had seen them both before in passing in one of my large lecture hall classes but had never actually interacted with them. I offered and made a few cocktails for all of us. Sarah and Gaby came on this trip together and were roommates back home. They were both smart and pleasant to talk to. Their average and unpolished appearances soon transitioned into halfway attractiveness the more they talked, the more I drank and the more the fire died down. By the end of the night, I was verging on being enchanted with the likes of these two.

"So are you guys going to go on the hike tomorrow morning?" Gaby asked.

I briefly tangled with the idea of seeing these girls in the harshness of the daylight, completely sober. I almost slipped and actually said that out loud. I was one or two more drinks away from the metastasis that always got me in trouble. There was a point where the alcohol morphed whatever little charm I had into something different. It's an unfiltered state of mind where my brain shoots words straight out of my mouth, bypassing the analysis and judgment department. In this state it'd make perfect sense for me to jokingly say to these girls I've just met, "The hike sounds alright but I'm a little scared about seeing you two in the harshness of the daylight, completely sober." Thankfully, that switch in personality hadn't been reached just yet.

Wynn answered, "I'm definitely going. I had already read about that particular two-mile side excursion Orif mentioned for tomorrow's hike. It leads to a natural pool that's fed by a twenty-foot waterfall. I was planning on doing that hike myself if it wasn't a part of the planned itinerary."

Sarah said, "Great. Something about Orif rubs me the wrong way so I would rather have you be our tour guide than him if you're okay with that."

"Of course. It's nice to finally be around people with an actual interest in biology. The whole flight here I had to endure the embarrassing ramblings of an alcoholic."

"Shut up, Wynn."

"And what about this alcoholic? Will he be joining us on the hike tomorrow?" Gaby asked.

I continued to wrestle with it. My body felt a mess. A day of quiet stagnation was what I really desired. I was a simple sloth-like creature that only responded well to words and phrases like *lounging, open bar* and *disease-free.* A phrase like *early hike* didn't do anything for me. But I did like these two girls and Wynn was so excited about this place it was kind of contagious.

"I guess so. Might as well see some trees and bushes and shit while I'm here, right? Hopefully, we'll get to see some kind of creature jump out of the jungle and tear out Wynn's voice box."

"I call dibs on his remaining stash of beer if that happens," Gaby said.

"I'll take his camera, I guess, if he dies. You have anything else worth taking when you die Wynn?" Sarah asked with a smile.

"Take it easy ladies. I said tear out his voice box, not kill him. He would survive but would just be really quiet for the rest of the trip."

"Well, if that's the case, we'll still take his beer and camera, I guess. I mean, what's he going to say about it?"

"I'm sure he'd still find a way to be annoying. Trying to communicate making weird squishing noises with the blood bubbles dripping from his neck hole."

"Really? I formally withdraw my acceptance of being your tour guide tomorrow. I'll alert Orif that all three of you have a crush on him and see who he chooses to mate with."

"I think Orif's the type of guy who'd prefer a bubbling bloody neck hole over any lady holes."

A collective groan. Damn you metastasis.

"Ooooh, maybe you should stay back at camp tomorrow and work on your twelve steps or something," Gaby said.

"Sorry. I've never been good at spotting lines. I always seem to be stumbling over them. Orif having sex with Wynn's menstruating neck hole seemed a perfectly reasonable thing to say to people I've just met for some reason."

"It's alright," Sarah said. "You'll need to take a lot longer strides to cross any of our lines."

Thank you, Zeus. Cool girls. Our conversation wrapped up thankfully before I had another sip of that cheap Australian rum and really started to probe their thresholds for indecency. Everyone agreed they needed to get some rest. We said goodnight and I retired to my tent to sleep my last night on this particular level of ignorant contentment.

Chapter Seven
Bowels of Destiny

A person's life is nothing more than a string of decisions and consequences, unless of course that person is a vegetable or in a coma or something, I guess. Let me restate: A fully conscious and functional person's life is nothing more than a string of decisions and consequences. I know it can seem like my infatuation with Ariel was kind of the starting point of my current situation, but as far as decision making and timelines go, that last night around the campfire with Sarah and Gaby was as much a catalyst to what happened to me as was the first day Ariel walked into my side-view. The more relevant question now deals with the influence involved with these decisions and the reasons behind wanting a particular fucked-up consequence.

That next morning, Wynn and I joined eleven others from our group for the morning hike. I was a bit in a fog still from the jet lag and rum.

I had no appetite but forced down the packaged breakfast that was given to me. It was going to be a long hike and I was already dehydrated from last night. I figured the food was necessary if I was going to last more than ten minutes on the trail. I think it was supposed to be some kind of oatmeal but the texture and color of it was more of a sewage varietal. From the first bite it just wasn't sitting right. When I was done, I felt a cautionary whisper in the depths of my digestive system which almost made me drop out of the hike before it even started.

As I was starting to consider just returning to my tent and going back to sleep, Sarah and Gaby walked up and joined us. They both had their hair pulled back and were wearing somewhat hip-looking hiking outfits. They both actually looked really attractive in a sporty bookworm sort of way. They greeted Wynn and me with such a genuine pleasantness that it was enough for me to ignore what my body was warning me might happen in the near future.

Orif briefed us before we headed out, going over a hiking protocol for all of us to adhere to. The trail we were to start on for this hike was a popular one that was only a five-minute walk from our campsite. It was one of the main arteries running through the Daintree and was well traveled by other visitors to the park. The scenery was way beyond what I imagined. Wynn had showed me some images on his tablet on the flight but they were just pictures on a screen.

Physically standing there, completely engulfed, it was incredibly impactful. The canopy of surrounding trees made everything feel comfortable and inviting. The sounds of nature, running streams, birds and the occasional buzz of an insect all made it feel like you were in an adventure movie. We were in it for real. The inner-nerd of Wynn got the best of him as he took every opportunity to point out some plant or animal species he recognized. Sarah and Gaby kept pace with us and kept a pleasant conversation rolling. These girls had edge. If anything, they'd eventually cross one of my lines if I even had any to cross.

I spent the first couple of miles of the hike admiring the scenery while contemplating whether to pursue Sarah or Gaby or even if I should bide my time and try for something more monumental with both of them. The human male mind consists primarily of ego and sexual fantasy and both were bouncing off the walls of my thought process during the hike.

After two hours, we made a turn off the main hiking trail onto a less-travelled pathway. The main hiking trail was a cakewalk. It was low-energy, wide and relatively flat. The terrain of this new path was a different beast. It was narrow and rough and for the most part required us to walk single file. We were forced at certain points to climb over large rocks and protruding root systems. This gave me the opportunity to hold hands with both the girls in helping them maneuver over the occasional obstacle while giving them the illusion of chivalry.

Thirty minutes had passed on this new hiking trail when things started to go wrong. The main trail was a casual stroll and I was feeling energized by the experience. This new path was uneven and difficult and was knocking my body around. That whisper I heard earlier in the morning had returned and suddenly turned into moody banter. Within another fifteen minutes, the moody banter turned to a team of squids playing angry drums with my intestines. There was no way I was going to make it back to base camp. The cold sweat started to build on my forehead and on the back of my neck as I fought through the first contraction. The gut-weasels were closing in on me and there was no outrunning them. Almighty Zeus, what have I done to displease you?

I slowed my pace and one by one allowed everyone in our group to pass me by. I was eyeing the sides of the trail for any kind of favorable clearing when another contraction hit me and stopped me dead in my tracks. I held my breath until it passed. I looked up ahead and the group had just rounded a corner and was out of sight. I surveyed the immediate area and spotted a small break in the foliage. I decided this would have to be my escape hatch.

I ducked under and plowed through some tree branches, then trudged through some thigh-high thick plants. As I was plowing my way through this unmolested piece of rainforest, I heard something fairly sizable scurry off in the opposite direction from me. I then stopped briefly to brace myself against a tree to fight off another contraction. I was close to losing it right there but I needed at least a fifty-yard buffer between me and the pathway. I needed to feel absolutely certain that nobody, especially Sarah and Gaby, could track me down if they noticed I was missing.

Finally, after five more minutes of fighting through the haphazard topography and a couple more contractions, I found a safe spot in the middle of three massive trees. We were all given a little hiking kit that morning by Orif. It contained band aids, hand sanitizer, a pack of granola, a small hand-spade and a roll of toilet paper. I came really close this morning to ditching the kit so I didn't have the extra weight in my backpack. Thankfully, I was too lazy to walk back to my tent to drop it off.

I quickly took the hand-spade from my backpack and dug a quick hole. I fumbled with my belt then removed my shorts completely as I didn't want any collateral damage. Once everything important was off and clear, I used the trees to brace myself up as I squatted over the hole I had just dug. The release was nothing short of violent. The relief was nothing short of orgasmic. A few tears rolled down my cheek as my body rejoiced from the deliverance. I spent close to ten minutes making sure I was exorcised of all demons. Once done, I buried the crime scene. I used up half the bottle of hand sanitizer and ended up rubbing it on my arms and legs, worried about parasitic odors much more vile than the hobo couch odor from that taxi. When I felt halfway clean and had reassembled myself, I started heading back towards the path trying to think of a believable excuse I could tell the group to why I disappeared.

As I made my way back to where I thought I entered the untamed forest, I realized I must have used the wrong tree in my makeshift outhouse as a point of reference for which direction I came from. Nothing in my current surroundings sparked any recognition. This feeling, something long ago buried into my subconscious, started to stretch its legs and make its way into the daylight. I slowly started to recall a time when I was seven years old and got separated from my parents at a mall. It was a slow suffocating pressure that pressed down on the chest with each passing moment. A shower of anxiety sprinkled down on me until I was all but drowning in it.

I scrambled around for another ten minutes trying to find any point of reference, with no luck. I was swallowed up by my surroundings. I tried to make my way back to the three trees in my outhouse but only got more turned around. I could now hear the faint sounds of running water from a stream and knew that just meant I was in a completely new area and even more lost. Panic had arrived and I was almost at a point where I was going to start screaming out in hopes of someone hearing me. Then I remembered the base camp beacon.

I dropped to one knee then rummaged through my backpack. The contents of the hiking kit were jumbled in with some water and some other shit I had brought with me. I was frantically stirring everything around in there until my hand settled on and pulled out the locator clip. I clicked the red button and said a quick prayer to Zeus that this thing would power up and work. After twenty seconds of watching a single dot blink on and off, it got a ping from the beacon and a small arrow appeared next to some very small text that read "8.5 km." Pompous science-department dicks, too good to use miles. What's a kilometer again? I felt a wave of relief hit me, different but equal in magnitude to the relief I had just felt in the middle of those three trees twenty or so minutes ago.

Chapter Eight
The Dainbow Connection

I headed in the direction of the LCD arrow on my locater clip. The going was slow and shitty as I was forging my own path through the dense unmanaged rainforest. There were no trails out here. It felt like each kilometer was at least seven miles. With 6.1 km reading on my locator clip, I wandered into a bit of a clearing where the trees were spaced more generously and I didn't have to constantly climb over shit to move forward.

It's then that I noticed the color purple. It started off gradually but then soon was all around me. The rainforest floor was covered with these extremely peculiar looking flowers with vibrant purple petals. The landscape looked like it was draped in velvet. I'd had a course in botany and had seen a host of different flower variations, but there was something unique and foreign about the architecture of these flowers.

I bent down and plucked one of the flowers from the ground to take a closer look. There was a faint sound like a whiff of air being squeezed out of an already deflated balloon. Then the flower collapsed. The petals just broke apart in my hand and fell to the ground as if the whiff of air it released was glue holding it together. This was something unfounded, I thought. I was surrounded by a flower that quite possibly had yet to be discovered. And there I was without a camera or anyway of taking a sample with me. Fuck!

My camera was also my phone which had been turned off and packed away since stepping on the plane to come to Australia. Wynn offered to take all the pictures I needed on his almost obnoxiously awesome SLR camera with four different lenses. Way to feed the stereotype, Wynn.

How was I going to get a sample of this flower back with me? If I plucked it, it disintegrated. I had my hand-spade. I could possibly dig out a chunk of soil with one of the flowers in it to keep it from collapsing but there was no way I'd make it another six kilometers cupping dirt in my hands while traversing this kind of terrain. Fuck! After thinking the situation over, I decided I'd have to just make it back to base camp, gather the troops and try to retrace my way back to this area of the rainforest. Not fucking likely, seeing I couldn't even retrace my way from the tree outhouse back to the hiking path, but it was my only option at the time.

So I continued walking in the direction of the arrow on my locator clip, trying to discern some possible method of finding my way back to this area once I reached base camp. I did have a little notepad and pen in the smaller pocket of my backpack. I pulled them out and wrote down the position of the arrow and distance to base camp for future reference as some sort of cheap coordinates if I did indeed try to make a return trip.

I continued on, lost in thought. I plowed forward another quarter kilometer when something caught my eye and broke my train of thought. It was the color orange. Off to my right, the purple landscape was being encroached upon by another flower. I made my way to them to take a closer look and saw that these new orange flowers were almost identical in structure to the purple ones. There were slight variations in the thickness of the stem and length of the petals but they were definitely of the same family. The only sizable difference was this one had fiery orange petals. I plucked one up by the roots and got the same exact results. There was a sound like a whiff of air and then the petals detached and fell from the stem.

This situation was a perfect mix of exhilaration and frustration. It was kind of like those almost-wet dreams where you're about to have sex with a super-model but she decides to grow tusks and dolphin fins right when you are about to penetrate.

I was still at a loss for any kind of game plan. I couldn't take any proof of what I was seeing back with me. And the likelihood of retracing my way back here once I reached base camp was going to be ridiculously hard. I thought of Hansel and Gretel and their trail of breadcrumbs. I considered ripping my t-shirt up into as many pieces as possible then tying the strips to different plants as markers, but I didn't think the amount of clothes I had would equate to six kilometers of breadcrumbs even if I reached base camp butt-ass naked. I could use up all the band aids and other shit in my hiking kit but that still wouldn't cover even a fraction of the distance. Fuck! I had to settle on writing down the position of the arrow and distance which I did again to mark the position of the orange flowers.

I trudged ahead, walking the mingled divide where the purple flowers met the orange flowers. I again got lost in thought. There had to be some money in this, right? Or do finders of new plant species just get to name them? How about the Serin-gas flower? That'd be a huge hit on Valentine's Day. It would actually be a great metaphor for the usual romantic relationship. The closer you examine it, the quicker it withers and dies.

I glanced at my locator clip and I was within 4.8 kilometers of base camp. That's when red decided to invade the upcoming horizon. About fifty yards in front of me, the ground was awash with blood red. The purple and orange flowers were still running parallel to the path I was forging and it looked as if the three different-colored flowers were shortly going to converge.

But with each step, I noticed an aberration in the color pattern up ahead where the colors looked to intersect. I picked up my pace to close the distance between me and the field of red. As I got closer, the aberration I saw from a distance became clearer until I reached the area of the color convergence.

I knew at that very second, I had stumbled upon something so significant to the world of botany, that my life was about to be altered in significant fashion. I was thinking talk shows, book deals and access to young celebrity whores. This was big. This was celebrity-whore big.

It was no more than a three-foot rough circle bordered on all sides by the red, purple and orange flowers. Within this patch was some kind of crossbreed of all three flowers. They were stunning. They were twice the size of the surrounding flowers. Their petals were a gradient of all three colors. Purple was closest to the base which bled into an orange middle. The orange middle bled to red which ran to the tips of each petal as if dipped in old coagulated blood. The flower petals looked like they were drawn by a four-year-old kid. They belonged on a piece of paper hanging from a refrigerator and had no business existing in reality. Aside from the amazing colors of its petals, there was an ominous and uninviting structure to the flower itself. It was like looking at the segmented tail of a giant scorpion.

I walked around this patch of crossbreeds and made my way over to the red flowers. I figured I was technically on a biology trip and might as well apply some scientific method by testing all subjects. So I took a good look at one of the red flowers. It too shared similarities to the purple and orange types but did also have its own unique differences. Its petals were definitely the shortest of the three and it had what seemed to be miniature thorns like on a rose but ten times smaller.

I reached down and plucked one from the ground and the results were slightly different. The red flower didn't expel any whiff of air but its petals did break apart and fall. What was different also was that the remaining center of the flower broke apart like blowing on a dandelion. Little flower remnants floated away in the light breeze. Three flowers down, all impossible to transport back to civilization.

One flower yet to try.

Chapter Nine
Money Shot

I approached the small, rough, three-foot circle of these hybrid alien scorpion flowers. There was no way I could leave without trying to bring one of these back with me. Maybe I could dump out my backpack, fill it with dirt and use it as a make-shift flower pot. Possible, I thought, but more than likely would result in a filthy backpack with disintegrated flower parts inside. First things first though, a test to see if it was possible to pick one of these crossbreeds without it withering and dying.

I kneeled down and grabbed the stem of one of them and held it up. I remember hearing a unique whiffing noise, much more resonant than the purple or orange flowers. Something wet hit my face and that's the last thing I remembered.

M. J. WATERS

Chapter Ten
Novum Organum

I woke up on my back staring up at tree branches through dim light. I looked at my watch which read 5:43 am. I'd been out for close to twenty hours. I got to my feet and was hit by a searing pain in my head. I also felt something gripping my face like a weak piece of tape. I peeled off what felt like long scabs but they were transparent. That fucking flower had jizzed all over my face. The term *flower porn* flashed through my disoriented mind.

I looked around and saw that when I passed out, I had landed and crushed the entire patch of hybrid alien scorpion flowers. I must have been rolling around as there wasn't a one that was still intact. There was nothing but dismantled stems and pieces that had already turned brown and lifeless. None were spared. Great Zeus, why do you continue to mock me?

I took a closer look at the area and my heart sank further as I confirmed there were no more of these flowers alive. My mind began analyzing what was most important. I wondered would the surrounding red, purple and orange flower species be enough to merit celebrity whores without the clout of the alien crossbreed. I feared not.

I grabbed a seat on a nearby rock and grabbed some water and the pack of granola from my backpack. My stomach was yelling at me as if I hadn't eaten in a week and my lips were cracked and peeling. I finished up the food and water then decided my only plan was to continue back towards base camp. I peeked at my locator clip and had a quick flash of panic as the little LCD screen was blank. What if the battery was dead or if I landed on it wrong and messed up the circuitry inside. I hit the power button and was relieved when I saw the flashing dot. Twenty seconds later I got a ping and the little arrow popped up. I got my notepad and pen out and made a note of the arrow position and distance, then I started walking.

After fifty yards or so, the red flowers became less and less dominant and eventually gave way to a green forest floor. I made a note of where the red flowers started disappearing, then kept going. The terrain became less accommodating and I had to climb over rocks and massive root systems. At certain points, the way became impassible with walls of thick foliage. I had to maneuver in different directions, other than the arrow on the locator clip was dictating, just to continue on at certain points. I twisted around the uncharted rainforest for an additional two kilometers.

When my locator clip read 1.6 km, I almost lost my mind when I connected with the original hiking trail and recognized where I was. I half-jogged the remaining distance to the base camp and was doubled over with cramps. My legs felt weak and my body as a whole felt hollow like after a round of flu-driven vomiting. I pounded the remaining water in my backpack then walked towards Wynn and some others who I spotted by the fire-pit.

"Hey, Wynn," I called out. "I need a breakfast beer."

Wynn looked up, as well as the others, and ran over to meet me. "Where the hell have you been for the last two days?"

"Two days? What the fuck are you talking about?"

"Where were you? The entire group has been combing the trails for you since you disappeared. Orif has the park rangers involved."

I stood there befuddled. Two days? That flower that ejaculated on my face was a product of millions of years of undisturbed evolution. I could very well have been exposed to some new type of plant STD. An electric spider of hysteria slowly descended my spinal column down to my inner taint.

"Where is Orif? I think I need to get to a hospital."

Chapter Eleven
Auspital

One of the guys in our group ran down the beach a ways to flag down Orif. Orif was having a discussion with two park rangers. When they heard I was back at camp, the park rangers used their walkie-talkies to cancel the search and to summon a jeep down to our camp site.

Fifteen minutes later I was in an official Daintree park ranger jeep and was driven back to civilization to a hospital. I told the park rangers and the hospital that I got lost and was poisoned by a plant that knocked me out for two days. They all looked at me the same when I told them, as if they were struggling to keep the word "bullshit" from spilling from their mouths. I'm sure they figured the American took some LSD and had a bad trip in the rainforest or something of the likes. I'm sure it wasn't the first time a dumb American did something stupid in their rainforest.

They put me in a room and ran all the toxicology tests they could. They gave me a full physical and had me sit for a couple of hours hooked up to an IV. Aside from slight dehydration, they couldn't find anything abnormal. All the tests came back negative. After six hours, I was released with a clean bill of health. No signs of plant chlamydia or anything.

Out in the waiting room were Orif, Wynn, Gaby and Sarah. Gaby and Sarah looked happy to see me and greeted me with hugs. Orif, on the other hand, looked at me with an unfiltered disgust as if he just caught me jerking off to animal porn. I do believe he was pissed. They had a van waiting outside and we got in and headed back to base camp.

I hadn't really explained in detail what happened to me yet to anyone. I could tell there would be nothing short of an interrogation on the long shuttle ride back to the campsite. I decided to be ninety-five percent honest about what happened, only changing the insignificant detail of why I originally wandered off the path and into the raw jungle. Wynn pressed me to recount the experience as soon as we got in the van. Sarah and Gaby faced me, eager to hear what happened. Orif sat in front, blatantly ignoring all three of us as he read through an Australian travel book.

A couple of days earlier, Wynn had mentioned a tree-lizard named goanna that inhabited the Daintree. So that was the only change to the story I had. I told them I spotted what I thought was a goanna and I followed it off the trail trying to get a better look at it. I figured wandering off the path to look at an interesting indigenous lizard was a more elegant reason than having to take an explosive shotgun shit out the butthole. If a guy shits in the forest and nobody is around to see him do it, did that shit really happen? Philoshitfy 101.

So aside from that one slight rewrite, I continued to tell them what happened. I told them I followed the lizard for a while then got turned around and couldn't find my way back to the path. I then explained that I eventually gave up on finding my way back to the group and sought out returning to base camp using the locator clip. I told them how the locator clip pointed me through uncharted areas of the rainforest and how I stumbled upon the uniquely colored flowers. Then I mentioned the crossbreed alien scorpion flower that knocked me into two days of hibernation.

I realized as I was explaining all of this that if I was the one listening to myself, I wouldn't have believed it. After I wrapped up my story ending with me finding my way back to base camp, I quickly added,

"I know what I just told you is insane and I don't blame any of you if you don't want to believe me. It really happened though and out there is an expanse of rainforest with three types of flowers I think haven't been seen by anyone else but me. When we get back to base camp, I intend to try to retrace my steps back to the field of flowers to take pictures. Any or all of you are welcome to go with me if you want. It's a shitty hike but if you're a fan of flowers it might be worth it."

Wynn looked at the group in the shuttle then said, "As farfetched as your story sounds, I can't figure out any possible reason for why you'd be making it up. I mean it'd be different if there were some kind of brothel or massage parlor in the near vicinity, and then I could easily see you disappearing and then crafting this tale to cover your proclivity for debauchery."

"Shut up, Wynn." Sarah and Gaby giggled at Wynn's stupid joke.

Wynn continued, "But based on the circumstances that you disappeared during the hike, and it's obvious by your filthiness and abhorrent odor that you were in fact in the wild for the last two days, I'm going to have to go ahead and half-heartedly believe you."

Sarah chimed in, "Can you look me in my eyes and swear to me that what you just told us is true?"

All except for the lizard-chasing part, I thought. "Sarah, I swear to Zeus and on Wynn's eternally nerdy soul, that I got lost in the forest, stumbled upon an unknown species of flower that poisoned me and knocked me out for the last two days."

Sarah looked at Gaby who shrugged as if she had no rebuttal. "Alright, lost boy, I guess you can count us in. Let's go tomorrow morning, and if we do find these undiscovered species of flowers you're talking about, you let us get a co-discoverer credit in the botanical records."

I smiled and looked at Wynn who said, "Count me in, though I will amend Sarah's conditions. In addition to receiving a co-discoverer credit, I will require that you bathe before we go tomorrow. Your stench is repugnant."

"Shut up, Wynn." I looked up towards the front row of the shuttle at the back of Orif's head. I asked, "Hey, Orif, any interest in joining us tomorrow and becoming a part of botanical history?"

Orif turned towards us, looking irritable. He surveyed the members of the van then put his hawkish eyes on me and said, "Do you have any idea the amount of work that went into organizing this trip? No, you don't. You are one of eighteen people in this group. I don't know what your agenda was coming here but seventeen of us just wasted two days of our trip being a search party instead of being a Biology Club. When we get back to base camp, feel free to disappear again. There won't be another search party, just so you know. "

"So, what are you saying, Orif, are you coming with us tomorrow or not?"

The girls giggled. Wynn shook his head and addressed Orif.

"Look, I know you can dismiss Serin as being irresponsible for wandering off the path, but from what I know of him he is honest to the point of embarrassment. Do you know what he told me was the reason he came on this trip in the first place?"

"Shut up, Wynn."

Gaby jumped in, "No, Wynn, do tell."

Wynn looked at me and smiled, then turned back to Orif. "Regardless of the reason, I'll respect his privacy and just tell you I was embarrassed for him and that only a completely honest person would admit to something so pathetic, especially to someone they barely knew."

"Keep it up, Wynn, and I'm going to knock you out for two days myself and let the rainforest wildlife have an orgy with your unconscious body."

Wynn finished by saying, "Basically, I don't blame you for being upset with him and this situation. His bad decision, which any of us could have made, resulted in a big distraction. I do, however, think that what he's told us is more than likely true. If in fact we can retrace his steps and find and catalogue these new species of flowers, it'd kind of make it all worth it. A Biology Club trip you organized resulting in the discovery of new species of flowers is a pretty good selling point for next year's Biology Club trip, right?"

"Orif, listen to Wynn. I have no reason to bullshit you. When we get back to base camp, I'll apologize to the group and hopefully we can all go back to enjoying our trip. And if you'd like to join us tomorrow, you'd be more than welcome, disgruntled-pissy attitude and all."

Orif mulled things over, then looked at Wynn. "When we get back to base camp, I will resume the planned itinerary for the group. You, Sarah and Gaby, as well as everyone else in the group, are free to join the daily planned activities or do your own thing. If you decide after this point to get lost in the rainforest with him, I will no longer claim responsibility for you. I want no part of anything involving him and I'd hope you'd keep your reckless excursions to yourselves and not try to encourage anyone else from our group to join you."

And with that, the shuttle went silent for the remainder of the return trip to home base. I couldn't decide, between Orif and I, which of us was the biggest dick. Probably me. We arrived back at the base camp around dinner time as most of the group was gathering around the fire-pit. I made my way around and addressed everyone, apologizing for disrupting their vacation, and gave them a barebones interpretation of my ordeal, basically just saying I was lost. Nobody in the group held any Orif-style animosity towards me, at least not to my face.

People ate. Orif announced the planned excursion for tomorrow. The vans would be returning and taking whoever felt like going to a different area of the rainforest to explore that included zip lining. I hit the portable shower and washed off two days of dirt, funk and scorpion-plant jizz. I almost felt human again. When Wynn handed me a beer upon returning to the fire-pit, I was back to one-hundred percent. We stayed up with Sarah and Gaby planning things out for the next day's venture. Our cameras were charged. We had two days' worth of food and water in our backpacks, just in case things went sideways. Everyone tested out their locator clips successfully. We were ready.

We called it a night and retired to our separate tents. I was surprisingly tired for just having recently slept for two days straight. Even though I was fatigued, I couldn't get to sleep for a long time. A lingering spark of paranoia kept my brain occupied. I knew the hospital said I was fine but I couldn't help but think that the crossbred alien scorpion flower shot some exotic unknown plague into my system that the tests at the hospital had no way of detecting. An army of mutant pathogens acting out domestic abuse on my cells, leaving them with black eyes and unwanted kids.

Turns out, my paranoia wasn't ill-conceived.

Chapter Twelve
Back into the Fray

Orif and the majority of the group were loaded into the vans and off on their excursion by 8:30 am. There were three others besides us who stayed behind but they left even earlier to hike down the coastline. Wynn, Gaby, Sarah and I met by the fire-pit at 9:00 am. We ate the breakfast packages that were left for us. I couldn't help but cringe a little at the thought of what happened the last time I started a hike eating one of these things. We double-checked that we had everything we needed, then headed off down the main hiking trail. There was an early morning fog that kicked up off the water and weaved its way inland through the trees and plants, giving the rainforest a supernatural quality. I knew I was 1.6 km from base camp when I re-entered the main hiking trail yesterday so between the locator clip and my memory, I had no problem recognizing the opening that I came through when we reached that point on the trail.

"This is the spot, guys. This is the doorway I made to get back on the main trail. Everyone still sure they want to go through with this? It gets really shitty in there at parts."

They looked through the spot and got an idea of the kind of terrain we'd be venturing into.

"Sorry to say it but knowing that you were able to get through it gives me all the confidence I need," Gaby said.

"Same here. Maybe if it was someone a little more manly that was warning us about it. But seeing it's you, I'm good to go," Sarah added.

57

"So it's like that, huh? What about you, Wynn? Got any weak jokes you'd like to add before we go in?"

"Nope, I think they said it all."

With that, we stepped off the trail and pushed our way onto the rough path I forged the day before. When I was lost, I had one eye constantly on my locator clip following that LCD arrow as best as I could. The reverse strategy was what I was using now. Now I was using the tail end of the LCD arrow as a guide, trying to keep the angle of the arrow the same that it was for the majority of my return trek to civilization. I knew we'd eventually reach the few impassable spots I had to traverse around, but by those points I was fairly confident I'd be in familiar enough territory to get us back on the correct trajectory. For the most part, my trip back yesterday was apparent by the rough path I had created. Stomped down plants and broken limbs were the breadcrumbs I had left.

An hour passed and Wynn was in nerd heaven once again. Just like the previous hike, he was pointing out different plant species and the occasional sighting of a bird or animal. Gaby and Sarah were following behind a bit, lost in a private conversation. Wynn nudged me and pointed to a lizard on a log off to our right. "There is your goanna."

I looked at the lizard Wynn was pointing at and replied, "Yep, stupid forest rat almost got me killed. I should shank that one for payback and make some friendship bracelets out of it for you to give to Sarah and Gaby. My point being, friends is about your only option with the opposite sex as long as you keep pointing out plants and animals like a kid at the zoo."

"Well, that is a foolish hypothesis that women aren't attracted to intelligent men. But I'd bet if they had to choose, they'd choose the intelligent man over the liar any day of the week."

"Am I supposed to be the liar in this scenario?"

"I'm not positive you are specifically lying for a reason or just out of ignorance. That lizard I just pointed out to you is not and looks nothing like a goanna. So either you lied about why you wandered off the path or you actually saw a lizard and having no frame of reference of what kind of lizard you were seeing, you just called it something you heard me say days before. So which is it? Are you a liar or just ignorant?"

I looked over my shoulder to make sure Sarah and Gaby were still lost in their own conversation and out of earshot then said, "Alright, you inquisitive dick, you win. While we were on the hike, my guts went liquid on me and I had to run off the path or I was going to shit myself. It's an insignificant detail that isn't relevant and needn't be shared. And just so you know, if you do decide to open your mouth about it to anyone, I will go back out to that spot in the forest, dig up the horror that came out of my ass that day, bring it back to camp and smash it into everything in your tent including your pillow, clothes and collection of anime porn."

"So, just so I'm clear on this, if I turn around right now and tell Sarah and Gaby you got lost because you had to defecate in the woods, you would in turn go dig up that particular defecation and hike for hours with it on your back? Sounds like a harsh punishment but one I think I'd like to see carried out."

"Just shut up, Wynn. Everything I said beside that was the truth. Let's focus on business for a second. What can we expect for discovering a new species of flower? Do we sell to the highest bidder or what?"

"If you are thinking there is some kind of monetary compensation for discovering a new species, I'm afraid you are mistaken, as usual. Current estimations figure that less than twenty percent of all animal and plant species on the planet have actually been catalogued. Thousands of new species are discovered on a monthly basis. The only thing in it for us is recognition and the gratification that comes with knowing we brought a new species to light."

I sighed loudly. "You're telling me, that even if we find another alien crossbreed with the knock-out gas, we can't sell it to the Department of Defense or something?"

"Wow, your delusions run strong, don't they? But no, please, I beg of you, I'd love to hear your planned course of action. Is your plan to somehow smuggle this extremely fragile specimen through customs and thousands of miles of travel unscathed, then do an internet search when you get home for the nearest biological warfare office?"

"Actually, I think my plan is to knock you out the old-fashioned way and bury you with the remnants of my three-day-old shit."

Suddenly, I was overwhelmed with the desire to turn around and head back to the base camp and get drunk. I guess the prospect of my being a co-discoverer of a new plant species lost its shine seeing there'd be no money attached to it. I then realized Sarah, Gaby and Wynn all probably knew there wasn't any prospect of money in this from the start and still held an explorer's enthusiasm. So I tried my best to mask my suddenly stricken case of apathy and depression and trudged forward.

We walked for hours and for the most part my memory and the locator clip kept us on track. By early afternoon, the first glimpses of red were in sight. A buzz generated between Sarah, Gaby and Wynn the closer we got to the crimson horizon. My mind was disenchanted and lazy and all I could think of as we approached the red flowers was a field of used tampons. That's what these stupid flowers were worth to me.

We reached the first of the red flowers and my merry band of bio-nerds was frenzied. Wynn used an app on his phone to lock in and record our exact global coordinates for any return trips for the official cataloguing and study of these specimens. I should have brought some alcohol to abate my boredom and melancholy. Wynn also had a two-gig app that had images and information of all known plant species. The app allowed you to take a picture of a plant and then it would try to match your picture to its database and bring up info of the plant you just took a picture of. Wynn was super excited when the app produced zero results.

"I updated the database on this app right before we got on the plane. I'd say the chances are pretty good that this is an undocumented species of flower."

Sarah and Gaby both were snapping away with their cameras. Wynn got down on his knees and elbows and was taking ground level snapshots with his SLR. You'd have thought the flower had fake tits the way Wynn was eye-banging it. I, on the other hand, was looking for a way to speed things along.

"Hey guys, I know this is a cool flower and all, but not too far up ahead is a spot where this one meets up with the orange and purple versions. Why don't we move on so you can see all three at once?"

It was like pulling kids away from a cotton-candy buffet but they reluctantly started following me as I started marching forward without them.

Another fifteen minutes or so passed and we were standing at the exact spot where I woke up from my flower coma. All the alien scorpion crossbreeds were dust just as I observed yesterday. There was nothing but a flattened area of dirt and rotted remnants of flower parts that weren't distinguishing in any way.

"This is it. This is where I was for two days."

They were all awestruck by the sight of these three unique flowers covering the entire area. Wynn did his thing with his phone app. Sarah and Gaby were filling the memory cards on their cameras with pictures and video of the area. I found a tree with some large protruding roots and sat down to let them do their thing.

My thoughts drifted. I was bored and still a bit worried about what that plant did to me. I was also exhausted from everything. I put my face in my hands and leaned forward and was close to nodding off. A small branch fell from the tree above me and stabbed me in the back of my neck. I looked up at Wynn, Sarah and Gaby and that's when the stability of my known reality began its gradual dissolve.

Chapter Thirteen
Blown Pixels

Sarah, Gaby and Wynn were still taking in the scene and not paying any attention to me. It was subtle, but there was something definitely wrong with what I was seeing. I opened up my backpack and pulled out a water bottle. I poured some water into my hand then splashed the water into my eyes. I used my shirt to dry my face then looked again at Sarah, Gaby and Wynn.

I got up with a hint of unease starting to claw around the insides of my heart valves. This wasn't right. I slowly circled the three of them. I looked away and saw nothing abnormal, just the regular old rainforest. But when I turned back to look at Sarah, Gaby and Wynn, each of them had a faint grayish blotch hovering above and behind them.

I watched Sarah and Gaby who were walking around still snapping photos and these blotches followed them as if they were little ugly kites tethered to the girl's necks with invisible string. Wynn was kneeling down taking a closer look at one of the orange flowers. His blotch was at eye-level for me so I approached him as casually as I could on increasingly unstable legs.

I looked up to see the girls looking off in another direction. I was now right behind Wynn and was face to face with this gray thing that was somehow invading my reality. I reached out and my hand went through it with no sense of anything. I waved my hand back and forth trying to fan it out like smoke, but it just held its form with me having no kind of effect on it.

It reminded me of the screen on my laptop back home. It has a couple of blown pixels. Two dots on my computer screen not doing their job and causing an insignificant but continuous imperfection with whatever I was looking at be it porn, world news or porn.

But these were blown pixels in the screen of my reality. I thought of asking Wynn if he saw anything out of the ordinary near Gaby or Sarah but figured if he could see what I was seeing, he'd soon enough make that apparent the next time he looked their way. I remembered I had my shaving mirror in my backpack and stepped away from Wynn and pulled it out. I held it up and angled the mirror so I could look behind and above my back but didn't see anything above me. A stupid and temporary relief hit me as I thought that if it was some weird rainforest ghost cancer, I hadn't caught it because I didn't have my own blotch. But then I turned the mirror so I could see Wynn, and his blotch was not reflected in the mirror either. Shit, rainforest *vampire*-ghost cancer.

I took out my phone that I decided to carry with me for the rest of the trip, and clicked on the camera. I snapped a quick shot of Wynn's vampire-ghost cancer. What I saw with my eyes wasn't in the picture I just had taken. The girls made their way over to where Wynn and I were and their blotches followed them.

"We're thinking maybe it's about time to start heading back. We have plenty of daylight left but just in case something happens, we'd prefer not to be hiking back in the dark," Gaby said.

"Yeah, we heard there are a couple of perverts out in these parts who try to lure girls into the forest with promises of rare flowers. They sound gross," Sarah said.

Wynn hesitated for a second then said, "I guess I got everything I need. I have the coordinates and have taken enough pictures."

I had been ready to go before we even got here. Now that I was seeing these things, I desperately wanted to get back to my tent for a drink to settle my nerves. I mustered up a fake smile and said, "After you guys." I held out my arm allowing the girls and Wynn to walk in front of me so I could stare at these things floating above their backs for a while. None of them seemed to notice anything peculiar. Apparently this was my own personal insanity to deal with.

The walk back was for the most part uneventful. My three companions were lost in their own conversations and didn't take notice of my silence and newly acquired staring problem. I walked behind them, hoping the whole way these blotches would disappear and I could begin denying to myself that they were ever there in the first place. But no, the blotches were constant in their appearance and proximity to each of the girls and Wynn.

A slow and steady dread built as we approached the part of our journey where we'd exit the rough rainforest and re-enter the main trail.

Chapter Fourteen
Concordance

I'm not sure what I thought would be the best outcome upon re-entering the main trail back to base camp. Since we arrived, the trail that led to our base camp and the beach was pretty well frequented by other people out hiking and exploring. I knew at some point we would pass another person on the trail on our way back. If that person also had a gray blotch hovering above and behind them, then my new insanity was epidemic. On the flip-side, if we passed another person and they didn't have a blown reality pixel above and behind them, then that might mean Sarah, Gaby and Wynn did have some kind of rainforest vampire-cancer. It was a lose/lose scenario with nothing to really hope for.

It didn't take long. After a couple of minutes of being back on the main trail, a group of three middle-aged women doing that irritating ski-pole hiking passed us going in the opposite direction.

All three of them had blotches.

Chapter Fifteen
Camp Blotchy

We made it back to base camp as the sun was sitting low in the sky. Orif and the rest of the group had already returned from their day trip and were preparing dinner. Wynn, Sarah and Gaby excitedly approached some of the others and started showing them pictures and telling them of our day. I bailed to my tent and got out the bottle of rum and spent about half an hour in solitude, numbing myself. First, Ariel goes to Paris. Then I get lost and taken advantage of by some crazily evolved demon flower. Now I was seeing little gray pieces of shit floating over everyone and invading my reality. What a shit vacation this was.

There was a knock at my tent flap. It had snapped me out of a trance of rising inebriation and dark thoughts. Wynn's voice passed through the nylon wall and asked, "You masturbating or something worse?"

I unzipped the tent door and held up the half-empty bottle of rum, inviting Wynn inside. He grabbed the bottle and knocked back a sip and sat down. "So what's really going on here? I know it's more than just the disappointment about there being no financial gains involved in discovering the flowers. The entire walk back to camp, you were acting odd. I'd occasionally look back at you and see you gazing into the sky with a look like you were in an alien strip-club trying to make out what you were seeing on stage."

I grabbed the bottle back from Wynn and took a sip, while taking a quick glance at his gray blotch which was half-way in the tent with us. Should I try to explain my current situation to Wynn or should I keep it to myself and give it some more time to resolve itself? "Alien strip-club? That's not just a spontaneous metaphor is it, Wynn? I bet if I checked your laptop, you'd have a treasure trove of bizarre animated porn."

"Nice deflection but I'll ask one more time then leave it alone. What's really going on? Maybe I can help?"

If only you knew what you were signing up for Wynn. Not yet though. "Look, I got some shit going on, possible side-effects from getting date-raped by a flower. It's nothing sinister yet so if you don't mind, I'd like to keep things to myself. I promise you, you're on deck. Soon as I need a second opinion, you're the first on my list."

"So I take it it's of the venereal variety of side-effects then?"

"And here I thought being an asexual nerd would inhibit a sense of humor. Good for you, buddy."

"So, is this your final destination for the night? Drinking in solitude?"

"No, I just needed a break from seeing people. Is there any shitty food left to eat out there?"

"Yeah. I'll walk over there with you."

Wynn let me leave it at that. We emerged from my tent and made our way to the fire-pit. And there they were. Every person in camp had their own gray blotch, crystal clear in the night sky. They were like huge splattered fire-flies hovering above and behind each person. It was somewhat psychedelic with the number of people and it being night time to where the blotches were more prominent against a darkened background.

I grabbed some food and a beer and took a seat by the fire, trying not to look obviously aloof as my eyes followed the dance of the blotches. The booze was finally starting to run strong enough to where the scene before me became more amusing than terrifying. As the night wore on, I almost convinced myself that upon awakening tomorrow, everything would be back to normal. All my brain needed was a nine-hour stimulus-free reset to correct my current optical debilitation.

Booze sure can make the ugly girl pretty.

M. J. WATERS

Chapter Sixteen
Vacate the Vacation

I awoke from a drunken slumber. From outside my tent, it sounded as if most of the camp had already started their day. For the first twenty seconds of consciousness, I completely forgot about my situation. Then the dread and apprehension slowly cemented itself in my core. I looked at the zipper to my tent flap. This was all that currently separated me from the rabbit hole. A stupid strip of metal interlocking teeth easily disarmed and spread open with a thumb and index finger. This reminded me of pudgy Brenda and I quickly changed thoughts before I barfed in my tent.

I took a long deep breath as if I were about to dive to the bottom of a pool. I unzipped the tent flap and peeked outside. Fuck! I could see a guy walking to his tent. His blotch was not only still visible to me, but had grown about fifteen percent. I retreated back inside my tent and zipped up the flap.

I closed my eyes and put my face in my hands. This wasn't happening. Yes, it was. What can I do? A steadily growing drumbeat in my bladder told me what I needed to do first. I really didn't want to leave the tent just yet but after a night of drinking, morning priorities were not to be ignored. So with my head down, I slinked off to the bathroom, trying to come up with some kind of game plan. After a good, solid forty-five seconds of powerful urination, I came to a decision.

I made my way back to my tent and packed up all my shit. This crap vacation was over. My problem wasn't going to find an answer by riding things out here pretending everything was normal. After packing, I made my way through the camp and hunted down Orif. I told him that I was in need of returning to the airport to go home early. He radioed for a van to come get me without hesitation or inquiry. The only thing he said was for me to return the locator clip and hiking kit before I got on the van. Fuck you, too, Orif.

I found Wynn finishing up breakfast with the girls. I sat down with them and said, "End of the road for me guys. I've got a van coming to pick me up and am heading back home. Just thought I'd say goodbye and give you my email and phone number just in case you feel like hanging back in the States."

Gaby asked, "Why are you going home? We still have three more days left."

"I just have this nagging fear that the plant that knocked me out also infected me somehow. I've been feeling off ever since it happened and the way my mind works, I don't think I could enjoy staying here another day while worrying about what kind of exotic disease could possibly be violating my blood cells right now. Plus, I really can't stand that guy Wynn."

"Funny," Wynn said.

"Well, that sucks," Sarah said.

"Yeah, I'm sorry you got bullied out of your vacation by a little flower," Gaby said.

"Really, Gaby?"

"No, I'm really sorry. I hope you are alright. You going to try a different doctor when you get home?"

"I haven't thought that far ahead. I'm a five-minutes-in-front-of-me kind of guy. I just know getting home is my next step, then I'll figure it out from there."

"Well, I hope you are okay. If you get home and get a clean bill of health, maybe we all can hang out when we get

74

back. If you do find out you have some kind of disease, then let's not bother," Sarah said.

"Really, Sarah? I can say without a doubt it's not the best three thousand dollars I've ever spent, but I had a good time hanging out with you three. And as I said, here is my number and email. When you get back, hit me up and fill me in on what I missed. Hopefully, something entertaining happens like Wynn getting violated by a tree snake."

"If you leave us your remaining alcohol, we'll pretend to be sad when you go," Gaby said.

"Deal. I left the bottles in my tent. Some fake tears would be nice when I look back at you through the van window."

"Fake tears would cost you a lot more than a few drinks. All you get for your remaining booze is one of us will give you a small wave goodbye," Sarah said.

"Just as long as the wave goodbye comes from you or Gaby, then we still have a deal."

We hung out until the van arrived. The driver's blotch breached the roof of the shuttle. I said my goodbyes and was off to the airport. I closed my eyes and tried to think but no ideas populated my hazy brain. All I could think was that somehow I'd be able to figure things out once I got back home. It was a long ride and I was still tired so I passed out for the remainder of the drive.

When I finally got dropped off at the airport and entered the terminal, I couldn't help but stare at the hundreds of people all floating a blotch behind them. It was like an ugly miniature balloon parade. I snapped out of it and made my way over to the counter for the airline I was supposed to take home in three days from now. Thankfully there was a flight back to the States leaving in four hours that had some seats open. Unfortunately and unsurprisingly, it cost an additional $352 to make the change to my itinerary. Everyone is a fucking money vampire.

By the time I got done with all my airport work, I still had over two hours to kill. It was only 11:00 am but I ended up at the bar anyway. I'm by no means an alcoholic (I tell myself) but this situation was cause enough to act like one. Three beers and two cocktails were consumed while waiting for the flight to arrive. In those hours of drinking, I had started to form a loose game plan for how to try to deal with this plant disease. By the time the plane was boarding, walking was bit of a fun challenge.

Making my way to the back of the plane towards my seat was also interesting, passing row after row of people and their blotches in such a uniform positioning. Zeus granted me a small respite from the shit-storm in the form of a window seat with an empty middle seat between me and some older guy plugging away at an inch-thick book of sudoku.

Before the flight even took off, I was asleep.

Chapter Seventeen
Straw Grasping

The flight home got painful as a pounding dehydration headache woke me up about five hours in. In a daze, I stumbled back to the bathroom to wash my face in the little sink, then grabbed a bottle of water from an unmanned drink cart before heading back to my seat. The remainder of the flight was an unrelenting string of uncomfortable mind-numbing hours, tossing and turning in my seat, unable to return to sleep.

By the time we landed, there were radiating sciatic pulses shooting down my legs. After making my way through customs and retrieving my luggage, I headed outside and grabbed a taxi. I stone-walled the taxi driver's attempts at idle chatter with one word answers and a few disinterested grunts.

Once back at my apartment, the first thing on the agenda was the mandatory post-flight shower to get off the airplane film you get on extended flights. It's that lovely mix of germs and filth from sitting in a chair and surroundings previously occupied by countless bodies of all shapes and sleaze. Once cleaned, a call to the University's Health Services was made. Granted they mostly treated the overly abundant river of STD cases college campuses tend to generate, but they did actually have reputable non-genital-related services, too. So I made an early appointment for the following day with their ophthalmologist.

There was nothing else this day had to offer me. I microwaved and forced down a frozen burrito for the sole purpose of having something in my stomach before popping a Valium and the last of a cheap fifth of vodka that was in my freezer. Within thirty minutes, the self-medicating had dimmed the lights on the day. For sixteen hours I slept uninterrupted and heavily.

The initial waking period was almost refreshing and pleasant but that was short-lived. It was like waking up from a bender in Vegas feeling good then remembering the three cash advances you made on your credit card the previous night. The wind gets sucked quickly from your sails when you know you're fucked in so many ways.

Rolled out of bed, got put together, then walked over to Health Services which was on the outskirts of campus. In the waiting area were all the usual health services suspects: a bunch of nervous-looking frat boys and some shamed-looking half-way-hot girls. Forty-five minutes passed until my name got called. Another twenty minutes passed before the doctor made her way into the room.

The bare white-painted room with the sterile fluorescent lighting amplified the doctor's blotch. I could see a more detailed composition hovering over her than any others before. It was still mostly formless but there was some semblance of symmetry to the outer edges. There were also the faintest hints of color. It was like ninety-eight percent gray mixed with two percent crimson. It was nearly undetectable, but I could swear that the two percent of color was definitely in there.

The doctor was in her forties with glasses and a butch haircut. She gave me the once-over then asked, "So what brings you in today?"

"I just got back from Australia. While I was over there, I got some pollen or something in my eyes. Ever since then, I'm having issues with my eyesight. Sort of like spots in my vision."

"Let's have a look then."

She approached me and checked both of my eyes with her scope.

"Cover your right eye. Do you see any spots in your vision?"

Her blotch was hovering behind her.

"Yes, I do."

"Okay, now cover your left eye. Do you see any spots now?"

"Yes, I do."

She writes some quick notes on her clipboard then fills out a prescription and hands it to me.

"I'm prescribing you a saline solution. Flush your eyes with it three times daily for ten days. If after that your symptoms persist, call us back and set up another appointment."

"Saline solution? That's it?"

"Your eyes look fine. You aren't in the susceptible age-range for macular degeneration which isn't something that just shows up over a weekend. And, a macular hole wouldn't affect both your eyes unless you had one in each eye, which is incredibly unlikely. Saline, three times a day for ten days. If symptoms persist, make a return appointment."

She jettisoned out of the room followed by her blotch. I crumpled up her prescription and tossed it in the garbage. All doctors have their shortlist. If it's not on their list, throw some antibiotics at it and hope it goes away. I guess for eye doctors, saline is their antibiotic. Fucking worthless.

I left Health Services feeling deflated. I knew the chances were slim to none, and slim got jizzed in the eyeball by a demon flower, but I did have a glimmer of hope the eye doctor would see something. Anything. Nothing. Back to square fucked. What was my next move? I didn't have one.

CT scan?
Exorcist?
Liquor store?

Chapter Eighteen
Liquor Store

It was less than a ten-minute walk from the Health Services building to Campus Liquor. Most people were grabbing coffee and overpriced toiletries at this hour. I, on the other hand, made my way to the wine aisle and grabbed a bottle of cheap Lambrusco with a screw-top. I'm really not an alcoholic, says the young man at the liquor store at 10:00 am, but circumstances demand wine at the 10 o'clock morning hour. Not a big fucking deal if you've ever been to brunch. Mimosas are socially acceptable early in the day but sipping a cheap red wine with a screw-top from a paper bag for breakfast makes you some kind of degenerate or something?

Paid for the wine after grabbing an empty soda cup by the self-serve machines. Walked over to the Commons on campus and found a quiet spot on the grass under a tree and sat down. Open brown bag. Twist off screw-top. Pour wine into soda cup. Twist on screw-top. Close brown bag. Phase 1: *drink in public like a transient*, complete. Phase 2: *what the fuck is my next move*, commencing.

So there I sat, in the middle of the lawn on the Commons of my school campus, sipping wine from a soda cup while watching a fraction of the school population meandering across campus during the summer session. Despite my situation, it was technically a nice day. Sun was out. Everyone's blotches were looking more defined.

Considerations were made about making another appointment with Health Services. Maybe just a physical or something and see about getting the blood work done again. That idea soured quickly. If the tests in Australia didn't raise any red flags, then why would the tests here find anything?

What to do? What to do? Sip. Sip. Fuck. Fuck. The wine bottle gradually got emptier and ideas became harder to summon. There was something about drinking wine early in the day and outdoors. It was an uncommon event that had a different kind of feel to it. Things started to get a bit glazed. I wondered what/who Ariel was doing. What was I doing? What the fuck was happening to me?

Amidst the wandering wine-minding, something caught my attention. I didn't know if it was the angle I was sitting at or the position of the sun but something didn't look right. I tried to focus in but between the wine and the amount of space between me and the scene I was seeing, I couldn't be sure. Off in the distance was a small cluster of people. This was different. What was going on here?

There were seven or eight people but only two fucking blotches.

Chapter Nineteen
The Down and the Pit

The people in the group were moving somewhat peculiarly. I grabbed my cup and brown-bagged liquid breakfast, then stood up. Getting to my feet too quickly caused the daylight to dim and I came close to fainting. No food combined with morning wine made for a shaky ground control. I closed my eyes and took a few deep breaths and waited for my blood to regain traction and bring my senses back online. Re-opening my eyes, I waited for the stars in my vision to fade away. Once stable, I started to make my way towards this peculiar looking group of people.

I dumped my cup and brown-bagged bottle in the first trash can I passed. Sorry earth, no time for recycling. It was quick work catching up to the group I was pursuing who were moving slowly and a bit disjointed. On approach, it was verifiable that there were eight people and only two of them had blotches. I walked up behind them and the situation became clear. Two chaperones with blotches. Six people with Down syndrome with no blotches.

I kept on walking, not wanting to be the slack-jawed asshole gaping at a group of people with Down syndrome. They had no fucking blotches. Whatever this was, it had to mean something. If only one of them were missing a blotch, then that would have left a wide-open margin for argument and interpretation. But here there were six of them, all without blotches. This had significance. Whatever I was dealing with had at least the hint of being systematic.

I found a nearby bench and sat down to take a last look at this group. This was at least something. Five minutes ago I had nothing but grass on my ass and a brown bag. This was something real I could use. If there were rules for what I was seeing, then this had to be some part of some kind of system. If I can learn the system, figure out the working parts, maybe I could escape from it or destroy it or find the eye of the system and jizz on it like it did me.

Scientific method 101, start with a question. What is this world of blotches? Once the question is established, time for research. Research, that's the next move. Stop scrambling around, sit back and observe things. Take notes and compile a big picture before constructing any hypothesis. Yes, this was a tangible course of action. Take some notes. Note number one, Down syndrome equals no blotch. I needed a notebook.

Revitalized with a fresh sense of purpose, the campus store was the next destination. They had quizzical summer hours but it was almost 11:00 am which felt like a necessary hour to be open regardless of the day or time of year. The campus store was on the border between the actual university and the real world. Across the street from it was a gas station and a shitty sandwich shop. It was in front of the gas station where I saw the second abnormality of the day.

In front of the gas station was a bus stop with a couple of green iron benches bolted to the pavement. Sitting on one of these benches at the bus stop was a ratty-looking skater kid smoking a cigarette. Wrapped around his hand was a thick leash. At the end of the leash was a pit bull. Two students with their backpacks and coffees were walking on the sidewalk behind the bus stop. The pit bull made an aggressive lunge in their direction only to be yanked to its hind legs by the skater kid. The dog did a snakelike head motion trying to break free from its constraints but then settled for some powerful barking and teeth gnashing. The skater kid gave it another yank and told it to shut up. The two students walking by made a wide arc away from the dog and looked annoyed and scared at the same time.

I stood across the street staring at the scene, looking at another noteworthy observation. The pit bull had a fucking blotch.

Chapter Twenty
Recon Z

People with dogs were a dime a dozen around here. There was a girl by the shitty sandwich shop who had a stupid little dog. Stupid little dog didn't have a blotch. Up over the street were a row of pigeons poised on the telephone line, readying their little white shits for the next car to come along. No blotches on the pigeons either. I looked back to the skater kid at the bus stop, and his pit bull unmistakably had its own blotch. Notes.

The campus store was open. I had made their strange summer hour window of 10:30 am – 3:30 pm. The place was dead aside from a couple of staff and three customers spread out on different aisles. One of the aisles in the middle of the store carried a majority of their paper products. There was a stack of cheap spiral notebooks for $1.79 each but I reconsidered and kept walking. The info I'd soon be recording would be of great significance towards my current fucked-up state of being. This info deserved a better home than a $1.79 spiral notebook. Further down the aisle in a different section I picked a clean, fake-leatherbound blank journal. $8.99 was more of a legitimate investment for something of this significance.

Grabbed a two-pack of pens, a pack of mechanical pencils, paid, then returned to the campus Commons. There was an empty table in the shade where I sat down and started writing. I recounted the genesis of my madness in the Daintree step by step. Once again I made the slight omission as to why I left the hiking trail. Stupid lizard. There was no current plan on letting anyone ever look at this journal but small details tend to get changed when writing history.

The pages started to fill with the descriptions of the flower, getting knocked out for two days, a trip to the hospital and so on and so on up until that current point in time with the group of Down syndrome people and the pit bull. Once the summary was complete, I then jumped to the halfway point in the journal. The first half of the journal would be an ongoing day-to-day recap like you would in a normal journal. The second half of the journal would be for specific notes and sketches about things that were notable.

So far the middle section of the journal included the group of Down syndromes sans blotches. It also had the aggressive pit bull with a blotch while other dogs/animals in the area didn't have one. Another note was about the hint of crimson color that was noticeable in the eye doctor's blotch. In the same section of the journal, using one of the pencils I had just bought, I made a sketch of the crossbreed, alien, scorpion flower. Finally I made a drawing of a person with a blotch hovering above and behind them. Granted, I wasn't the greatest artist but it was good enough to convey the idea.

Once my drinking hand started to cramp up a bit from all the writing, I decided the day was still young and I should find my way to a more populated situation. Observation and documentation would be my main course of action. Just needed to find a better place for people watching. Campus normally would be great but seventy percent of the school body was enjoying the summer elsewhere. Where to go then? Briefly considered the mall but I hated the mall. Where? Had to be someplace with a guaranteed wide variety and dense amount of people. Someplace maybe with some animals, too. Beach? Dog park? Tijuana?

It then came to me out of nowhere: The perfect place for crowds and animals. I glanced at my phone to get the time. It was still early. On the walk back to my apartment I made a quick stop at a little hole-in-the-wall coffee shop. Pounding down a tall iced-coffee helped clear out the lingering cobwebs of my wine-head.

Once back at my apartment, I loaded up my backpack. Packed up my new journal, a couple of pens and pencils, a bottle of water and three mini-bottles of vodka I had kept from the flight back from Australia. Spot number twenty-three in the parking lot was where my beat-up Honda had been sitting for the last ten days. Thankfully, it started up with no issues. The way things had been going for me, I all but assumed my car would have had a dead battery or sugar in the gas tank courtesy of a disgruntled pudgy Brenda or something. An eighth of a tank would be plenty to get to today's destination.

Twenty minutes up the interstate brought me to the parking lot of the zoo. Parked, threw on my backpack and then off to the main entrance. Forty-six fucking dollars? Price of research, I guess. Paid for a ticket then entered the park. The place was packed with the summer crowd. Adults, elderly, kids from all corners of the planet converging to see some animals in cages. This would do nicely.

I took one of the park maps even though I'd been there many times, usually high or drunk or both though. The goal was to be thorough and see every animal they had while simultaneously people-watching to compile at least forty-six dollars' worth of notes.

The first attraction through the front gate was the foul-smelling flamingo pit. It was just a baffling decision to have this particular attraction as the first thing people were going to encounter on their day at the zoo.

There were about a hundred flamingos in a six-inch-deep lake that was literally a lake of flamingo shit. The smell couldn't have been worse as there was minimal shade and the lake of shit was heated by the sun all day causing the fumes to expand and rise. Who was the guy on this zoo's planning committee who proposed, "How about at the entrance, as people walk through the gates, we greet them with the crippling odor of a desert outhouse?" Genius idea. While holding my breath, I did a quick walk-by of the flamingos. No blotches. Moving on.

I started on the northern outskirts of the park first which housed mostly birds and little uninteresting animals. Nothing struck me as notable on a normal or metaphysical level. After twenty minutes I was already starting to mourn the loss of my forty-six dollars.

There was a bench next to the restrooms which was a proper location for a water break and to do some people-watching. The flow of people was constant. There was a high volume of parents with strollers and I soon put it together that none of the strollers had blotches poking through their canopies. I sat and focused on just strollers for a while. Upwards of thirty strollers went by in a five-minute span. Retrieving my journal from my backpack, I flipped to the halfway point and wrote: *Babies = No Blotches.*

Next, my focus turned to the kids. Things were a bit more muddled in trying to decipher a definitive pattern concerning the children. For the most part, the kids around and under four years old didn't have any blotches. But once in a while a two-year-old would stumble by and have a blotch. Not sure what to make of it. Wrote a new note in the journal: *Kids four and under, mostly no blotches with a few exceptions.*

Older kids and adults all were tethered to blotches. There weren't any exceptions here so far. Got up and walked over to the water fountain to refill my now-empty water bottle, then decided to return my focus to the animals. Hours melted away as I systematically checked every animal exhibit they had to offer. Bears nothing. Zebras nothing. Rhinos, elephants and giraffes, nothing.

My legs were starting to wear out and I was running out of animals. I was pretty much resigned to this zoo trip being a failure when I hit a cage with a single mountain lion in it. The mountain lion had a blotch. What the fuck, mountain lion? Hundreds of animals today and you're the only one with a blotch. A girl in a green safari zookeeper outfit was coming out of a gate behind the neighboring exhibit to the mountain lion. I walked over to her and asked, "Could you tell me if there is anything special about this mountain lion over here?"

She looked me over one time, then at the mountain lion and replied, "He is a new arrival. Came in two days ago."

"Any idea where he came from? Another zoo?"

"No. He was spotted in the vicinity of a local hiking trail. Department of Wildlife resources tranquilized and captured him. They checked with us to see if we could temporarily hold him until they figured out what to do with him. Anything in particular you were hoping to find out about him?"

"No. He just struck me as a bit peculiar for some reason. Different from the other animals I've seen today. Thought I'd ask. Thanks for the info."

I returned to the front of the cage and stared at the mountain lion and its blotch for a minute. Just another piece in a mind-fuck of a puzzle. Jotted down a note in my journal about the mountain lion then continued on to the remaining exhibits I hadn't seen yet. The tour of the entire park finished up with no other noteworthy encounters.

With nothing more to see, I made my way over to the area near the park exit and bought some orange juice at a snack bar.

Drank down a third of the o.j. I had just bought. Covertly, inside my backpack, I proceeded to pour two of the three mini vodka bottles I brought into the o.j. container. A couple of shakes and so began happy hour at the zoo. One last session of people-watching before calling it a day.

I had spent four and a half hours walking the zoo and I was beat. It looked like most of the park visitors were also beat as they were steadily walking by me towards the exit turnstiles. Strollers were a staple of the exiting park goers and all were consistent with my earlier observations.

When my zoo cocktail was finished, the decision to leave was made. Tossed the o.j. bottle in a blue recycling garbage can, then slung my backpack over my shoulder. That's when I noticed the geezer.

There was an older couple who was leaving the zoo. They were in their mid-sixties, I'd guess. The man was pushing a wheelchair with what looked to be a corpse seated in it. It was probably his father or even his grandfather in the wheelchair. He looked catatonic. I'd have guessed he was dead. His face was slack and expressionless. His eyes were crystal blue and vacant. The only sign that he wasn't dead was his hands. They were in his lap and doing a palsy shake of some sort.

The geezer in the wheelchair didn't have a blotch.

Chapter Twenty-One
Crimson

I made my way back to my apartment after grabbing five rolled tacos with guacamole at the dirty Mexican joint down the street. Threw on the TV, sank into the couch and ate. My head was running full speed but my body was beat from the day of walking, early wine and the remaining touch of jet lag. It wasn't even six o'clock but I decided to be done with this day. After the food was consumed, I drank the remaining mini bottle of vodka and popped another Valium. By seven o'clock I was passed out.

Fifteen hours later, I slowly got up and made my way to take a shower. A new day with some new horrors in store for me no doubt. There wasn't much of a game plan for me other than being out in public with my journal and observing and documenting. Shit had been steadily progressive with what I'd been able to see. No doubt in my mind that I was in for something new with each passing twenty-four hours.

After cleaning up I decided to walk to a bagel shop that was three blocks away for some coffee and breakfast. The walk was quiet, as the route from my place to this bagel shop was all back alleys. Arrived, then went up to the counter and ordered a coffee and a jalapeño bagel egg sandwich. After the food was ready, I settled at a table outside and began to eat while studying the bagel shop patrons.

It was instantly obvious that since yesterday the different blotches people had were more defined. It reminded me of some stupid game show I watched once where one of the challenges was they'd put up a blurred picture on the screen then slowly bring the image into focus. First person to ring in and identify the picture would get points. These blotches were the same thing. These gray shits hanging over people were slowly coming into focus and I wasn't sure I'd want to see them at full resolution.

Must have missed the morning rush as the current foot traffic at the bagel shop was thin and sporadic. A guy and two girls came out of the bagel shop and took a table near where I was sitting. They were all somewhat facing away from me so I didn't worry about staring at them. The girls were young, constantly checking their phones, and were pretty much ignoring the guy. The guy seemed almost obligated to be there, as if it were a study group meeting or something school related.

The girls seemed your run-of-the-mill dimwits. What struck me was that their blotches seemed almost identical in size and shape. This wouldn't have been a big deal if it were yesterday, but yesterday wasn't today. Today the resolution was turned up. Their blotches held the same proportions and both had similar symmetrical angles. There were also hints of appendages almost. It was as if the true forms of the blotches were trying to press through a thick wall of gray cotton. There were forms within the formless. The girls' blotches were definitely different from the guy's. I probably wouldn't have even registered it if it were just the two of them but the guy's blotch stood in definite contrast to the girls'.

Despite my shitty drawing skills, I grabbed a pencil and attempted to sketch out the shapes of their blotches and jotted down some notes about how the dimwits had almost identical ones. As I was putting this new info down in the journal, an older guy sat at another table to the right of me. He seemed familiar and I recognized him from around campus. Pretty sure he was a professor who taught over in the philosophy department. His blotch was different in shape and size than the ones I had just sketched. It was also undeniable—his blotch had color.

It wasn't a solid color, still ninety-percent gray, but it looked as if it were rolled one time through some crimson sand. I sketched out the shape and added notes about the color. I decided it was time to also start adding notes about the actual people tethered to the blotches. This guy is a professor and has this particular shaped blotch with some crimson. These girls are dimwits and have this particular shape with no color yet.

The wheels then started spinning. I wondered if Ariel had the same blotch shape as the two dimwits. She was a dimwit. Maybe all dimwits had similar blotches. The eye doctor I just went to had some semblance of red in her blotch like the professor sitting next to me. Maybe red equates to being educated or being a pompous prick or something. I'd need more observations and notes but my gut told me that these things weren't random. There would be definite identifiable patterns once things continued to come into focus.

Focus was the current problem. Things just were too fuzzy at the moment. It was like trying to make out porn on the scrambled pay-per-view channels. I knew something awesome was going on but I just couldn't see it clearly enough to make out what. So what to do? Slip into a vodka and pill coma for three days so I could fast forward and wake up to some higher resolution? Sounded fun but there had to be something somewhat constructive to be done even with these things still out of focus.

Think! Patterns are what I needed to concentrate on. Study the patterns of particular groups of people who are of the same mentality. Like the dimwits, I needed to find a concentration of dimwits in one place and see if their blotches match.   The bagel shop was too general and random in its clientele. Where was a location that attracted a specific kind of person? It didn't necessarily have to be dimwits, although a frat or sorority might be hotspots. Where? Where do people of a similar character go and come together in bunches?

Chapter Twenty-Two
Strip Club

Believe it or don't, I hate strip clubs. A lot of things are lost on me. Tattoos, stretched-out earlobes, moustaches, roller-blades, pop music, hand-jobs. These are all kinds of things in which any appeal is enigmatic to me. Just don't get it. Strip clubs are one of these things. There was no kind of happiness or entertainment for me to extract from going to these places. I always would feel embarrassed for everyone involved and abused by the overinflated drink prices.

Regardless of my dislike for these places, I did happen to know for some reason that Angel's Cabaret opened at 11:00 am and had a free lunch buffet with paid admission before 2:00 pm. Just some random strip club information that men inherently know, like shoe sale information is inherent to women.

So that would be the next move—a trip to Angel's Cabaret for some field research. After finishing up the bagel sandwich, I walked back to my apartment to get my car. Stopped by an ATM to make a forty-dollar withdrawal so as to avoid the eight-dollar surcharge at the strip club ATM. A quick trip to Campus Liquor to break a twenty on a pack of gum. Three singles was about all I was planning on spending once inside the strip club. Fifteen minutes later, I was in the parking lot of Angel's.

Angel's was one of the seedier strip joints in the city, with a one-and-a-half-star rating on the strip club review forum. The girls were all busted. The ambiance was sullen. The sound system never really worked correctly and fell victim to random crackles of static. There was really nothing to hang your hat on. I figured this to be ideal seeing the so-called nicer strip clubs closer to downtown catered to a younger, hipper and more diverse clientele.

The shithole I was about to walk into was on the outskirts of an industrial area and catered to a specific type of person. The people that went here were the same ones you'd see walking into the adult book store at one in the morning by themselves. These guys were all local, had at least one or two hustles going on at any given time and treated this strip club like a charging station for an electric car. This was their church, of sorts, where their blackened spirits fed off the greasy energy this place generated.

Locked my car and made my way to the entrance. The huge and angry-looking doorman patted me down. Paid my ten-dollar admission that got me in the door with a red wristband for access to their shoestring lunch buffet. It was almost a criminal use of the term buffet. It consisted of cheap potato chips dumped into a bin, a heating tray full of hotdogs and what looked to be microwavable pizza rolls. The food did fit the overall quality of this place though.

They didn't appear to have a cleaning crew and the place felt saturated with years of filth and stripper sweat. As soon as I walked in, the smell of the room slapped me in the face kind of like the flamingo smell at the zoo slapped all the park visitors in the face. The smell inside the main room of Angel's was different but equally as rancid as the flamingo shit-lake. If the smell of this place was bottled and sold as a perfume, it'd be called *Raw Wolf-Pussy*. The red wristband to the lunch buffet would not be utilized.

The place was like any other strip club but with an extra layer of clam-slime and despair. It was dark with a walkway and stage in the middle. There were chairs and small tables running parallel to the stage on both sides. Against the walls were sticky-looking booths with strips of duct tape used for patchwork on the split vinyl. There was a bar on one wall and the rest of the walls were all mirrored. There was pink lighting above the mirrors that gave the entire place a fuzzy atmosphere. There was one dimly lit hallway by the bar with an ATM at its entrance. The hallway led to the restroom. Past the restroom the hallway led to the champagne room or, more accurately for this place, the crystal meth room.

I took a seat towards the back, away from the stage, in one of the booths. The place had only been open for thirty minutes or so but there were at least twenty other patrons scattered around the room. The girl on the stage was at least sixty-five pounds overweight. She had glitter on her large stomach that reflected the stage-lights in a way that highlighted her C-section scar. The other girls working the floor were all either sloppily overweight or had a drug-weary thinness to them. The girls were a wide array of unhealthy.

The other patrons were all men and all by themselves. This place didn't attract the frat boys or chicks who think they are cool for going to a strip club. No, this place remained open thanks to the lone degenerate locals. Thankfully, the strippers were all occupied with the regulars, leaving me free to observe without distraction.

I started with the girls and for the most part my hypothesis wasn't satisfied. The girl currently on stage with the glittered C-section scar had a distinct blotch shape that I hadn't seen yet. While facing her directly, her blotch was wide at the top and narrowed down like an upside-down triangle. There was no mistaking that I saw hints of yellow. I opened my journal and made a quick sketch of her blotch and made a quick note, "overweight C-section stripper," underneath it.

I surveyed the other girls and found a match. There was one other stripper with the exact same blotch hovering over her. There were twelve strippers total working here. There was only the one match amongst them and the other ten all had unique blotches from one another. Even though there was only one true match, the other blotches all kind of seemed to be from the same ethereal dumpster. It was kind of like how an orangutan and a baboon aren't identical, but they both kind of feel like they're in the same animal category. That's the vibe I got from all of the stripper blotches.

Well, there was one exception. There was one stripper who was completely out of place. She was by far the most attractive girl in there. It wasn't even close. She hadn't talked to anyone since I arrived as she just sort of strolled around the perimeter not coming too close to anyone else. She and her blotch both gave off a different vibe than all the others. Her blotch had a form kind of like an upright cocoon with vertical rows of something. I couldn't make it out but it reminded me of an elongated ribcage. It had a bluish tint. I sketched out her blotch and wrote down some notes about her.

After I was done sketching and taking notes on the other stripper blotches, I then concentrated on the patrons. There were twenty-three total. They were different types of guys.

Some seriously slimy-looking, like they'd have no problem masturbating in public through a self-made hole in their pants pockets.

Then there were some small foreign-looking jittery guys who looked like they had cooking oil seeping from their pores.

Then there were a couple middle-aged overweight guys.

Those guys all seemed to be there not out of entertainment or horniness but more on the side of a necessity for human contact. It was a charming group.

Out of the twenty-three of them I found two blotch matches. So nineteen out of the twenty-three were unique from one another. So the thought crossed my mind that I was possibly dealing with an incredibly large pool of blotch variations.

Wrote down my notes and made some sketches. As I was involved with my journal, I didn't notice that the one attractive stripper who was roaming the perimeter had approached my booth and slid in on the opposite side of my table. She asked me, "What are you doing here?"

Up close and under the lighting above the booth, she was actually really pretty. Too pretty for this place even with the shit tribal tattoo she had that started from her shoulder and ended up halfway up her neck. Her eyes were sharp and unglazed, unlike the other strippers who all seemed to be on pills of some sort. I closed my journal and responded, "Sorry, is this a VIP booth or something?"

"No, I mean what are you doing here at Angel's?"

"I just had some time to kill and was in the neighborhood."

"Seriously, why are you in here?"

"I'm not following. I got my wristband, see? I paid my admission and just want to hang out for a bit and kill some time."

"Here's the deal, this place runs off the money of regulars. You're not a regular. This place doesn't attract non-regulars. So when a non-regular comes in and sits down and starts writing in a book, that's something that might make my regulars feel uneasy and that's not good for business. So I'll ask you again, what are you doing here? Just be honest with me and I'll see about not having the bouncers take you to the parking lot and do things to you."

"Are you serious?"

"I don't know, what do your kidneys tell you?"

I glanced around the room. The bartender was a big muscle-bound fucker. The doorman consisted of more fat than muscle but stood about six-foot four. I didn't know if this girl was kidding or not but I didn't feel any need to roll the dice with my kidneys.

"Alright, you win. I'm not a strip club patron. I hate strip clubs."

"And you are here because . . . ?"

"I'm a psychology major with a minor in journalism. I figured a story on the strip-club scene would make a good paper that I could use for my major and minor at the same time."

Pretty good fucking lie if I don't say so myself. She looked at me, then at my journal.

"So what's the paper about?"

"It's about the different psychological profiles of strippers and strip club patrons. I'm trying to paint a picture of how similar types of people are drawn to be strippers while other types of similar people are drawn to patronizing strip clubs habitually. It's kind of a symbiotic organism made up of broken people."

"Did you just call me broken?"

"Honestly, I don't know what you are. You don't seem like you belong here either."

"How is that?"

"Five of the girls working the room are sloppily overweight and appear to be pilled-out on OxyContin. My guess is that they are embarrassed about how they look in general, but working here and being pilled-out while guys actually pay attention to them gives them a sad sense of self-worth.

"The three girls with the cancer-physiques working the floor are obvious tweekers. If this were Vegas I'd give them the benefit of the doubt and say they might be on coke, but you and I both know girls who look like that and work in a place like this can't afford a coke habit.

"Then the other three girls don't appear drugged but stink of depression. Maybe they have an abusive boyfriend at home or even worse a couple of kids that they have no other way of supporting. Whatever it is, they are an unhappy bunch, completely different but equally broken in one way or the other. Then there's you."

"Do tell."

"You don't fit. If you are on anything it is probably either an energy drink or coffee. If it weren't for the tattoo on your neck, you could probably be a model. You walk around the room with a confidence and stability none of the other girls have. You don't fit at all. So why don't you answer your own question and tell me what you are doing here?"

"So you are a journalist, huh? How much cash do you have on you, journalist?"

"Why's that?"

"How much?"

"I've got like twenty-eight dollars and some change. Why?"

"Give me the eight dollars."

"Why would I give you eight dollars?"

"You're a journalist, aren't you? Eight dollars will buy you some information and a trip to the champagne room."

"Champagne room? Isn't it like a two-hundred-dollar minimum just to go back there and sit down?"

"You are starting to bore me now with the questions. Give me eight dollars and follow me to the champagne room or take your little book and walk out the front door. Those are the only two options you have. Make a decision."

I glanced towards the door, trying to hide my undeserved excitement. Here I had a beautiful stripper offering me an eight-dollar trip to the champagne room. I pulled out my cash and counted off the five and three ones, returning the remaining twenty-dollar bill to my pocket. I handed her the money.

"Here you go."

She took the bills and got up and walked over to me. She grabbed my hand. I grabbed my journal with my free hand and got up from my seat. She led me down the dimly lit hallway and made a left after the bathrooms. We continued down a shorter hallway ending with a door with a tinted window. She opened it up, flipped on the lights and led me in, closing the door behind her.

The room looked like a large version of the backseat of a limo. There were a lot of mirrors and a lot of vinyl bench seating. She took me to the back of the room and pushed me down onto the seat. I looked up at her in anticipation of I don't know what. Even with her blotch hovering over her and the shitty tattoo on her neck and shoulder, she was absolutely stunning. After looking at me for ten seconds or so, she smiled and sat down across from me. I guess a smile is all you got for eight bucks in the champagne room.

She asked, "So what's your name, journalist?"

"Serin."

"Serin? Unique. I like it."

"And your name? Are you allowed to let me know your real name or do I have to call you by your strip club alias? Destiny? Felony?"

"My real name is Evelyn."

"Pretty. And what's your strip club name?"

"Joy."

"So Joy, are you going to tell me what I get for my eight dollars?"

"Don't get too excited. I can't be seen talking to anyone for too long or the regulars will wonder why I don't talk to them at length. It's a rare occasion that this room gets used with this clientele, so it's the best place to have a conversation."

Conversation. Damn!

"You were relatively spot-on out there with your observations. Although the bigger girls are on Xanax and the skinny ones are snorting Ritalin. One of the regulars is a pharmacist of sorts and takes care of the girls with pills."

"And you?"

"Just coffee."

"But why are you here? I was right that you really don't belong here, correct?"

"You're not too far off on me either. I was never a stripper and currently am not a stripper. You'll never see me up on stage or giving anyone a lap dance or wearing less than what I'm wearing now. I'm more of a strip club muse."

"A strip club muse?"

"Basically, I was recruited by the owner whom I met through mutual friends. He offered me a percentage of the nightly take for just hanging out. He said his pool of talent wasn't so talented and if I were around for his regulars to look at then that would get them more active with his girls."

"That's fucking nuts. Does that even work?"

"I guess. Two months in and I'm still getting a paycheck."

"Is it worth it? It seems sort of a depressing place to be working."

"I was a barista for seven months before I started here. That was depressing, how much I was getting paid. I just treat this as an acting job that pays really well and nothing more. I mean, what I'm wearing now is actually something I usually wear to the beach so it's not really a big deal to me."

"Not to sound like a douche but it seems like you got your shit together. Can I ask why the tattoo?"

She smiled and moved her shoulder strap down to the side of her shoulder. That small act set fireworks off in my chest and elsewhere. She licked her finger then started rubbing the part of the tattoo that had just been covered by her shoulder strap. After about ten seconds she removed her finger exposing a now blank spot in her tattoo. She leaned in so I could get a better look at it then returned her strap to cover the erased spot of the tattoo.

"It's an airbrushed stencil. My friend majors in art and has all kinds of art supplies including non-toxic body paints. Under the dim lighting of this place it looks pretty real. Looking trashy is just a part of the act."

"So you're just as much of an imposter as I am."

"I think you are more of an imposter than you are letting on. I'm not buying the journalist angle. You've got something else going on."

"Why would you say that?"

"Can I have a look in your book?"

"I'd probably have to say no."

"Need I say more?"

"No. You're right. I've got a situation which is a bit beyond explanation right now. I'm not evil or anything, it's just that you're a strip club muse I barely know and this situation is a bit out of the range of a getting-to-know-you conversation."

She looked me over and seemed to be contemplating some kind of decision in her mind.

"Give me your pen."

I handed over my pen and she picked up a cocktail napkin and wrote her name and number on it, then handed the pen and napkin to me.

"You're giving me your number?"

"I don't know. You coming into a strip club mid-day doing God knows what, making up lies about being a journalist should be a blazing red flag. But you did say you thought I could be a model and said it not in a sleazy pick-up way but in a matter-of-fact kind of way. Might just be a side-effect of being in this creep-infested environment but if you want, give me a call and I'll treat you with your eight dollars to some coffee and maybe you can tell me something that's not a lie. As for now, I have to get back on the floor and muse it up."

I was stunned. Girls who looked like this didn't do things like that to guys like me.

"Could you do me a favor and tell me now when I should call you. If you don't, I'll probably call you from my car in the parking lot in five minutes."

"Wow, a liar and kind of pathetic. I'm busy tomorrow, so the day after. Call me in the morning."

She smiled and left the room, followed by her blotch. Sexy blotch.

I sat there in shock for a minute then made my way out the front entrance and out to my car. Plugged her number into my phone with the name *Evelyn the strip club muse.* Ariel who? Elation. The power of a pretty girl. My whole blotch world situation temporarily lost some virility. Focus, my son, focus. A pretty girl is great and all, but your world is still fucked. Keep the focus on the issues at hand and not your hand on the rising issue in your pants.

Chapter Twenty-Two
Focus

The exhilaration from my encounter with Evelyn needed to be put on hold as I settled myself down and tried to think of my next move. Sitting in the strip club parking lot wasn't an ideal spot for peaceful thinking. The neighborhood riff-raff seemed to ooze out of the shadows like worms from dirt. My thinking needed to be done elsewhere, so I buckled-up and made my way back to my own zip code.

With the stench of the strip club fading from my nose, my appetite resurfaced. I made my way to the parking lot of Los Jalapeños, the shitty Mexican joint with cheap shitty Mexican food I always ended up going to. Got the usual, a carne asada burrito and a beer, then posted up at an outside table to eat and people-watch.

What next? It was hard trying to focus after the encounter I just had with the stripper muse. Evelyn was a spray of stripper-glitter across my thought process and made it impossible to concentrate. At that moment, I couldn't see past her.

The struggle to think strategy lasted for about fifteen minutes when my stomach interrupted to tell me my new strategy would be to quickly close the gap between me and my own bathroom. This food was nothing more than a delicious broadband laxative. Not even halfway through the carne de burro burrito I could already feel the newly ingested food starting a revolución in my guts. Well, what better place to do some thinking than the porcelain library.

Took a last bite, pounded the last of the beer, then had a race with the devil trying to get home before the revolución spilled across the border. Shuffled into my apartment then disrobed, seeing as how I was pretty sure I'd need a second shower once I was done. Fifteen minutes of porcelain followed by ten minutes of showering led to two ideas.

Idea #1 – no more eating at Los Jalapeños. I'm not sure if I have IBS or something, but Los Jalapeños doesn't mesh well with my digestive sensibilities.

Idea #2 – visit people I knew already. I wasn't complaining about how things went at the strip club but I should have thought of this to begin with. Friends, family and acquaintances. People I knew for better or for mostly worse. I guess I was assuming all the strippers and strip club patrons had the same exact personalities but there was no real way of knowing for sure. No, this new idea was a better route. Visit people I already had relationships with and whose personalities I needn't assume anything about.

Toweled off and got dressed, then slumped onto my couch with my journal. Started writing profiles of people I knew personally and were within driving distance. Most of my family were up North but my Uncle Chester was only a thirty-minute drive away. My mother's brother Chester was a degenerate gambler and alcoholic. He'd been divorced twice. His license had been restricted because of two DUIs. He had three illegitimate kids he never talked to. Cool guy, actually.

I turned the page and wrote a profile for Angie. Angie was a lunatic masquerading as a sorority girl. We met at a house party and went on a handful of dates. I don't know how or when, but she had managed to install a GPS tracking app on my phone when I wasn't looking so she could keep tabs on my location without me knowing it. I also started noticing texts and emails I hadn't read yet were marked as read. In less than three weeks of dating she already let the facade slip, exposing a paranoid, jealous, intrusive serpent. I took the mature route with Angie and blocked her number, blocked her email and told my friends to tell her an emergency came up and I had to move to Panama.

I continued writing profiles in my journal until I had twelve solid personalities of people I knew and could track down. It was as good a plan as I could come up with. Grabbed my backpack, threw in my journal, then headed back out into the blotch-filled world.

First stop, Red's Tavern.

Chapter Twenty-Four
McBride

Red's Tavern was a shitty dive bar. The only reason it was in business was that it was within walking distance of campus. This place was a hundred percent location and zero percent aesthetic. The booths were dirty and beat up like at the strip club. The floor was sticky from all the spilt drinks and the décor on the walls consisted of a couple of broken strings of x-mas lights and three unframed posters of skateboarders, two of them with long tears in them. The only upside, apart from the location, was that I knew one of the bartenders who poured most of my drinks for free.

I walked over to Red's Tavern which was just over a mile from my apartment. It was a little past 4:00 pm when I arrived and walked through the door. The place was pretty dead as it usually was that early in the day. I grabbed a stool at the bar and spotted McBride by the floor, changing out a keg.

McBride was a fringe friend I just sort of came to know through knowing the same people and being in the same partying circles. Still, to this day, I don't know his first name. McBride is what I'd call a wound-up East Coast goon. I liked him because he was funny and a good guy to have on your side. But the guy had an instigating violent nature about him. He was always the first guy at the party to rip his shirt off and jump into the static if any situation ever arose. If there were no situations for him to tangle with, then he would tend to create a situation so he could satiate his thirst for disorder. His blotch loomed over him, neon greenish with what looked to be wing-like structures coming from its sides.

He was still focused on the keg, so I pulled out my journal and flipped to the page I had just created for him back at my apartment. I drew a quick sketch, then added notes on the color.

It kind of hit me then that if I were to continue cataloguing people and seeing if certain personalities and their blotches matched others, I was going to need to have a streamlined and uniform description setup. A personality cheat sheet. I could take as many notes as needed but I wanted a simple *quick-trait* identifier for each blotch. It needed to sum up the person's personality in five or less words.

Like for instance, if I ended up cataloguing Ariel's blotch, her quick-trait would be something like *vapid twat*. Then, moving forward, every time I saw someone with the same blotch, I could go straight to the quick-trait and say, "Hey, there goes another vapid twat." At the top of McBride's page I wrote *The Violent but Loyal Jester*. I finished writing my notes and closed my journal. McBride finished with the keg, stood up and noticed me at the bar.

"Aye, yo, Serin, what up there, bitchy-lips? I knew you was a sissy and all but didn't know you kept a diary. What you writing about there, all the pricks that visit ya mouth?"

"McB, you know they offer elocution classes at the university right? A couple semesters of hard work and maybe you can get rid of that half-rat accent of yours."

"Aw, tough guy, uh? What you want, little girl, wine coola o' somethin? Tampon?"

"A Severus should suffice, preferably in a glass not exposed to your Hep-C."

"Aw, bitch-nutz, it's you I heard got them monkey herpes. How much that Valtrex costin ya?"

He poured me my beer and walked to the back. I slipped my journal in my backpack so as to avoid any more inquiries. He walked back over to me and slapped a piece of paper on the counter.

"Check this out, Gladys. Gonna be mad chickies at this."

I looked at the cheap-looking flyer. It read, "Party at the Lex. Dj Methmerize with Yellow Pony."

"The Lex is a shithole. You work in a shithole and choose to go to a different shithole after work? Why you like shitholes so much, Shitty McShits?"

"Ya betta watch your shithole, Herby Herb, before I take your manhood from ya. What, you don't like honeys or somethin? Lex is going to be snatch-packed tonight. What you got betta? Watchin fuckin dat fatty-foot porn and wackin off?"

"Sounds better than going to that shithole Lex and navigating through all the junkies."

"What you got against junkies, you fucking drunk? At least them drugs keeps them girls skinny."

"And less teeth to worry about while getting blown, right?"

"Got that right, Susie."

Two girls and a guy walked in and sat down at the other end of the bar. McBride made his way down to them and got their drink order. I got what I came for and knew if I stayed any longer I'd get strong-armed into going to the Lex with McBride. I pounded my beer which wasn't the easiest or wisest way to drink a Severus, having an alcohol percentage of nine and a half. Got up and grabbed my backpack and started walking to the door.

"Later, McB. Try not to step on any hypodermics at the Lex tonight."

"Outta here already, puss?"

"Nine minutes is all I can handle of you and this place."

"I got nine inches you can handle wheneva you ready, jerky jerk."

I walked out of Red's and broke the tractor beam of McBride. If I had another beer he would have convinced me to go to the Lex. I liked hanging out with him but it was almost a guarantee at a venue like the Lex that McBride would be starting some shit with some other degenerates just for the sake of starting shit and I'm never in the mood for that. I'm what you would call an apathetic pacifist with a strong confrontation aversion.

Five steps out of the bar and the beer injection gave me a head-change. Things got glassy and smiley. The temptation was strong to walk right back into Red's for another but I resisted. It was still early and I wanted to catalogue one more of the dozen personalities I had outlined before the day was up.

There was one more out of the twelve that was within walking distance. This one still resonated echoes of confusion and embarrassment for me. The frustrating desire for some closure had never subsided after all this time. I was hesitant but if I was going to pursue this cataloguing idea, then this one made sense and needed to get done. The thought of seeing her again still made me feel awkward though.

At least I was hungry.

Chapter Twenty-Five
Pizza Slim's

After a seven-block hike from Red's Tavern, I was walking through the entrance of Pizza Slim's. It was kind of an oxymoronic name but Pizza Fat's didn't have that appetizing of a ring to it, I guess. P-Slim's was once one of my favorite spots, back in the day. Dim lighting, cheap but good food, solid beer selection, acid jazz playing just loud enough and a handful of old-school video games and pinball machines in the corner. For twenty bucks you could get fed, buzzed and play pinball for a couple of hours. Loved me some P-Slim's.

There was only one thing that kept me away from this place over the last year, that one thing being Loren, the girl working the counter and the person I was here to see. Loren was dirty-pretty.

She had tattoos on both of her upper arms and four or five piercings in each ear and a stud in her nose. There wasn't any kind of uniform for P-Slim's employees so they dressed however they wanted. Loren dressed in ripped up old concert t-shirts with the sleeves cut off and the same weathered black shorts every time I saw her. She wore minimal make-up and had dyed purple streaks coursing through her hair that she usually put up in pigtails.

Somewhere in there, behind the layer of bad decisions, was a strangely attractive girl. I'm just talking about her exterior. It was her exterior that caught my attention at a house party about a year ago. Her interior, from what I had glimpsed, was a hellish carnival of fuckery.

117

I had seen her at P-Slim's on many an occasion as I used to go there all the time with my friends. I didn't pay her much attention at first but on some days, in a certain light, usually two to three pitchers of beer deep, I started to see the diamond in the rough. There was something about her you couldn't quite put your finger on but were drawn to. The more I frequented the place, the more she became someone I caught myself stealing glances at. Then one night our paths crossed out in public and I'd been sort of emotionally scarred ever since.

So one night last summer, I ended up at a house party with some friends. It was your typical college affair. A couple of kegs, loud music, drinking games and a long line at the bathroom. This house had a decent-sized backyard where most of the people were hanging out. Inside, on the kitchen counter, was where all the alcohol bottles and mixers were set up. I had been at the party for a while when I had noticed Loren had entered the party through the backyard gate. She was an easy person to spot in a crowd, with her unique style and purple-streaked hair. She arrived with a small group of people that all kind of looked and dressed like her.

I had made my way into the kitchen at some point to mix myself a cocktail. At that same time, Loren walked in by herself with the same intention of making herself a drink. I was somewhat buzzed and decided I'd try talking to her as she was literally right next to me. She was dirty-pretty so I didn't feel the same intimidation as I would have had if I were striking up a conversation with a girl that was clean-pretty.

"Hey. You work at Pizza Slim's, right?" I asked her.

"Yes I do. You work at NAMBLA, right?"

"What was that?"

"You work at NAMBLA. I've seen your picture on the website. You work to abolish laws that prohibit you from legally having sex with little boys."

"Why would you say that?"

"Why do you want to have sex with little boys? This isn't ancient Greece, Socrates. Try fucking boys your own age."

I was lost and a bit scared. All I could manage was, "Alright. You win."

I finished mixing my drink and walked away from her a bit shell-shocked. I didn't know if she was serious or just fucking with me. With each step I took away from her, I considered walking straight out the door and away from this party just in case she was fully cracked-out and was going to call the cops on me or something. It was a weird encounter and I was rattled. I walked outside and was ten feet from my friends, and five feet behind them was the gate that led out of the backyard and out of this party. I was leaning more towards escape than friends.

While maneuvering past some people, someone grabbed my shoulder. I turned around and saw it was her. She leaned in close to me and kissed me on the cheek.

"Why did you run away so fast? A gentleman would have waited for the lady to finish making her drink."

I was frightened yet intrigued. No matter the circumstances, if a girl you don't know kisses your cheek, your dick hits override on the brain and takes the wheel. Didn't they make that into a country song? *Penis Take the Wheel* or something?

"I'm not much of gentleman, I guess. Any particular reason for what you were saying back in the kitchen?"

"I thought it'd be fun to see how you reacted."

"Fun?"

"Plus, you carry yourself like a pedophile."

I considered walking away again but she leaned in and kissed my cheek again and grabbed my hand. I reluctantly let her lead me past my friends and out the backyard gate into the dark and quiet surrounding neighborhood. We got out to the curb and she sat down on the sidewalk with her feet in the gutter. She was wearing a sleeveless vest, kind of safari-like but grungy with a couple of sewn-on patches and some random drawings and words in black marker. It looked like it was designed by a hipster street dweller.

I took a seat next to her, somewhat amused, somewhat curious, and somewhat excited as to what was coming next. She reached into a vest pocket and pulled out two pills. She put one in her mouth and followed it with a sip of her drink. She put the second one into her mouth then turned to me, grabbed my hair and kissed me, transferring the second pill to my mouth with her tongue. What was this, cyanide? Cialis? My fight-or-flight instincts kicked in and I was milliseconds from spitting the pill into the gutter. But in the dim light of the street, I looked into her deeply confident eyes and swallowed. Buy the ticket, take the ride.

"My hero."

"Any chance you'll tell me what that was?"

"Mescaline."

Mescaline! Fuck! Have I ever taken mescaline? Is that an upper, downer or side-wayser? The anxiety must have been easy to spot on my face. She grabbed my hand and kissed the back of it.

"Don't worry, it's nothing violent. It'll just put a nice glaze on things for a couple of hours."

"Okay. So now what?"

"Now, we walk."

"Where to?"

"Somewhere with trees."

She got up and started walking down the street, away from the party. Induce vomiting and go home or a trip down the rabbit hole with this slippery weasel of a girl? My fingers slowly started to creep upwards towards my mouth to tickle my uvula. She looked back at me.

"Is your cowardice getting the better of you?"

She continued walking backwards while looking at me. She held out her hands and waved them inwards, beckoning me to follow her. Penis took the wheel. I caught up to her and she turned around and led the way. We walked for twenty minutes or so. The conversation consisted of her singing under her breath some off-key dark melody you'd hear come out of a broken pipe organ in a haunted pagan church.

The minutes passed by and the glaze from the pill she force-tongued me started creeping in. The street lights started glistening and vibrating a bit. The strange melody she had been singing the whole time transitioned from mildly annoying to hauntingly beautiful. I spotted a cat lying underneath a parked car across the street, casually watching us walk through its territory. That cat knew something. My thoughts started to get away from me. Something about that cat. Who is he to be judging me? He's just a stupid cat.

I was getting lost in my head and almost didn't notice that this girl I was following had stopped walking. I stopped and looked to take in where we were. We were at the end of a cul-de-sac.

"Where are we?"

"Almost there."

"Almost where?"

She walked up to me and gave me a hug. I hugged her back. It was a comforting drug-hug. I was back in the womb, completely enveloped and safe from the world. She stepped back and stuck her sharp fingernail in the center of my chest

121

then quickly sliced downward. Did she just draw blood? I grabbed at my chest to feel for wetness. She smiled and started walking towards the house at the end of the cul-de-sac. I followed. She headed off to the side of the house when I noticed the trail. A dirt patch that headed down a small ravine and into the darkness. I hesitated a second even though she didn't.

I took a breath and then caught up with her. It was a narrow three-foot-wide trail with weeds and brush on both sides. We walked. Behind us was the cul-de-sac. Up a ways ahead I could see lights from other houses. This trail was a shortcut between neighborhoods.

We got about halfway down the trail when she stopped. To our left was an incline covered with ice plants. To our right there was a wall of trees leading down into an absolute darkness. The moon was out in full and gave the only light in this part of the trail but no light penetrated the wall of trees and it looked like the world ended about three feet past them. It made me uneasy, like standing near the edge of a cliff. My mind was conjuring dark thoughts of unearthly hands shooting out from the darkness and pulling me into the void.

She walked off the trail and up the incline about fifteen feet, then laid down on the ice plants, looking up at the sky. I wanted nothing more than to get away from those trees, so I quickly headed up to where she was and laid down next to her. The sky looked fantastic. Did it always look this great? It looked like someone polished it up with some industrial glass cleaner. The moon was amazingly white and radiating. It was the greatest sky I had ever seen. I couldn't remember the last time I even bothered looking up at our part of the universe.

It kind of made me feel uneasy again, as if gravity might stop working and I was going to start floating up into space. My right hand instinctively grabbed a handful of ice plant just in case the gravity thing happened. I tried to shake off these thoughts and focus on the girl next to me who had me out here on this strange expedition.

"So what's your name?" I asked her.

"Why?"

"Why? I don't know. Customary getting-to-know-you type of stuff?"

"You want to get to know me? Why?"

"Why not? We are taking drugs together on the side of a hill. Is asking your name really so intrusive?"

She rolled over on top of me and pushed herself up so she could stare into my eyes. Her eyes were wild. If she had pulled out a knife and cut off a slice of her own cheek at that moment, I wouldn't have been surprised.

"My name is Loren. There. You happy now?"

Before I could say anything, she grabbed my face and kissed me. The drugs, the girl, the location, sparked a parade of adrenaline and electricity down my spine. I put my hand on the side of her face and was pricked by one of the many earrings in her ear. Without warning, she broke the kiss and rolled off me and stood up.

"I live right over there in that neighborhood. I'm going to run home real quick and get something. I'll be right back."

"Can I go with you?"

"No, wait here for me. Give me fifteen minutes."

She shuffled down to the trail and started jogging down the dirt path and quickly faded into the darkness. My heart was tingling. I looked at my phone for the time. 9:45 pm. Okay, she'll be back by 10:00 pm. I laid on my back, staring up at the sky, replaying that kiss. I felt like gravity did weaken a bit and that I was almost hovering on the tips of the ice plants.

After ten minutes went by, I turned on my side so I could monitor the trail for her return. It was dark down the path and the shadows were playing with my mind. A dozen different times I thought I saw movement but it was only the shadows.

After twenty minutes went by, I walked down to the trail and just stared down it. The void behind the tree to my right was really bothering me, especially now that I was by myself. I stood on the ice plant side of the trail trying to keep my distance from the wall of trees but still be able to see down the trail.

After thirty minutes went by I decided to walk in her direction and meet her halfway.

I reached the end of the trail which deposited me into the middle of a street. I looked in both directions but saw zero activity. I took a seat on the ground near the trail entrance and waited another ten minutes. Nothing. Twenty minutes. Nothing. I thought maybe she somehow took a different route and was waiting for me on the side of the hill in the ice plants. So I headed back down the trail to the spot of the kiss. Nothing. I felt a steel-toed boot of despair kick me in the chest. Any delusions of her coming back dissipated.

I eventually gave up hope and made the long walk back to the house party. That stupid cat was still under the car across the street and was mocking me.

Once I made it back to the party, I did a quick walkthrough as a last desperate attempt to see if maybe she'd come back to the party looking for me. She wasn't there. I resigned myself to the disenchanting probability that I got ditched or possibly she fell victim to a werewolf or something that lived in the ravine.

I walked back to my apartment and rode out the remainder of the mescaline high in a miserable funk. The following day I felt depressed. What happened last night? I had to get some kind of an answer. I cleaned myself up and waited around until

11:30 am then walked over to P-Slim's. And there she was behind the counter.

I waited in line behind a couple of other people ordering food. When it was my turn, she registered no signs of recognition and simply asked, "What can I get for you?" I ordered a slice of pizza and a beer and sat at a table facing the counter hoping to catch her looking my way at some point. She didn't. She did, however, walk around the counter and went outside to talk to some guy who pulled into the parking lot on a crotch-rocket and had two sleeves of tattoos. After a couple of minutes of talking to him, she stuck her tongue in his mouth for a good twenty seconds before returning to work.

That was my Loren experience. Just a random encounter at a house party generated an avalanche of mixed emotions and memories. I stopped going to P-Slim's after that because I didn't want to be around her. She had stuck her hooks into me that night with the drugs, her erratic appeal and the spontaneous affection. It was the perfect chemical and psychological spell she cast on me. She was something out of ancient mythology. The greasy siren.

So a year later, there I sat at P-Slim's at a table closest to the counter. I got a slice of pizza and a beer and once again no recognition from Loren who had changed the purple streaks in her hair to orange. Her new hair color was close to the color of the blotch that was hovering over her. It had strong and distinct angles and appendages to it. It was still out of focus but what I could see strongly resembled something insect-like. It fit her well, like a tick that burrowed its way into my brain and refused to leave. I sketched it out and took my notes while eating and drinking.

Next to her sketch I wrote, "Dirty-Pretty Temptress."

M. J. WATERS

Chapter Twenty
Strobe-Effect

When I was done with my pizza and beer, I threw out my trash and headed towards the door. Before heading out the door, I took one last look back at Loren. After walking outside, I felt a small pang of sadness. It didn't seem like this Loren thing deserved to be classified as legitimate. I mean if you took a second to analyze it, whatever relationship we had lasted a total of forty minutes. Apart from our house-party adventure that one night, she'd only previously been a pizza restaurant worker I occasionally looked at from a distance. There was no denying what she made me feel though. For some fucked-up bizarre reason, this was definitely a heart crush.

I had planned on going to try and hunt down one more person on my list before the day was over, but being around Loren again kind of got me sulking and robbed me of any ambition I might have had. So instead I decided I was going to grab some wine at Campus Liquor then go back to my apartment and tune out for the rest of the night.

The route to get back to my apartment took me across the foot bridge near campus. This foot bridge created a walking path over the always-busy four lanes of traffic that travel north and south on College Avenue. Looking down, I could see each vehicle had one or more blotches spilling through their roofs in correlation to the number of passengers each vehicle had.

I was almost all the way across to the other side when I picked up something out of the corner of my eye. For a

127

millisecond, my brain processed it as some kind of police or fire engine light. I turned towards it and realized it was something else completely.

A new low-profile black BMW with tinted windows was about to pass under the foot bridge. It was weaving through traffic and going fast. I couldn't focus in on it quick enough and had to run to the other side of the walkway to catch it as it came out from under the bridge. When it reappeared, I saw what had caught my eye. There were two blotches coming from the roof of the BMW. The driver's was normal but there was one in the back seat that was flickering like a strobe light at a dance club. I watched it for about five seconds before it disappeared down and around the bend in the road. Looking around at the other cars and people walking over the foot bridge, no other blotches were flickering. What the fuck was that?

When I got back to my place, I wrote some notes in my journal about the flickering blotch I had just seen. A half of a Valium was then washed down with some of the wine I had just bought. After the last couple of days full of zoos, strip clubs and seeing Loren, I felt used up and exhausted. I zoned out on TV and tried to pretend things were normal. It was nice that the blotches only appeared in person, so everyone on TV looked clean.

My mind still dwelled on my situation though. I wondered if anyone else out there could see the same shit I was seeing. I mean, something in my brain, something that processes the visual spectrum was switched on or some kind of filter was switched off. You'd have to figure this even being a possibility of the brain, it had to have happened to someone else before me.

Maybe this change in perception could be triggered by some other means and not just some ancient rainforest flower ejaculate to the eyeball. Maybe it'd been triggered before in others with a blow to the head or a bite from a plague-monkey or something. I couldn't be the only one who's ever seen behind this curtain. Maybe there was a whole community of people out there with the same dysfunction I had. Maybe they had their own website and message board. CrazyShitIAmSeeing.com. Might be worth checking out. Some internet spelunking. Not tonight though.

The eyelids were losing the fight against gravity.

Chapter Twenty-Seven
Angie, Me and Uncle C

Awoke around 9:20 am and laid in bed a minute staring at the ceiling, recalling bits of a dream I had last night that involved Loren. We were back on that ice-plant-covered slope. I remember being hit with fear as I looked down the slope and saw the wall of trees. There was definitely something unnatural moving around in the shadows, like black hairless human-sized monkeys all staring at me.

I suppressed that part of the dream and managed to turn and concentrate on Loren. There was a time-skip and when the dream picked up it seemed like we were in the middle of a yearlong conversation that was really deep and involved. Fragments of the conversation skittered across my brain.

She said something like, "I need the tide to reverse. There is no space for us under the bridge."

I replied, "Can you just stay here with me and not float away again?"

I reached for her face but noticed her earrings were a mix of rusted nails and shards of glass. She reached out and held my hand and I felt every molecule of myself flush with a pulsating warm emotion. It was the type of overwhelming powerful feeling you could only experience in the dreamscape.

In dreams, an emotion like fear can be more primal and savage than anything you could experience in the waking world. It was this type of power I had just felt when the dream-Loren held my hand. But it wasn't fear I felt—it was an all-consuming desire to be with her. As I laid awake in my bed, the wonderful comforting afterglow of the dream lingered. What the fuck is up with that girl and her hooks in me? It's some kind of black magic I tell you. Voodoo enchantments of some sort.

I shook off the dream haze, showered, then got dressed. Today's agenda involved visiting as many people as I could on my list, starting with my Uncle Chester. Chester was a creature of habit, so tracking him down was never an issue. He either was sleeping off his hangover in his shit apartment or was at the poker tables at The Flats, an Indian Casino that attracted more local degenerates than tourists.

Then, once his money ran out, he'd usually make his way to the Sleeping Fox, a dive bar a couple of miles from the casino where he could get drunk for twenty bucks. Once he was properly intoxicated, he'd then float his '82 Thunderbird on a drunken voyage home. Catching him early in the day before his fourth beer was the sweet spot to interact with him.

Grabbed my backpack and journal then hopped in my car and headed east. On the drive to Chester's, I noticed that the blotches had taken a significant jump in clarity overnight. Yesterday it was like their true forms were trying to push through a wall of cotton. Today it was as if their true forms were pushing through a half inch of plastic wrap. I could see their colors. All the vague details were now almost clear and the forms I was seeing were unnerving.

Seventeen miles of interstate followed by three twisting miles into nowhere delivered me to the Songbird Manor Residences. This was the shithole apartment complex where my Uncle Chester lived in the middle of a low-rent wasteland.

As I pulled up to a parking spot, I already spotted Chester sitting in his ragged lawn chair on his three-foot by three-foot concrete porch with his apartment door wide open behind him.

He was reading the sports page while sipping what looked to be a cheap beer and tomato juice breakfast smoothie.

His blotch was a new one to me. Dark green and mangled looking. There were large random clumps protruding asymmetrically. In my journal, I sketched out his blotch on the profile page I had already created for him.

Uncle Chester hadn't looked up from his paper when I pulled in. Even though I already had what I came for, I wasn't going to bail without saying hello. He was a fuck-up, but aren't we all in one way or the other. He was just kind of an all-star at being a fuck-up which can be admirable when someone is so unapologetic about it. I got out of my car and made my way to the stairs leading up to his mini-porch.

"Yo, Unk!"

Chester looked up from his paper, then stood up to greet me as I ascended the fourteen stairs.

"Nephew. What you doing out here in the Beverly Swills?"

"Nothing good, Unk. Met a girl on one of these dating apps on my phone. Her picture was an eleven so I rolled the dice and came all the way out here to meet her for coffee. Turned out she was just really good at Photoshop. Total bust. I figured since I was out this way I'd check to see if you got any locks for today."

"Aw, you came on a good day, nephew. I got some picks in baseball today guaranteed to hit."

"You talk to Mom lately?"

"If I want to hear a woman tell me I need to find a girlfriend, stop drinking and stop gambling, I'll go to a psychic and talk to your grandma's ghost. That's women for you, always trying to nag a circle into being a square."

"She's just looking out for you, Unk. Nothing criminal about giving a shit about family, right?"

"You're right, nephew. I was planning on giving her a call on her birthday."

"That's two months away!"

"Fine kid, I'll call her tomorrow. I just get shitty reception out here."

The thumping bass of a car stereo came into earshot. I looked and saw a ghettoized Mazda with mismatched paint on the doors and an extra-large spoiler on the trunk. It was exiting the far end of the apartment complex. It had a flickering blotch coming out of the roof just like I had seen on the foot bridge. I was too far away to chase it down or make out the driver.

"Hey Unk, you have any idea who is in that Mazda over there? A neighbor of yours or something?"

"This place is a shit-nest, nephew. It only houses shit-birds. That there is a shit-bird driving that car. I'm just a quiet spectator in the shit-nest who avoids the shit-birds by all means necessary."

Damn. That strobe effect has got to mean something. I considered hopping in my car and following the Mazda but I wasn't in the mood for tailing a shit-bird. I figured this is becoming a more commonplace phenomenon in my realm of insanity and I'll come into contact with one soon enough without having to chase one down in my car. The Mazda chirped out into the street and peeled off with one of those extra loud engines that sounded like a thousand-pound lawn mower.

"Hey Unk, you should think about finding a girlfriend and stopping the drinking and gambling."

"Screw you, too, nephew. You got time for a beer?"

Chester had a small cooler next to him that he opened to reveal four cans of the cheapest beer sold in stores. I ended up having a beer with him as he explained to me why the Indians were a lock tonight against the Tigers in the late game. He said he heard the rookie starting pitcher for the Tigers got a DUI two nights ago so his head isn't going to be in the game tonight. He also had a lock on the horse races for me.

"I'm telling you, nephew, third race today at Saratoga. Take the number four horse to win and use him as your winner in exactas across the board. The name of the horse is Thishful Winking."

"Thishful Winking? This isn't another one of those crazy long-shots you tried to get me to bet on last time is it, Unk?"

"This is completely different than that last one. This one is a certified lock. It's a perfect storm, nephew. The trainer, the jockey and the race is on grass just like this horse loves. Odds are starting at seventeen to one. Go make some easy money, kid, and when you win, you can buy your uncle some of that snooty college craft beer you're always telling me I should be drinking."

Chester was convincing. From listening to him with such certainty in his voice, you'd think he was a sports guru who had all the angles figured. Too bad I knew the guy. I'd say he would hit about ten percent of his bets. His angles were shit-bird angles.

Finished my beer, said goodbye to Chester, then headed back to my car. It was time for another person on my list. I whipped out my phone, then scrolled through my contacts that I had never bothered editing in all the years I've had a cell phone. It was just a numeric junkyard of mostly people I'd never talk to again and names I didn't even recognize. I found and dialed the number labeled *U-Skate*.

"University Ice Rink. Rachel speaking. How can I help you?"

"Hi, Rachel. Could you tell me if Angie Hallenbrat is working today?"

"Yes, she's on the ice right now. Do you want to leave her a message?"

"No, thanks. It's not important. I'll try back later."

I hung up and started the drive back to the less-depressing parts of town. Chester's neighborhood was the land of broken dreams. He wasn't a bad guy unless you looked at his life directly. He never set out to hurt anyone but his self-centered lifestyle seemed to leave behind a long trail of destruction and casualties. I always gave him a pass though because he was family.

The anxiety of my next stop started to slowly build the closer I got back to my own part of town.

The University Ice Rink wasn't really a part of the university. It was just like all the other surrounding businesses leaning on their proximity to the school and using "University" or "Campus" in their business names. There was University Subs, Campus Dry-Cleaning, University Car Wash and my most-frequented place of business, Campus Liquor.

When Angie wasn't stalking her boyfriends, she spent all her time at the University Ice Rink either working or skating. Maybe it was the constant cold she was around that froze the part of her brain that regulates jealous rage and insecurity.

Twenty minutes after leaving Chester's neighborhood, I had arrived at Angie's work and pulled into the parking lot. There were two goals for this stop. Get a sketch of her blotch and don't let her see me. I hadn't run into her since I phased her out with my email and phone blocking and the bullshit story about Panama. I had no idea if she even cared or if she was walking around with a hate-dagger sharpened just for me.

I walked up from the side of the entrance doors and peeked through the tinted glass. She wasn't at the reception desk area so I walked in. The ice was fairly packed. There were a lot of little kids mixed in with the douches who took skating really seriously and were doing leaps and spins amidst the normal people who were just trying to have a good time and not fall and crack their skulls.

One of the douches flying around the ice was Angie whom I spotted zipping around and weaving her way through the crowd. I made my way to a three-foot gap by the ice rink window between a soda machine and a claw game. It was as good a spot as any to try to do what I needed to do and not be spotted by her.

It was an interesting scene, watching the blotches float around the ice above everyone. I locked onto Angie and sketched out her blotch as best I could. Angie's was a messy orange-yellow like the piss you take when you're infected with something and your body needs to release extra loads of contaminants. It was small but dense with jagged appendages pointing downwards from its midsection. It was ugly but at the same time kind of powerful looking.

I finished my sketch and wrote out as many details as I could to supplement my shitty drawing. Once done, I closed my journal and was about to turn around and leave when I heard a loud banging on the glass in front of me. Fuck.

Angie was on the other side of the glass, just staring at me. My instincts screamed at me to run and flee this place. My penis said stick around and see what happens.

Out of my peripheral I registered that the break in the rink wall where skaters entered and exited the ice was just on the other side of the claw game next to me. I decided to smile and wave a weak hello. Her expression was blank although the flush of her cheeks from the cold of the ice made her blank expression look angry. With eyes still locked she pushed off and skated to the break in the wall then walked over to me. With her skates she was almost my height. She had me trapped between the claw game and the soda machine.

"Hi, Angie. How's it going?"

"What are you doing here?"

"Nothing. Just in the neighborhood and had to use the bathroom."

"Was that you who called here looking for me about half an hour ago?"

"Wasn't me. I forgot you even worked here. I was just passing by and remembered the bathrooms here were relatively clean."

"Sure, just like you moved to Panama, right? What the fuck are you doing here, you fucking liar?" Voice definitely rising.

"I…uh…mmm…look, I was driving by and I was just curious to see you. I always felt kind of shitty for how I handled things so I came in here to see about maybe apologizing. But then I saw you on the ice and chickened out a bit and was about to leave when you knocked on the glass."

"Fuck you and your bullshit apology. I've got a real man now who would kick your ass if I tell him I was being harassed by some asshole from my past."

"Look, I'm sorry about everything. I'm leaving."

"You better leave. My man's going to be here any second and I'm going to tell him what a piece of shit you are."

"So I guess he hasn't found out you've bugged his phone yet or read his texts and emails behind his back. Nothing quite as sexy as jealous insecurity."

She took a swing. I ducked and her fist slammed into the plastic side of the claw game. I skirted around her and sped towards the door. She was taking long carpet strides in her skates towards me. She was a demonic locomotive with kill in her eyes.

"Get back here, you asshole!"

I bailed out the door. There was no way she would scuff up her professional skates on the gravel and asphalt of the parking lot. Wrong. She continued out the door yelling at me. I did a half-skip half-run to my car then jumped in. I must have subconsciously known something might go wrong because I had parked backwards in a spot facing the parking lot exit. Got my car started and sped away.

Angie stopped and looked around her for something to throw at my car. All she could find was a crushed up soda can. She bent down and picked it up then threw it as hard as she could and almost toppled over in her skates with the effort. Holy fucking skate psycho.

Although, I still probably would have slept with her again if she accepted my fake apology and things went differently.

Chapter Twenty-Eight
Krueger

After a couple of blocks, I pulled into an empty parking lot of a little strip mall. The encounter with Angie had me on edge and I needed a minute to let the bad vibes dissipate a bit and to plan my next move. Flipped open my journal to the list of names. I crossed out Uncle Chester and Angie, then scouted the remaining names. Who should I see next?

I realized everyone on my list so far had either left me depressed or rattled. I needed someone with a different vibe right at that moment. After scanning the remaining names on the list, I saw the perfect anti-venom to the Angie toxins that were clouding up my head at the moment. Picked up my phone and scrolled through the contacts. When I got down to the K's, I stopped and dialed the name Krueger.

"What up, fool? Thought you was in Alabama or some shits."

"What up, Kruegs? You around? Can I swing through?"

"Sho. Lounging. You know the cost of admission."

"Be there in fifteen."

"Cool."

Hung up and headed towards Campus Liquor. Krueger was my weed guy as well as my pill guy. You could technically say we were friends, too, but it seemed like every time we talked or hung out, some kind of drug transaction ended up taking place between us. Krueger was the mellowest person I had ever met in my life, probably because he was always high. He had this apathetic blissfulness about him that made any worries you might have had seem irrelevant. Never had I seen him get worked up about anything and being around him gave you contact mellowness. Krueger was the perfect chaser for the Chester and Angie shots I just had.

Arrived at Campus Liquor, then walked to the back corner where they housed the shittiest of the chilled alcoholic beverages. Grabbed a forty-ounce of malt liquor, paid, then went back to my car. Cost of admission to hang out at Krueger's pad was a forty. For some reason, all he ever drank when he drank was malt liquor. He had no desire to drink anything else. I brought him some tall cans of Severus once and he wouldn't even take a sip. Every time someone came over to his place, they brought him a forty of shitty malted piss. To each his own, I guess. Who was I to criticize?

Pulled in to his apartment complex and got lucky with a guest parking spot which normally are all taken. If you can't get a guest parking spot at his huge complex, then it is a quarter-mile hike from the street parking to his unit. I made my way through his building to his apartment, then knocked on his door.

"Who dat?"

"It's Serin."

"Door's open, man."

Opened the door, then walked into his apartment which had its own weather system. Outside, it was a beautiful clear day. Inside Krueger's apartment, it was overcast with a thick skunky cloud cover. Krueger always seemed to be wearing a bath robe and was always parked on his couch. His blotch was new to me. It almost seemed aquatic. A light-bluish streamlined form, covered in upward-pointing webbed structures. It seemed mellow like he was.

"What up, boy? Throw your admission in the box."

Walked to his kitchen and put his forty in a fridge half-filled with other forty-ounce bottles of all the shittiest varieties. The other half of his fridge was filled with take-out boxes from different restaurants. Krueger didn't venture out much aside from occasionally going to school. His main world was within these walls. People came to him. Food was ordered, then delivered to him. Money came to him through his apartment doors. He was the happy king of his one-bedroom kingdom. I took a seat in a chair by the couch. He had a football game on the sixty-inch TV that dominated his living room alongside a very nice sound-system and three different video game consoles.

"So what's the deal, boy? Weren't you rolling to Albania or some shits?"

He handed me his little handheld vaporizer and I took a pull then handed it back.

"Australia, man. The place got me sick so I came back early."

"Oh, yeah? What'd you get, that Ebola or some shits? That's why I don't go no place. Too much shit out there always fucking with people."

"It's not all bad out there. I met a superhot strip club muse yesterday. You can't meet one of those sitting in your apartment all day."

"I don't know what the fuck a strip club muse is, but I had three strippers over here last weekend buying pills. Outside world is for suckas. So what you need, boy, or you just miss me?"

Shit. I didn't really think through this visit aside from wanting to catalogue his blotch. I did have a twenty-dollar bill left over from my ATM withdrawal before the trip to the strip club.

"I got twenty dollars I don't want. What you got for me?"

"High roller. What you want, a speck of weed or half of one pill, poor-boy?"

"Whatever is in that vape should suffice."

He opened up a wooden box on his coffee table and pulled out a little plastic bag of weed and threw it at me.

"Shit's nice. Shit's also kind of pointless these days. Everyone and their grandma got their cards now and just go to the dispensaries. Trying to put this soldier out of business. Lucky I still have you and another dozen monkeys too lazy to get a card."

"It'll be completely legal soon enough, Kruegs. Better get your resume put together for Walmart."

"Yeah, fuck that. As long as they don't start dispensaries for pills, I'll be just fine."

I took a long hard look at Krueger's blotch, then told him I had to bounce. Five minutes was the average visiting period for all of his guests/customers so it wasn't a big deal leaving so soon after arrival.

Walked to my car and took care of the sketch and notes while his blotch was still fresh in my mind. The hit I took off his vaporizer was starting to grab a hold of me and I caught myself getting way too involved in sketching out his blotch. The shit was potent. A bit of paranoia started to creep in about me sitting in my car in this guest parking spot. I felt some evil imaginary forces closing in on my location. I needed to leave. Opened up my journal back to the list and crossed out Krueger. Scanned the other names on the list that I hadn't visited yet but I was having trouble concentrating.

All of a sudden I was starving.

Chapter Twenty-Nine
Lunch

The weed had me thinking, which was never good. A voice was telling me I needed to wean myself off the delicious but dirty Mexican food and pizza I'd come to rely on as my usual sources of nutrition. I had to accept that having to shit midway through most of my meals wasn't normal. My digestive tract was temperamental and I was constantly massaging it with Mexican napalm.

So what now, weed-conscience?

Started my car and made my way to a little shopping center a couple of blocks from campus. Amid the nail salon, dry cleaner and frozen yogurt store was a small restaurant. *Fresh Fills* was the name of the place which I'd passed a thousand times but never considered going into.

Parked, then made my way to the store front and checked out a menu that was taped to their entrance window. The tiny type on the menu was swimming around on me and my brain was having trouble putting meaning to words. I finally composed myself and walked in. It was a tiny shop but it felt clean. Everything was organic and supposedly fresh, hence the name of the restaurant.

I practiced the order in my head a couple of times then approached the guy at the counter and ordered a chicken-vegetable pita. No booze at this place so I settled on a glass of water infused with mango. I already hated Fresh Fills. Waited at a stool by the window and stared out into the parking lot until my order was ready. Grabbed my food and headed outside to one of the three small tables they had out front.

The food wasn't bad. No taste substitute for the low-grade mix of carne asada, sour cream and neon-orange cheese I got at Los Jalapeños but still not bad. My mind was scatter shot. Girls, blotches, tapped-out credit cards and booze. Did I really go to Australia? Was I really seeing what I was seeing floating in the air above people? Did I really meet a stripper muse who was interested in me?

This shit can't be real. I'm not really eating a chicken-vegetable pita right now. I died in the rainforest after getting sprayed by that demon flower and everything after is just my brain in its death spiral scrambling while trying to interpret this new experience of death. This is my death, a sci-fi adventure intertwined with people and imagery from my life. Holy shit, I'm high right now. This pita was fucking awesome all of a sudden.

Deep breath. Back to center. Focus. Wiped my hands and checked my phone for the time. 1:49 pm. Why were there only 60 minutes in an hour? Wouldn't it make more sense to just go to a hundred minutes in each hour? So I'd look at my clock and it'd be 1:98 pm. Two minutes till 2:00 pm. Then we'd have fourteen-hour days.

Holy shit. Back to center, asshole. This fucking weed had unlocked the insane asylum in my brain, letting all the crazy ideas out to play.

I had a couple more people on my list that I wanted to get to but weed is great at erasing any ambitions you may have had. Fuck it. I needed a break from all the madness of the day and my new life. Finished up my food and got back in my car. It hit me then that I made it through an entire meal and there was no kind of intestinal uprising taking place. Maybe Fresh Fills would be my new Los Jalapeños.

Started up my car and drove over to the campus parking lot. Got out and took a walk over to the rec hall. The university had a decent-sized arcade and bowling alley that mostly was frequented by the Asian exchange students. I had an old rec card from my freshman year that had a balance on it that I had never bothered to use.

I made my way over to a machine and swiped my rec card. The machine spit out forty tokens that were good for all the video games, pinball, air hockey and miniature basketball machines.

The place was relatively dead which was nice. They had music playing and the lights dimmed at fifty percent for a more comfortable gaming environment. There were eight bowling lanes but none of them were being used. This was my detox, even though I was high. It was my detox from this other world reality. I got lost playing pinball as there was nobody else around me and no blotches to invade my vision. This must be how chicks felt after a two-hour yoga class. I was centered.

When my tokens finally ran out and I came up for air, my clock said 4:74 pm. No it said 4:47 pm. What time would it be in thirteen minutes?

A good time to start drinking, I suppose.

Chapter Thirty
McBride Revisited

Exited out of the rec hall and into the harsh remaining light of the day. Walked across campus and drove my car back to my apartment. I went inside to wash my face and brush my teeth, which felt hyper-sensitive at the moment. Changed my outfit, then headed back outside on foot and made the walk over to Red's Tavern.

Arrived at 5:28 pm, with an unbelievable cottonmouth. It felt like the roof of my mouth was made of cheap leather that'd been left in the desert for a year and was about to start flaking off in bits and pieces. I went inside and took my same stool at the end of the bar. It once again was pretty dead. Not much action at Red's until around eight o'clock usually. McBride was loading canned beers into the small refrigerators below the bar.

"Aye, yo, is that some fruity ball juggla that just sat at my bar? Sorry, we're all out of coladas, Missy."

"McB, you surprise me. A trip to the Lex last night and you're not in jail right now?"

"Always bringing up dat old shit, ain't ya, Gladys?"

McBride poured me a beer of which I drank down half in one gulp. The leathery feel of my mouth started to subside a bit.

"How was it?"

"What, da Lex? Lot of ladies, not that you'd be interested in that, ya fuckin' Liberace. I had to slap around this one kid who spilt some beer on me. I didn't fuck 'em up too bad,

149

though. Took twenty bucks from his pocket. Dipshit clowny needed to be more careful."

"For fuck sakes, man, can't you ever just go someplace without slapping, beating, robbing or stabbing someone?"

"Naw, fuck that. Don't try to make me out to be a bad guy here. I don't fuck wit' no one on purpose. But if some dummy is gonna disrupt my shit, then they gotta be dealt with. That's them rules. You know that."

"You and your Least Coast rules."

"Betta watch yourself, little Miss. Don't disrespect the homeland of ya' lord and savior McBride."

I pounded the rest of the beer and slid the glass three feet down the bar towards McBride.

"You out already again? Going to go write some more poems in your diary?"

"Nope. Fill her up, bartender. I'm looking to ease the pain of living."

"What pain you got? Ass hurt from getting that train run on ya' the other night?"

He filled up another beer and threw it down in front of me. This one I'd sip more casually as the first one was starting to work. The illuminating glow of the first drink of the night was stretching out from my center to my extremities in a gleeful warmth. The first log was on the fire.

"If only you knew, McB, the shit that is going on in my world."

"What you got there? Limp-dick problems, I'm guessing."

"I just ran into Angie today. You remember her?"

"What, that crazy little blondy that tapped ya phone?"

"That's the one."

"Naw shit. My boy Brian's hitting that these days. I tell you that?"

"What?"

"My boy Brian. You don't know him. He goes to my gym and brought her around a couple times. That boy's a beast. Benching four-fifty or some shit like that. You don't wanna fuck with him."

Small fucking world. Note to self: avoid Angie and beast boyfriend.

"What, you still in love wit' her or sumthin? You like girls who fuck wit' ya privacy and shit?"

"No. Seeing her today was just symbolic of how my world currently has a dark evil cloud hanging over it."

"There you go again wit' ya poetry problems. Maybe you should take your diary over to the coffee house with all those other clowns, typing their books and movies on their laptops."

"You're the bartender, McB. It's your job to pour the drinks and listen to problems."

"Naw, fuck that. All you need to do is punch ya' fuckin problems in the jaw like I do. Then ya' other problems see you don't fuck around and get the fuck out cha way."

"I wish I could punch my problems in the jaw but my hand just goes right through them."

A couple of people walked in and sat down at the other end of the bar. McBride walked down to help them. I really wanted to explain what was going on with me to someone, but not McBride. McBride was a simple machine that only understood booze, drugs, sex and violence. Anything nuanced that didn't fall into those simple categories wouldn't compute with him. Or maybe I didn't give him enough credit but if I were to come out of the blotch-closet to someone, it'd have to be someone a little less likely to punch me for being stupid.

Looking at my beer, I came to a quick decision that this would be my last stop for today. Three, four, five more of these and I'd zig-zag my way back to my apartment and wait to see what nightmares awaited me in tomorrow.

Chapter Thirty-One
Coffee with the Muse

Ow! I rolled on my side and a marching band bass drum sounded off in my skull. Fucking McBride threw a half dozen shots my way last night on top of the beer. I must have been on auto-pilot walking home as I couldn't fish any images of that journey from the databanks.

My eyes were slow to focus as I lifted up my phone. Fuck, 10:27am. I was supposed to have called Evelyn. Alright, calm down. It's still technically morning. Don't want to seem too anxious. The right amount of dismissiveness works wonders sometimes with the ladies.

I put the phone back down, then took a deep breath before sitting up. The entire marching band played a few phrases then subsided after a minute. Made my way to the bathroom and relieved the pressure, then washed my face with cold water and brushed my teeth. After swishing around some mouthwash and drinking a half glass of water, I felt strong enough to make the call.

I thumbed through my phone and found the number for Evelyn I had plugged in the other day in the strip club parking lot. I was hung over but excited as I put my index finger on the phone icon by her name to make the call. It rang five times then went to voicemail. I had nothing prepared. You should have prepared. I was about to hang up but started talking instead.

"Hi, Joy. This is Serin, the fake journalist who was in Angel's a couple of days ago. I was calling because I was

153

looking to write a fake story about a fake stripper and was wondering if you were available. (*Stupid*) No, I know you said call you in the morning but sometimes this is about when my mornings start. (*Great, so now she'll think you're an addict of some sort.*) Anyway, if you are still offering coffee, my head could use some right about now. (*Wrap it up, gabby.*) Uh, em, alright then. Call me back…or don't. Later."

I hung up. Fuck. That was bad, right? Maybe not. Somewhat witty, I think. I felt it arrive as soon as I finished leaving the message. The anxiety of whether or not she'll call back would slowly heighten over the next hour, then would eventually transition into depression the longer she didn't call. Stupid. It's alright. Shake it off. We got bigger fish to fornicate. The perception of your entire world is eroding away and revealing terrors from different nightmarish realms, so let's not dwell too long on a girl who works at a….

My phone started ringing. It was her.

"Evelyn? Joy?"

"I should have mentioned that morning to me means around 8:00 am."

"So, did I miss the window? You already on your fourth coffee of the day and on your way to get some fake tattoos or something?"

"No. I'm free for now. How about meeting me at the Lamp Room around eleven fifteen?"

"For sure. Looking forward to seeing you with some clothes on for once."

Silence.

"Sorry."

"One thing. No lies today, alright?"

That might be tough.

"I'll see what I can do."

"Okay."

She hung up.

Butterflies in my stomach with blotches on them. The Lamp Room was two blocks from Red's Tavern which I'd assume means she lives in the neighborhood.

I took a quick shower at the hottest temperature I could stand in hopes of steaming out the alcohol from my skin. I rushed through my little regimen then decided I had enough time left to walk over to the Lamp Room instead of driving and trying to find parking. Headed out into the searing sunlight which sounded off like a high-pitched violin that could only play dissonant notes for my hangover.

As I made my way down the main avenue towards the Lamp Room, I noticed that the blotches that I was seeing hovering over people on the street had taken another leap in definition. We were in HD today and it was horrifying. I tried not to look too much but I caught glimpses of tendons and veins and semblances of eyes. The ones I saw were not normal everyday eyes but something like the dead-looking eyes of a shark.

My excitement at seeing Evelyn kind of ebbed a bit. How, even if I managed to get this girl to like me, could I ever get intimate with her while being watched by her nightmarish creature hovering over us? It was a permanent in-room chaperone. Fuck. Maybe with a lot of booze and my eyes shut? I don't know. I'd figure something out. Let's not get too ahead of ourselves just yet. There's little chance at anything with this girl anyway. If I lie, she walks. If I tell the truth, she walks.

I walked, slightly discouraged, but still about four percent optimistic. Reached the Lamp Room with three minutes to spare. Walked in, then did a quick tour of all the rooms but didn't see her. Went back up to the front and looked at their menu that was posted on large blackboards mounted above the main counter. Someone tapped me on the shoulder and I turned around. It was Evelyn, I think. Joy had been packed away in a closet. No tattoo, no bikini, little make-up and no glitter. Evelyn looked like just a girl. Just an amazingly beautiful girl.

"Hello, Evelyn."

"What's your poison? My treat."

"Iced – coffee should do the trick."

"Judging by your eyes, it looks like you need that plus a shot of espresso. Rough night?"

"Just a regular night. It's the days that are rough."

We ordered and waited in silence in the holding area until our drinks were ready. She just ordered a black coffee so it only took a minute. She grabbed her drink and walked outside to an empty table on the patio. I grabbed my drink then followed, sitting across from her, trying not to look directly at the creature floating above her.

"So are we telling the truth today or are we going to try to sneak some lies past me?"

Fuck it. I had the feeling she had tons of practice spotting lies with all the sleazy guys at the strip club. She could probably spot a lie as easily as I could spot a blotch. Lying wasn't going to work so then I might as well let the truth scare her away.

"You know what? Today I'm an open book. No more lies. Anything you want to know, you'll get an unfiltered answer."

"Wow, that almost sounded convincing. Shall we begin?"

"Sure thing, Joy."

She frowned at being called Joy but then smirked a bit.

"Why were you in Angel's the other day?"

"I wasn't writing a paper for school, that was a lie. I was, however, observing the people in the strip club and taking notes on the types of people they were."

"Why?"

Here we go. Hope your walking shoes are laced up, Evelyn.

"First, ask me what I was doing last week."

"Ok, I'm game. What were you doing last week?"

"I was in a rainforest called the Daintree in Australia."

She seemed to perk up with the mention of Australia.

"You really were? I watched a travel show that did a segment on the Daintree. What made you go there?"

"I'm actually a biology major. The Biology Club organized a ten-day trip that I decided to go on."

She seemed to lock in on my words. I could see she was running numbers in her head. She didn't believe I was the type of person who would just go on a Biology Club trip. You're about to lose her.

"Okay. It's not a lie, I am a biology student. I didn't necessarily go on the trip for the sake of biology though. The reason I went on the trip was because of a girl."

"There you go. Stick to the complete truth, buddy, and we'll be just fine. So what about this girl?"

"She was a girl I had a couple of classes with over the last couple of semesters. I found out she was going on this trip, so that's the real reason I signed up for it."

"And how did that work out?"

"It didn't. She went to Paris with her boyfriend instead."

She smiled at that.

"So, why did you have me ask you where you were last week? How does you chasing a girl to Australia last week have anything to do with you being in Angel's two days ago?"

"This is the point of no return, just so you know. What I'm about to tell you is basically impossible to believe and you will be the first person I've told any of this to. The only thing I can hope for is that your bullshit radar is so finely tuned that you'll at least see that I'm not lying to you. Not that me not lying to you will count for much once I'm done with the story, as you will most likely write me off as insane."

"I am so pleasantly intrigued right now. This is kind of a nice surprise. You've got my full attention. Spill it!"

So spill it I did. I covered the entire trip. Me getting lost. Finding the demon flower. Me getting poisoned and knocked out. Nothing found in the Australian hospital. Nothing found with the eye doctor at Health Services. The daily progression of what I'm able to see of the blotches. My decision to start cataloguing people and their blotches. My trip to Angel's and everything up until coffee today. My only omission was how I got lost in the rainforest. I told her I got turned around which is a truth of sorts. An omission is not the same as a lie. She didn't have omission-radar, too, did she?

I wrapped up my story and let her sit with it as I took a long drink from my coffee. It was a huge relief telling someone the truth, even knowing that I've more than likely made a beautiful girl think I'm a lunatic. She sat staring at me with a neutral look on her face and continued sipping her coffee. Fight or flight, Evelyn? What's it going to be?

"So, you won't hurt my feelings if you want to leave. I promise I'll erase your number from my phone and never will return to Angel's to bother you. You wanted the truth. That is the truth. Nice knowing you, Joy."

"What's mine look like?"

"What?"

"I'm around liars all the time. You at least believe you are telling the truth as far as I can tell. So if this is the truth of what you are experiencing, then what does mine look like? Did you draw it in your journal? Did you bring your journal?"

"I left it back at my place." *You want to come over to my place and look at pictures of your demon that I drew? Have a few drinks? Maybe dance a little?* "I didn't think you'd be around long enough to look at it after I told you my story."

"Describe it to me."

I looked up and took my first good look at it. Back at the strip club it was still mostly out of focus. Now, two days later, it was flesh, tendons and bones. It wasn't frightening like I feared it would be. Hers was somewhat, dare I say, attractive? No, that's just my little mind trying to see with one eye. It wasn't hideous though. As far as blotches have gone so far, it was the most fuckable I'd seen so far.

"Give me a second."

I got up from the table and walked back into the Lamp Room and went to the counter where they had a cup of pens for signing receipts and grabbed one. By the door was a pin board with random business cards and flyers. Grabbed a flyer for guitar lessons that was printed on one side and blank on the other, then returned to our table. Evelyn was sipping her drink while staring at me with amused eyes.

I started sketching out Evelyn's blotch, trying my hardest to improve upon my kindergarten-like artistic styling. It still had a cocoon shape and the blue tint was now a full-on Caribbean blue. It had a weave of interlocking appendages that gave the appearance that it was hugging itself. Towards the top there were three recessed folds. Buried in those folds were pure black orbs that seemed like eyes. I spent about five minutes sketching it out then turned it around and slid it towards Evelyn.

"As far as these things go, yours is almost attractive. I haven't seen any others quite like it yet. If my hypothesis is correct and these things correlate to a person's personality, then you must be really unique. Kind of like a stripper muse."

She looked at it for a while then back at me. Her guard was halfway down now. I must have done something right.

"Can I keep this?"

"It's all yours. Want me to sign it?"

She slid it back towards me and nodded. I signed it and slid it back.

"Your signature should help in me getting you committed."

"Sweet. I hear they no longer do shock therapy and just dose you up with the good pills. Hang out in my white pajamas all day. Maybe you can sneak some beer in to my padded room."

My phone rang. I didn't recognize the number so I muted it and let it go to voicemail.

"I tell you what. I'm going to go now."

"I figured as much."

"No, don't take it the wrong way. I'm not running away. I'm just meeting a friend at the gym in forty-five minutes and still need to go home and change."

Shit, hope her gym friend isn't Brian, Angie or McBride.

"So, if you are not running away, any chance we can hang out again? I didn't get to ask you anything yet. Do you go to school here? Do you live in the neighborhood? Do you like guys who see demons?"

"Maybe, yes, yes and I don't know yet."

"What?"

"Maybe we can hang out again. Yes, I go to school here. Yes, I live within walking distance. I don't know if I like guys who see demons yet."

"Well then, I was wondering if maybe tonight you want to have a drink at a dive bar with me."

"When? Where?"

"How's 7:30 pm? Red's Tavern down the street?"

"Bring your journal."

She got up, smiled, then dropped her empty cup in the trash bin and walked away. A ball of electricity was spinning in my chest, throwing off sparks. How the fuck did I come out of that with a date tonight? I guess being hung over and resolved to fail kept my nerves at bay. Why the fuck did I say Red's Tavern though? My mouth didn't get permission from my brain on that one. Oh well, she said yes. And I think McBride is off tonight. Fuck, I hope so.

I sat there in the Evelyn afterglow while finishing my coffee. I saw I had a message on my phone so I called my voicemail.

Chapter Thirty-Two
Wynn

The message was from Wynn who got back last night from Australia. I hung up my voicemail then gave him a call.

"How are things going with you? Sarah and Gaby made me promise on the plane ride home to give you a call and see how you were doing. I couldn't care less but felt obligated by them."

"Shut up, Wynn. How was the rest of the trip? Anyone else go missing?"

"Are you really interested in the trip? What's going on with your side-effects? Things better or worse? You ready to talk about it?"

Sure, why not. I already had spilt the demon beans to basically a complete stranger. A beautiful female of a complete stranger but a complete stranger none the less. Might as well let Wynn in on the party, too.

"You free at all right now? If you really want to know, I'll tell you what's happening although I will forewarn you, it's nothing short of unhinged."

"I'm a bit jet lagged but have no plans right now. Do you want to meet up somewhere?"

"Yes. I'll text you my address. I'll be home in twenty minutes, so head over."

"Okay. See you then."

I hung up, then texted him where I lived, then got up from the table, threw out my empty cup and headed back to my apartment. No real reason to keep Wynn in the dark. He was there from the beginning and had a hell of a lot more to go on than Evelyn did and she didn't run. She casually walked away but that's definitely not running. Even if Wynn didn't buy it, he'd at least have some ideas for me. The guy was nerd first. A problem needed a solution regardless of what dimension the problem was on.

Made it back to my apartment and spotted Wynn getting out of a Toyota. His blotch was fully-formed, of course, and I gave it a quick once-over. Wynn noticed me, then walked over. I opened my door and went in.

"What up, Wynn?"

He walked in and looked around, then took a seat on the couch.

"I expected posters on your walls of different alcohol brands and half-naked women."

"Those are in the bathroom. What, you think me classless or something?"

"All I know of you is what I know."

"Whatever, Confucius. Did you get to first base with Gaby or Sarah after I left? Figured once I was gone your chances skyrocketed."

"Look, I'm not lying about being jet lagged and you are a tiring individual to be around on a normal basis. So if we can bypass your nonsense and get to why I'm here, that'd be appreciated."

"Pissy little thing when you're tired, huh? You and Orif sync up your menstruations after I left?"

I walked over to my backpack on the kitchen table and pulled out my journal, then threw it on Wynn's lap.

"Your big problem is you need help with your homework?"

"Your jokes are dumb. Start at the beginning. That will pretty much sum up everything up until this point. After that, flip to the middle. That's where you'll see some additional notes and some sketches. I'm going to excuse myself and go look at my posters of alcohol brands and half-naked women. On top of all the shit that's going on with me, I think I got IBS, Wynn. Can't eat burritos. Can't drink coffee. Life is a cruel bitch sometimes."

I made my way to the bathroom. While I was in there, I heard the occasional mumblings coming from the living room. Wynn started to shout a question but quit after a few words. Ten minutes later I returned to the living room to see what his reaction would be. The journal was closed on the coffee table in front of the couch. Wynn was staring at it with his hands folded near his mouth and in deep contemplation about something.

"So what's the verdict? Are you trying to decide which loony bin to call or what?"

He just sat there, still staring and thinking, like it was his turn at the world championship match of the chess Olympics.

"You can't hurt my feelings, Wynn. I know the shit is crazy but I just told all of this to a stripper muse and got a date out of it. What have you got for me?"

He slowly looked up with a look of confusion and irritation mixed in with exhaustion from still being on Australian time. He looked back down towards the journal on the table.

"I don't see how it'd be possible. There is no way and even if there were a way you are not that resourceful. Nobody is. And what would be the point? I can't process it. My mind is too tired and I can't see the angles."

"What the fuck are you mumbling about? If you know something, anything, for fuck sakes spit it out!"

He looked up at me again and this time locked eyes.

"I know it's not really a possibility but I have to ask you anyway. Are you fucking with me?"

I was caught off guard. I think this was the first time I heard Wynn use a swear word. What did he see? What did he know?

"I don't know what you are asking me right now. Fucking with you how? Are you asking did I make up this entire thing, wrote all that shit down in that journal for some kind of a fucking joke? What a stupid fucking joke that would be. What are you even talking about? All that shit in that journal is what I'm experiencing. What is going on? Does any of this make sense to you? If so, you need to tell me right now."

"Alright. So I read what I could and got the gist of it. Your handwriting is atrocious but I could make out enough. The whole time I was considering your personality and assessed this was more than likely a joke on me or you'd been on something like a methamphetamine binge and this journal was the by-product. But then I flipped to your crude sketch work."

"And? You flipped to my crude sketch work and . . .?"

"I've seen similar sketches before."

My stomach dropped and my heart started pumping double-time.

"You've seen sketches like mine? Where?"

"My grandmother. She has this old book I used to look at all the time growing up. I couldn't read it because it's written in Bengali, but it had all these strange illustrations in it that I found fascinating as a kid. It's not a regular book you'd find in a bookstore. This book was handwritten on parchment and probably is two to three hundreds of years old. That is where I've seen sketches like yours."

"God, I hope you're not fucking with me right now."

"I promise you I am not."

"What's the book about? What's the story?"

"My mother just told me it's a book about the province where my grandmother was from. It's written in Bengali, like I said, so I never read it. Most of the book looks normal with a few drawings of villagers and fishing and other common things. But I just remember always flipping to the end of the book and being mesmerized by that section that had pages and pages of strange sketches like yours."

"Your grandmother never tried to translate and read it to you?"

"My grandmother never learned enough English. She came here when she was in her thirties and my mom was six years old. My grandmother worked in a sewing factory for forty years with a bunch of other women from Bangladesh she had come here with. She and her little community never bothered learning the language. My mother speaks both English and Bengali and has always been my interpreter with my grandmother."

"We have to go see her, Wynn. I need to see this book and get the story. This is my sanity we're talking about. Help me out here."

"I understand but going now wouldn't be productive."

"Why not?"

"We could go visit my grandmother and see the book but without my mother there to interpret, we wouldn't be able to learn what it's about. Plus, my grandmother doesn't like white people."

"I get it, all grandmothers are racist but I need to see this book."

"I haven't seen my mother since I got back and was planning on having dinner with her when she gets off of work. I'll see if we can stop by my grandmother's place and I'll meet up with you after to let you know what I find out."

"Cool. Do you think she'll let you take the book?"

"I probably won't even ask. It's not just a book she has sitting on a shelf. It's more like an heirloom which she keeps locked away in her armoire. I'll take pictures of the pages and see if my mother can translate the story. That's about the best that I can offer right now."

"Alright then. Come find me soon as you are done. You know where Red's Tavern is, right?"

"I've walked by it many times."

"I'm going to be there at 7:30 pm. Come find me there if you can."

"Why there?"

"I kind of got a date. I met a girl a couple of days ago and saw her this morning and told her everything. Australia and all the shit you just read in that journal."

"You told her all of this? Why would you do that?"

"I don't know. She has this thing about not lying. I'm a shitty liar so my only option was to roll with the truth or she never would have given me a shot."

"So she's fine with insanity, just not dishonesty? Sounds a bit off in her priorities."

"No, sounds like I've got a date with the hottest girl in this zip code. Seeing she knows everything already, it'd help me out to have you stop by and back up my story, especially if you get some new info from your grandmother."

"I am kind of interested in meeting this girl who's willing to overlook the unknown implications of your story and go on a date with you. Even more interested in seeing what kind of girl could overlook your personality and go on a date with you."

"Shut up, Wynn."

"I need to go and try to get some sleep before I meet my mother. I'll see what I can find out and will meet you at Red's Tavern after I'm done with dinner."

"Thanks. I'll call you if the plans change but if you don't hear from me I'll be at Red's.

"Alright."

Wynn got up from the couch and walked out. Now alone, I decided to lie down and go over this new development. Unless his memory was fucked up and he was recalling some Dr. Seuss book from his childhood memory banks, this was huge. What if there were some real information on what was happening to me and what I was seeing hovering over every individual I encountered? Well, almost every individual. Every individual except the pack of Down syndrome people I saw on campus and that deathly looking geezer in the wheelchair at the zoo.

Even more significant, what if there were real information in that book about a cure? I'd never be able to forget what I've seen, but what I wouldn't give to stop being able to see them in real time. I was kind of getting used to seeing them but how could I ever be with another girl again in my current state, seeing what I'm seeing? I'd have to be one of those blindfold fetish people or something. No way am I maintaining anything in the bedroom while being gawked at by a hulking demon from the netherworld or whatever the fuck they are.

Is there any position in existence where the girl's blotch wouldn't be in my line of sight? No. Not that one. No. Maybe a reverse pile driver but what are the chances of finding a girl outside the world of porn who would be cool with that?

I was screwed. I needed a cure. I needed to close my eyes. I had only been awake today for a handful of hours but I felt like Wynn's jet lag was contagious.

I'll just close my eyes for a minute and try to clear my head.

Chapter Thirty-Three
Group Date

6:47 pm. Shit. I fell asleep. Oh shit, I was supposed to be at Red's Tavern in forty minutes to meet Evelyn. Get up!

Rolled off my couch and made my way over to my closet to make some quick decisions. Changed, then hit the bathroom for a quick tune-up. Deodorant, fix the hair, brush the teeth and a rinse with mouthwash.

Grabbed my keys, money and ID and headed out the door. Wait. Ran back in and grabbed my backpack and threw my journal inside. Glanced at my phone and decided I could get to Red's by 7:30 pm on foot. I headed out feeling fresh and excited. Excited to see Evelyn. Excited Wynn might have some info for me on my condition. Excited that shit-talking McBride wasn't working tonight and wouldn't be there to embarrass me in front of Evelyn.

I walked at a measured pace. Not too slow that I'd be late. Not too fast as to generate musty swamp-nuts. My anticipation started to build the closer I got. How had I managed to get to this point with a girl like Evelyn? Aside from her suspect profession, she was still way out of my league. Maybe she had some huge dinosaur skeletons in her closet. What was it going to be? She had her first kid when she was twelve? Convicted felon? Snatch-rabies? From how she makes me feel, I'd be willing to overlook pretty much anything. Well, maybe not snatch-rabies, but pretty much anything else.

Made it to Red's Tavern with four minutes to spare. Walked in and the place was quiet with only a couple of guys sitting at the far end of the bar and a group of four girls in one of the booths. My usual stool was available so I took a seat.

I breathed a little easier when the bartender that wasn't McBride walked out from the back and came over to take my order. Her name was Effie and she was all business. No bullshitting with customers. Take your order, take your money, end of interaction. Most people would say a bartender is hurting oneself tip-wise by not schmoozing with the customers. I, on the other hand, could never stand the manufactured chit-chat of most service industry workers. Waitresses, hairdressers, supermarket cashiers. Just perform your service in silence, please.

Got my beer from Effie and tipped her forty-five percent for not talking. Ahhhh, that first sip of the day, I tell you. Warm and enveloping, like a fat-guy handshake.

Out of the corner of my eye I caught movement coming from the entrance. She was right on time. I loved punctual people. It takes close to no effort being on time for shit. She made the effort. She looked casual in a hooded sweatshirt and jeans. She sat down at the empty stool next to me.

"Started without me? And here I thought you were a gentleman."

She grabbed my beer and took a large sip.

"Sorry. I tend to lean on generalizations, one being that the prettier the girl, the longer it takes them to get places."

"So I must be ugly then."

"Only on the inside."

"Well, at least you have decent taste in beer."

Effie walked over and Evelyn just pointed to my glass and said, "The same."

"So, did you bring your journal?"

"I did. I also brought news of an interesting development."

Effie brought Evelyn's beer over. As I reached to pay, Evelyn pushed my hand down to the bar, then threw down a couple of twenties with her other hand and said, "Keep them coming." I'm back in fourth grade when holding a girl's hand was going all the way. My insides lit up like a box of cheap Fourth of July sparklers.

"Let me see your journal first, then tell me about your news after."

I dug in my backpack and handed her my journal.

"The summary of everything is at the front. I told you pretty much everything already but feel free to read it. Then if you jump about halfway, you'll see some specific sketches and notes."

At that moment, I realized I had written some notes about Evelyn next to the sketch of her blotch. What did I write? Ah fuck, I couldn't remember.

She started reading and I started drinking. I finished my first and Effie refilled it. Evelyn finished up the front of my journal then flipped to the sketches and notes in the middle. I tried to be nonchalant when she got to the page with her sketch on it as I was trying to make out the notes I had written through my peripheral. Shit, why's my handwriting so messy? She stopped on her page for a minute then skimmed through the other sketches, not spending too much time on the rest. She closed the journal and slid it over on the bar in front of me, then took a long drink from her beer. She finished her beer then made eye contact with Effie who came back over and gave her a refill.

"I like your notes about me."

"To be honest with you, I can't remember what I wrote."

"You wrote I was beautiful and confident looking. Then you wrote I was possibly half-a-retard based on my tattoo."

Ah, that's what I wrote.

"Well, obviously I wrote that before we ever talked. You can't hold that against me, right?"

"I can do whatever I want. Just so happens I find the phrase half-a-retard extremely inappropriate."

Ah shit. That's the skeleton. She's politically correct. Fuck!

"Well, um, look I...um, I..."

"If that tattoo were real, the appropriate term would be full-fledged retard, not half-a-retard."

Oh, I'm in love.

"So what do you think? Is my journal everything you'd hoped it would be?"

"I'm a little disappointed in how messy your handwriting is."

"And that's it? That's your professional review? I got shit handwriting?"

"I'm trying to figure you out. On the one hand, I can't see why anyone would make all this up. On the other hand, it's pretty impossible for me to accept it at face value, me being of sound mind and all. But you don't strike me as particularly crazy. I've known crazy. You don't have that kind of energy."

"I understand. I wouldn't believe me, but I'm living it so I can't really deny it."

"So what's this development you mentioned?"

"There is this guy, I guess he's kind of my friend now, who was on the trip with me in Australia. I mentioned him in the summary—Wynn. He's back now from the trip and came to see me earlier today. I let him read my journal, too. I didn't know what to expect in showing it to him but he said he'd seen sketches like mine before in an old book his grandmother has."

"You're kidding."

"I kid you not. Right now he's trying to get information from his grandmother about the book. He said he'd meet me here when he was done."

"Wow. Let me just say that if this isn't real, and you are pulling some kind of scam on me for some odd reason, I applaud the effort."

"It's not a scam. And what effort are you talking about?"

"Well, first the encounter at Angel's. Then the backstory while getting coffee this morning at the Lamp Room. The journal just now. And soon the introduction of a character witness. It's all very elaborate if it were a scam."

"It's not a scam. I wish it were a scam and I'd be on the verge of grifting you for all of that stripper muse money you've got."

I finished my second beer and signaled Effie. I should slow down a bit I thought. Usually, after my fourth or fifth drink, the brain and the mouth start to disconnect and misfire. The entrance door opened and Wynn walked in. I waved him over.

"What up, Wynn? This is Evelyn."

"Hello."

"Hi there, Mr. Character witness."

"Excuse me?"

"Nothing. Sorry. Nice to meet you, Wynn."

"You drinking? You want a beer?"

"Sure, why not."

Evelyn finished up her second beer and Effie set us up with three fresh ones.

"So you were in Australia with Serin?"

"Unfortunately."

"He told me all about the trip. Getting lost. Getting poisoned. You going to back him up on his story?"

"Depends. Did he tell you how he got lost?"

"Shut up, Wynn."

"Yes, I was there. He did disappear and showed up two days later. And he did lead me and some others back to where he said he was poisoned. All of that is true. Although the species of flowers that poisoned him were all destroyed, we did catalogue three new species in the immediate area. His story seemed legitimate."

"And did he mention why he went on the trip in the first place?"

"Really, Evelyn?"

"Yes, embarrassingly enough. He was pursuing an imbecile whom he was attracted to."

"You know her? What is she like? I'm just curious."

"Can we move on, please?" Last thing that needed to be brought up was Ariel.

"Oh, relax. Just give me a quick description, Wynn."

"From what I've experienced, her most striking characteristics are that she's incredibly shallow, conceited, shortsighted and obtuse."

"Oh, she sounds lovely. Was she at least pretty?"

"Enough! Wynn doesn't even like white girls. He probably thinks you're a dog. His opinion is moot on this."

"Is that true, Wynn?"

"If I'm honest, Evelyn, I think you are very pretty. Ariel, on the other hand…."

"Shut up, Wynn. Can we seriously move on here? You went to your grandmother's, right? Have you got anything for me? The book? Some insight? Anything?"

"I learned a lot of things, actually. Things I don't want to believe but can't seem to ignore seeing that it'd be a near impossibility that you've ever seen a book like this."

"Do you seriously still think I'm playing a joke on you? I thought we were past this."

"I know, I know. I just believe in science. I believe in facts based in reality. I'm not going to concede that there is a logical explanation somewhere in all of this. But what I learned at my grandmother's doesn't help things on the side of rational thought."

"Spill it, man. Evelyn has read my journal so there is nothing to hide here."

Just then the entrance door opened again. And then I heard his voice. Shit.

"Aye, yo, what've we got over here?"

McBride walked over to us and looked us over.

"What's going on, Serin? You and your cousin here getting tutored for math or sumthin?"

"Who's this?" Evelyn asked me, while smiling at McBride.

"Evelyn, Wynn, this is McBride. He's an East Coast delinquent turned West Coast bartender. I thought today was your day off?"

"What, you trying to avoid me there, Curly Sue? Just in to pick up my check."

"Excuse me, but did you refer to me as Serin's cousin?" Evelyn asked.

"Well, you're either his cousin or a sista I've neva heard about."

"Why would you say that?"

"Cuz my boy Serin here only brings around them beefy girls or them psychotic ones. I figure you two must be related cuz you ain't beefy. Or is you one of them psychos?"

Evelyn smiled, then looked at me. Fucking McBride.

"And who's this guy? What your name? Win? What you winning? How you know Serin here?"

"We had classes together. We also were on the same trip to Australia."

"Ah yeah? You gals get married over there? What you guys doing here? This your honeymoon? Oh, I see."

McBride spotted my journal still lying on the bar. He reached over and grabbed it before I could stop him.

"You and your fruity diary again. You guys doing poetry club or sumthin?"

"You got us, McB. Can I get my fruity diary back? We're just about to start a reading."

McBride looked at my journal and flipped through the pages.

"What pages are the flowers and unicorns on?"

He tossed the journal back on the bar. I guess if there were sketches of naked women he'd have paid more attention to the content.

"What you guys doing after your fruity book club here? Dirty Dan is spinning tonight at the Lex. Show up with me at 9:30 pm and my boy Rueben will hook us up with the door and drinks. What about you, girlie? I know Serin's scared of the Lex. What about you, guy? You and Serin going roller-skating later or you want to go have some fun with your Uncle McBride?"

I was about to shut McBride down when Evelyn said, "We're in."

"Alright. I like your cousin here, Serin. She ain't got the fear like you do. What about you, guy?"

McBride put a hand on Wynn's shoulder and leaned down to look him dead in the eyes like a used-car salesman. Wynn looked at me for answers to what kind of creature had just latched onto his shoulder.

"Come on, Wynn," Evelyn said. "Don't leave me alone with this undistinguished bunch. We'll try and make a good time of it."

Wynn looked torn. McBride was impossible to like. Evelyn was impossible not to like. I guess I was the tie-breaker.

"Yeah, come on, Wynn. I know you're jet lagged but maybe it'll be educational. Treat it as field study."

Wynn closed his eyes then said, "Fine."

"Dat a boy. I'll be back here at 9:15 pm then we'll roll over to the Lex together. And if Serin here pussies out like he probably will, you two are more than welcome to still roll with ya Uncle McBride. Now, if you'll excuse me I need to grab my check and go handle some business."

"Later, McB."

McBride grabbed my beer and drank half of it, then walked to the back and disappeared.

"Well, I like your friends so far," said Evelyn.

"That guy has too much erratic energy. I bet he becomes real unbalanced really easily, am I correct?" Wynn asked.

"Look, Wynn, as long as McBride is on your team, there is nothing to worry about. Now, back to grandma business. What have you got for me?"

Wynn took a drink from his beer, then retrieved his phone from his pocket. He opened up his gallery app and swiped through a bunch of pictures. He then handed the phone over to me and Evelyn.

"So, look at the first three images I took and you'll see the cover and a couple of pages and get an idea of the age of this book."

"Holy shit, what is this, the Book of the Dead or something? What's that made of?"

"It's just some really old parchment. You know, animal skin."

"What did you tell your mom and grandma?"

"What do you mean?"

179

"I mean when you went over there. What did you say was the reason you wanted to know about this book? Were they suspicious of you bringing it up?"

"I told them that I was doing a research paper on my own genealogy and knew the book had some connection to where my grandmother came from."

"Wow, Wynn, you didn't strike me as the type of guy who lies to his own mother," said Evelyn.

"I'm not. I don't lie to anyone. Serin put me in a position where it was impossible to tell the truth."

"Don't blame me, Wynn, you fucking liar."

"Shall I continue?"

"Yes, of course. I apologize for interrupting," Evelyn said while leaning over and placing her hand on his knee. All of a sudden I was jealous of Wynn's knee.

"My grandmother grew up in an isolated province of Bangladesh. Extremely remote. No technology. No politics. No known religion. No influence from any neighboring provinces. Their entire existence was dedicated to fishing and farming and nothing much else. She lived there till she was ten, then some kind of agricultural blight forced them to flee to a larger province. Eventually, decades later, my grandmother made her way to the U.S. The only thing she kept from that time in her original province was this book.

"She didn't elaborate on too much but just gave me broad strokes. She did mention they had a lot of rituals. A ritual for the harvest. A ritual for rain. A ritual for a healthy pregnancy and so on and so forth. I inquired about the last part of the book with all the sketches and she almost seemed embarrassed. She said those had to do with a ritual about choosing a new leader for each township. She said there were four townships in the province, each with its own leader. "Every twelve years there was some kind of election process where new leaders were chosen for each township. She said each township had a shaman. Some kind of healer, voodoo doctor or whatever you want to call them, and during this ritual they were able to see things nobody else could see. They could see the whispering phantoms.

"She was extremely dismissive towards this while she was talking about it. It was obvious she didn't believe any of it. I figure she was only ten when she was removed from that specific province's culture and that she more than likely wasn't around or could remember one of these rituals that only happened every twelve years."

"She called them phantoms?"

"My mother was translating and had to think about it for a second before she used the word phantoms. There might not be a direct translation and that's as good as she could come up with."

Evelyn asked, "Do you have any idea how your grandmother got a hold of this book? It'd seem like this was a one-of-a-kind type of thing."

"Yes, I thought the same thing and asked her. She said her grandfather was one of the last four shamans before the blight hit and they were all forced to relocate. Her grandfather refused to leave his home but recognized their province was going to disband so he gave the book to his daughter which then was passed down to my grandmother. On my phone, if you continue swiping, you'll see some of the phantom pages with illustrations and notes."

I swiped to the next couple of pictures and there they were: the same types of creatures that had been haunting my world and that I had been studying, there on the pages of an ancient book. Excitement and relief washed over me. I wasn't crazy.

"So did she say anything else about it? I mean, there's got to be more details in the book, right?"

"Remember, I told them I was doing a research paper on my genealogy. I couldn't press too hard on one particular thing, especially something like this."

"So where does that leave us? I mean this is the one and only source we've got. We need to know everything. I need to know everything."

"I will take care of it. I'm going back over tomorrow morning with my printer and laptop. I'm going to scan all the pages."

"And your mom is going to translate it for us?"

"No. I don't want to involve my mother any more in this so as to avoid any further dishonesty. I have a friend I grew up with who can translate it for us. I left him a message and hopefully he'll be available tomorrow. If not, it might take a few days."

"Thanks, Wynn. Drinks are on me tonight." Especially if drinks are on Reuben later.

"So either this is the most elaborate, pointless joke ever played on someone or this is really happening," Evelyn said to both of us.

"Every fiber of who I am is against believing any of this. But I can't ignore the facts that are currently available to us. Serin disappeared in the Daintree. He led us to new species of flowers which backed up his story. The chances are negligible that he'd ever come across this book, given its extremely isolated origins. I've got nothing to hang my hat on for an opposing position. The facts require me to treat the content of this book and Serin's journal as supporting evidence of one another."

"What are you saying? The science geek that sits before us is actually considering believing in ghosts?"

"If you spent more time reading books instead of destroying your liver, you might have a clearer understanding of the realm of possibilities within physics. We, as humans, only experience reality through three dimensions. Superstring theory presents the possibility of ten dimensions to the universe. Who's to say if sentient beings exist within these other dimensions and what their capabilities might be? We currently are only seeing through a narrow keyhole when considering the complexities of a near infinite universe and our limited abilities and tools to perceive it."

"So, yes on believing in ghosts?"

"You guys are interesting to hang around with," Evelyn said. "Let's try a little experiment. This morning Serin met me for coffee and after explaining all of this to me, I asked him to draw a sketch of my phantom. So if the door to this phantom world is still open to you, then you should have no problem sketching out my phantom again correct? I mean, from what you say it's hovering over me right now, right?"

"Your challenge is weak, strip club muse, but I accept."

I grabbed a pencil from my backpack and ripped a blank page from my journal, then went over to an empty booth so I could have a better angle of her phantom.

"So, just curious and you don't have to answer if you don't want to, but does the term 'strip club muse' have any substance or is it some kind of inside joke between you two?"

"Sure, it's kind of silly when I explain it out loud but, oh well. You'll keep all your dickish judgments concentrated on Serin, right?"

"Well, I kind of have to be somewhat judgmental about your taste seeing you are out in public with him, but regarding your job, if that's what it's relating to, I'll refrain from further judgments."

"Deal. I was hired to hang out in a strip club but I don't have to strip or interact with the customers if I don't want. The owner thinks having me around will make the customers want to spend more money with the real strippers."

"And that works?"

"I don't know. All I know is I make more working two days a week there than I did five days a week at the Lamp Room making coffee."

I finished up my sketch and walked back over to them and threw it down on the bar. Evelyn then reached into her sweatshirt pocket and produced the sketch I did earlier at the coffee shop and placed it also on the bar next to the sketch I just did. The sketches of course were almost identical. Wynn and Evelyn looked them over then kind of shrugged at each other as if to say "good enough."

"What now, kids? Are we really going with McBride to the Lex or should we escape before he gets back and forces us there at knifepoint?"

"Living in a world of floating monsters and you're most scared of going to the Lex? Why is that?"

"I'm not scared of going to the Lex. It's just kind of low-rent and the people who go there are generally low-rent. Not scared. Just not a fan of low-rent."

"Yet you had us meet you here?" Wynn said.

"Ok, Red's Tavern gets a zero for ambiance, but it's within walking distance and when McBride is working he usually gives me most of my drinks for free. So this place is a compromise for the sake of laziness and being cheap."

"Well, I'll pay for the taxi and your friend McBride said someone named Rueben would be covering the door and drinks. So you really have nothing to argue about unless you just want to admit you're scared," Evelyn said to me.

"I'm going, fine. And I'm not letting you pay for our taxi. Wynn here will pay for it."

"I'll pay for me and Evelyn. I'm assuming McBride has a motorcycle or drives around on a sled driven by abused pit bulls. You two can find your own way," Wynn said.

We managed to drink another two rounds while waiting for McBride to return. Red's was starting to get crowded and Evelyn and Wynn were getting chummy. I noticed a bunch of other guys in the crowd eyeing Evelyn on occasion. She was hard not to stare at, even dressed down in a hooded sweatshirt and jeans. Would this be the normal if we were to start dating? Everywhere we'd go other guys would stare her up and down then shoot me a dismissive glance of wonderment of how I possibly scored someone like her. I could live with that.

9:15 pm rolled around and McBride came through the door. For a brute, he was very punctual. He walked over to us and grabbed my beer and finished it.

"What up, pretty ladies? You ready to go get into some trouble?"

"How are we getting there? You calling us a taxi, McB?"

"Cabs are for chumps. So I guess you two can get a cab and me and your hot cousin here will meet you there. Just fucking around."

McBride grabbed Wynn's beer and pounded the rest of it. Evelyn, sensing a pattern here, put a stiff-arm to McBride's chest then drank down the rest of her beer before McBride reached for it.

"Alright, follow me, ladies."

McBride led us outside to a party bus that was double-parked with the hazards flashing. The doors swung inwards and McBride waved us on. There was a hulking guy behind the wheel who looked us over and nodded as we entered and sat down.

"This here's my boy, Brian."

McBride winked and smiled at me then mouthed the name "Angie" while gesturing with his thumb towards the beast in the driver's seat. This was who Angie's new man was, this fucking 'roided out pile of muscle? Fucking McBride.

"Brian, the hot one here is Evelyn, then over there you got her concubine, Wynn…."

McBride smiled wide as he pointed towards me. I tried not to look nervous. What if Angie had pictures of me in her phone? What if he knew my name? Of course he knew my name. Why'd you have to name me Serin, Mom? If you gave me a common name I wouldn't be about to get stomped to death on a party bus right now.

"And this clown ova here, we just call him clowny no-nuts. Ain't that right, clowny?"

"That's me," I said.

"My boy Brian here is hooking us up with a ride over to the Lex before he goes to work. Lucky fucka got a bunch of drunk sorority chicks to pick up later. We're on our own getting back."

"Thanks, Brian," Evelyn said.

Brian flipped off the hazards, closed the doors, then headed off towards the Lex. McBride just smiled at me with his shit-eating grin for most of the trip. Techno music came on full blast through the speakers, so nobody talked on the ride there which was ideal seeing if Wynn or Evelyn called me by name, Brian might snap many of my fragile bones. We arrived fifteen minutes later and all thanked Brian while exiting. He drove off, thankfully without further interaction. McBride slapped me on my back.

"Told ya' he was a beast."

"Why the fuck would you do that to me?"

"Do what?" Evelyn asked as she overheard us talking.

"That guy Brian right there, he's hooking up with one of Serin's ex-psychos. I like seeing my boy here sweat a bit."

"Ex-psycho, huh? Angie perhaps?" Evelyn said.

"Yeah, how you know Angie? You run in the same psycho-circles or sumthin?"

I had to catch myself for a second. How did Evelyn know Angie? Then it came to me, she read my journal. She knew some basic traits about the people in my journal that I had catalogued so far.

"Oh, I read about her today in Serin's diary."

"Oh yeah? Serin write any poems about me in that fruity book of his?"

"Maybe you should join our poetry club, McBride, and find out for yourself."

"Naw, me and poems ain't a mix. Ah shit, there's my boy Reuben. Let's go, cupcakes."

We followed McBride over to the entrance. There was a line to get in but McBride walked to the front and slapped the enormous bouncer on the back.

"What up, salty? I got these three ladies with me tonight. I know, those two are busted but the third one makes up for them."

"What up, McBride? Take these for you and your lady friends."

Reuben handed McBride four wristbands and unhooked the velvet rope to let us all in. McBride led the way inside.

The Lex consisted of one huge room with a stage at one end and the bar at the opposite end. In between was open space where people stood or danced or got into the occasional pushing match. The place was about seventy percent full with more people waiting outside. The inside was lit with x-mas lights that hung from every wall. There were additional lights around the stage where the DJ was currently set up.

McBride walked past the main room, through the crowd and out the back door to the patio, where weed and cigarette smoke filled the air. The back patio was large with couches, tables, heat lamps and a smaller bar. McBride handed a wristband to me and Wynn then helped Evelyn put hers on.

"These here are for the bar. Whatever you want. Just throw them a tip when you get your drinks and it's all good."

"Thanks."

"Why don't y'all grab some drinks and get comfortable? I got some shit I gotta handle."

With that, he disappeared back inside, doing Zeus knows what. We grabbed some drinks, then found a table in the back corner of the patio that was empty.

"Have either of you been here before? I'm assuming that's a no for you, Wynn."

"I tend to like going to places where the susceptibility rate for catching a transmissible disease is lower than what I'd assume this place's is."

"Bit of a snob there, Wynn?" Evelyn asked.

"If I were a snob, I wouldn't be associating with Serin, now would I?"

"Good point. I was here once with some co-workers from the Lamp Room but never thought to come back."

Evelyn turned to me and asked, "So who is Loren?"

Once again I had to catch myself before remembering they both had read my journal.

"Loren?"

"Yes, I'm just curious what a Dirty-Pretty Temptress is."

My reflexive impulse was to lie about Loren but Evelyn seemed to appreciate the truth-telling.

"She's just a girl I hung out with at a house party one night last summer. She has a bunch of tattoos and piercings but underneath all of that shit is a pretty girl. She gave me mescaline then ditched me soon afterward."

Wynn interrupted, "This is one of the people you chose to catalogue? Someone you barely know? It'd seem from a scientific standpoint that if one were cataloguing personalities, they'd start with people they actually knew."

"You can have an experience with someone and instantly know what kind of person they are. I've only known you really for a week or so and already know you've got a dickish personality. I mean, you've known McBride for about ten minutes now and I'm pretty sure you have got a solid take on his personality, right?"

"And what about me? Do you have me all figured out?" Evelyn asked.

"You, I don't know yet. I'm waiting for the tragic flaw to present itself."

"Her tragic flaw is all but obvious. It's her taste in men."

"Shut up, Wynn."

Something caught my eye from inside through the wall of glass that separated the patio from the main room. At first I thought it was just the lights by the stage but this was coming from the middle of the room. Someone's phantom was flickering.

"What is it?" Evelyn asked.

"I don't know how thoroughly either of you read my journal, but two times so far, once near campus and once at my Uncle Chester's apartment complex, I saw phantoms that were flashing like a strobe light."

"Are you seeing one now?" Wynn asked.

I stood up. "Follow me."

Wynn and Evelyn grabbed their drinks and followed me inside. I stayed by the wall and walked halfway toward the stage until I could get a glimpse of the person whose phantom was flickering.

"Which one?" Wynn asked.

"It's that guy in the middle of the room with the red shirt that's unbuttoned all the way."

Wynn and Evelyn understood who I was talking about and watched him. He was sort of dancing to the music but off-beat and kind of stumbling. He looked beyond wasted. At our current distance, I could see that his phantom wasn't just flickering. It was twitching in spurts. The whole thing would vibrate and temporarily stretch and blur before coming back into focus. Something was going to happen to this guy in the red shirt. But what?

"Something is wrong. I know this is hard to understand but from what I'm seeing, I get the feeling like something bad is going to happen to him."

"The other two of these that you've seen, how long were you watching them?"

"I saw the one near campus drive by for only about six seconds before it was out of my sight. The one at my Uncle Chester's place was also in a car and I only saw it for maybe twenty seconds before it drove off."

"If this is real, we need this observation to set a future precedent for this type of occurrence. You've only seen this for a matter of seconds without any kind of follow-up. This could mean almost anything or nothing. We simply need to observe. For all we know right now, this strobe effect might be temporary and will return to normal in a matter of minutes."

"If you guys were seeing what I'm seeing right now, you wouldn't have any optimism."

"So what do you suggest?" Evelyn asked. "To us he just looks like a drunk. But if what you are seeing is really that bad, what can we do?"

"I don't know. Maybe Wynn is right and we just have to wait and see."

McBride pushed his way through some people holding four shot glasses and spotted us by the wall. He headed over and held out the drinks to us.

"What up, ya wallflowers? Why ya look all sour? Serin here read you a sad poem or sumthin?"

Fuck, not now, McBride. Your timing is for shit. If I were ever going to try to explain things to you, this definitely is not the moment for it. What to do with McBride?

Evelyn spoke up, "McBride, do you see that guy in the middle of the room with the unbuttoned red shirt? The one doing the drunken dancing? You don't know him do you?"

McBride scanned the room and locked in on who Evelyn was asking about.

"Ah yeah. I've seen him around. Just some junky kid. Why, Wynn ova here looking for a date?"

"It could be nothing but we just think he's acting strange, like something might happen to him."

"You guys are sweet with all your caring and shit, but don't waste your time worrying about any of these junky kids in here. They don't give a shit so why the fuck should you?"

McBride raised his shot glass to us and we clinked glasses and drank. The three of us didn't take our eyes off the guy in the red unbuttoned shirt. McBride seemed agitated.

"You guys fucking high or sumthin?"

Just then the phantom hovering over the guy went from flickering to a nuclear flash. I jumped back and threw up my arms to cover my face. Evelyn and Wynn jumped at my reaction. McBride ducked, then looked around, then back at us, bewildered. I looked back and the phantom was gone. The guy in the red unbuttoned shirt was on the floor. The people in his immediate vicinity were slowly reacting to this guy who

191

collapsed to the ground as if they weren't sure what was happening.

Wynn asked me, "What did you see?"

"It went supernova. Just a huge bright flash and then it disappeared."

"What da fuck you queers rambling about? How you know that kid was gonna drop?"

Evelyn pushed her way past McBride and walked slowly over to the growing group of people starting to form around the guy on the floor. If she was holding onto any doubt about what I was seeing, the look on her face said her doubts were now at zero. One of the bouncers was called over and was kneeling next to the guy on the floor slapping his cheek and trying to get the guy to wake up. I felt ice coursing through my body.

"You chicks gonna fill me in or what? You a bunch of scanners or sumthin? Blowing people up with your minds and shit?"

"If you really want to know, McB, I promise I'll fill you in. The shit's a bit complicated though. This isn't the best time or place to get into it."

McBride glanced over at Wynn and Wynn nodded at him in agreement that this wasn't the time or place.

"I'll give you a pass 'til tomorrow then. I'm opening Red's around 3:30 pm. Swing by with some answers."

I nodded back at him. Evelyn walked back over to us.

"He doesn't look like he's breathing. I'm kind of freaking out right now. I think I need to get out of here."

"I'm thinking the same thing. You want to share a taxi or are you looking to get away from me, too?"

"No, you're fine. I just can't stay here. We can share a ride."

"I'm with you guys," Wynn said.

"All of you bailing on your Uncle McBride, huh?"

"Sorry," Evelyn said. "This situation is too much for me right now."

"It's alright, girlie. Do what you got to do. Yo, Serin, come with some answers tomorrow at 3:30 pm."

"I will McB. Thanks for getting us in. I'll hit you up tomorrow."

McBride slapped Wynn on his back. Evelyn gave McBride a quick hug. I could see McBride was confused by all of this but a few more drinks and we'd be in his rear view mirror for tonight. We walked outside and got lucky as a couple of girls were just getting out of a taxi. We jumped in it as the faint and distant sounds of an ambulance siren could be heard. We rode in silence, dropping Evelyn off first who lived four blocks from the Lamp Room.

"So, have I managed to scare you off for good yet?"

"I think the smart move would be to distance myself from you guys and pretend this never happened."

My chest started to constrict. Feelings akin to what I was feeling when Loren ditched me that night started to rise.

"How could I possibly walk away from this though? No, I'm not going anywhere. I've got a full day tomorrow but I'm going to see if I can meet you at Red's. If anything, I'd love to see McBride's reaction to you telling him about this."

She then reached over me and squeezed Wynn's hand.

"I liked hanging out with you, Wynn."

"Same here, Evelyn."

She surprised me with a quick kiss on the cheek. She got out of the taxi and before I could protest, gave the driver enough money to get us all home. She waved at us and headed towards her apartment.

"I am truly at a loss. She is beautiful, intelligent and thoughtful. You are none of those things."

"I'll let you have that one, Wynn. I really don't get it either."

The driver headed to Red's Tavern and dropped us off.

"I'm going to call my friend again when I get home. Hopefully, he'll be free tomorrow so I can expedite the translations. I'll head to my grandmother's first thing in the morning to scan the book and get the process going."

"Thanks. Let me know as soon as you've got something. I'm coming back here at 3:30 pm to try to explain this to McBride."

"You really think he's capable of processing something like this?"

"I honestly have no idea how he's going to react. As I told you before, though, he's a good guy to have on your team. So who knows?"

"I haven't asked yet because I was still on the fence about all of this until tonight."

"Do you want to know what your phantom looks like?"

"Well, I guess so. That can wait though. I was actually curious if you can see your own phantom."

I never really thought about it since I tried taking pictures of my blotch when it was just blown pixels in the rainforest that I was seeing. I just assumed no. But now that the pixels were full-fledged creatures, I never bothered trying to see if I could see mine. Now I was starting to feel anxious.

I slowly looked over my shoulder and up but couldn't see anything. I then tilted my head straight back as far as it would go but still couldn't see anything. What did that mean? Was I not able to process my own phantom or was I like that group of Down syndrome people or that old geezer in the wheelchair and simply didn't have a phantom? Shit, what if my phantom just went supernova and disappeared and I've got two seconds before I collapse?

"I can't see anything."

"Interesting. Alright, I'm going to head out. You want a ride home? My car is around the corner."

"No, I'm good. I'll catch up with you tomorrow."

"Okay."

Wynn walked towards his car and I started heading back to my apartment. I decided to make a quick detour to Campus Liquor to pick up a bottle of rum and some orange juice. It was still relatively early and I was starting to dry buzz. Two or three more drinks would be needed to nullify the vision of the spastic exploding phantom that was still fresh in my mind.

After arriving back home, I settled in with some cocktails and a boxing match I had on the DVR. I caught myself occasionally touching my face where Evelyn had kissed me. Her hooks were buried in me now.

Sorry, Loren, your spell has been broken and replaced by a more powerful sorcery.

Chapter Thirty-Four
The Brain, the Muse and the Brute

Up at 10:36 am. I was still on the couch and the TV was still on but muted. The bottle of rum was sitting on the coffee table, three-fourths empty. Another day in wonderland.

There was no agenda today aside from waiting to hear from Wynn and checking in with McBride at Red's later.

Grabbed my journal and flipped through it. I looked at the list I had created and the people I had remaining but didn't see much point in cataloguing the rest of the list if Wynn came through with the scans and translations.

Glanced at my phone and saw a text from Wynn. All it said was, "Check your email." Walked to the bathroom to relieve myself of the three-fourths bottle of processed rum, then returned to the couch and fired up my laptop. Once it was booted up, I opened my email. Wynn had written a long message with an attachment of a scanned image from the book.

His email read, "I've been at my grandmother's since 8:00 am this morning and am close to finishing up the scans. I have been emailing the scans to my friend as I have been going along. He's been translating the pages as we go and should be done in a couple of hours. This is a redundant and mundane process so I've had plenty of time to think this morning. I've been running searches trying to find some kind of reference to what is in this book.

"Aside from a brief mention of my grandmother's old province geographically, there is nothing to be found culturally specific to their people or rituals. I haven't been able to find

197

any mention of the mythology about the phantoms. What's in this book, as far as I can see, has never made it out into cyberspace. In all likelihood, there are probably only three more copies of this book in existence as I'm only assuming that each shaman had his own copy. Of course, that might not even be true and my grandmother is in sole possession of the one and only version of this book.

"So in taking into account the absolute rarity of this book from this isolated culture, I'm forced to have to consider something I don't want to. Keep in mind, I still want to believe that there is a rational explanation for all of this that has yet to present itself. But, putting that aside and working within the confines of what we know and assuming this is all real, the following seems inescapable. You and I were somehow brought together.

"You and I are both extremely rare individuals in our own ways within the context of this situation. You, through poisoning of a sort, are now able to see things nobody else can see. I, because of where my grandmother was born, have a genealogical tie to an almost unknown sub-culture and access to a more-than-likely one-of-a-kind book that just so happens to relate to your situation. The laws of probability would say that we meeting each other would be an almost impossible occurrence. Mathematically it just can't be a coincidence.

"My grandmother said they were whispering phantoms. What if they can actually manipulate us somehow? Get in our minds and pass off suggestions as our own thoughts. If all of this is true, then somewhere along our timelines, you and I were both influenced into meeting each other. It is futile looking back and trying to decipher when and where each of us was being pushed towards each other. Too many factors over too much time involving too many decisions. But if I'm working within what we know, I'd say that you and I were manipulated by these things into coming into contact with each other so you'd have access to what is in this book.

"It all seems the more ludicrous as I try to type out these thoughts. But these are the ideas I've been wrestling with this morning and thought I'd present them to you. Attached to this email is a scan of one of the pages. I can't be sure, as your sketches are the work of a five-year-old, but the attached scanned page has an illustration that resembles the sketch you did last night at Red's Tavern. I think this is Evelyn's Phantom."

I opened the attachment and there it was on my screen. It was Evelyn's Phantom. The drawing was a hundred times more skillful than my sketch but I didn't need to compare this scan to my sketch. I had seen the real thing in person last night and this was what hovered over Evelyn.

Maybe Wynn was right. Maybe he and I were pushed together somehow by these things. Who knows how intricate a system was involved on that realm. He's right. It hurts my head to try and look back and find particular points of where I could have been influenced.

The most obvious thing I could think of was Ariel. She could have been placed in front of me all this time to eventually lure me into chasing her to Australia. How long had she been influenced to be a part of this? Was she manipulated into pursuing a biology major for the sole purpose of being a part of this larger plan? Was the ticket agent manipulated into putting Wynn and me next to each other on the flight to Australia?

How deep can it go? How much could they orchestrate? Were there opposing forces up there working against one another trying to sabotage each other's influence and perpetuate their own agendas? What was motivating them?

What was their end game? My head was starting to really hurt and not from last night's rum.

Too much thinking. I'm much more functional when the thinking is minimal.

Shower. Shave. Fresh start. Coffee was the next short-term goal. Grabbed my backpack, threw my laptop and journal inside it, then headed out for a low energy stroll over to the Lamp Room. The streets were relatively quiet which made it easier to try to ignore the phantoms that I was seeing and just relax my mind a bit.

Made it to the Lamp Room which was also quiet. There were only a handful of people in the entire place. The Lamp Room was a non-corporate coffee joint with five different rooms. Each room had some random furniture in it. Couches, lounge chairs, different tables and lamps. It was like a furniture outlet that served coffee.

I grabbed a large iced-coffee and talked myself out of their microwaved breakfast burrito and settled on an oat muffin and a banana instead. I was trying to mend relations with my long-disgruntled digestive system. Sat down at a quiet spot in the back room on an unoccupied love seat next to a coffee table. Booted up my laptop then connected to their free wifi. I reopened Wynn's email which I reread while eating my breakfast.

After I finished off the oat muffin and banana, I launched my own investigation. I searched Bangladesh rituals, religions, provinces and mythologies. I did image searches on phantoms, spirits, ghosts, demons. There was nothing I could read or see that had any connection to what I was experiencing. The only thing of interest I found was during an image search for demons, a few images for "sexy demon costumes" popped up for an online Halloween outlet. Those were pretty cool.

The coffee was starting to work and the neurons were starting to fire. I re-opened the email from Wynn and downloaded the scan of Evelyn's phantom to my desktop. I then edited the scan in Photoshop, isolating only the image and erasing everything else in the background. I then saved the edited version of her phantom and then uploaded it for a similar-image search. The results were shit. This world of phantoms was an exclusive club.

It's been what, half a century or more since that province was abandoned because of the blight? Hadn't anyone from that province moved on and shared their traditions? Or what if the whole phantom thing was only known to the shamans? Possibly the common townsfolk were oblivious to what the ritual really did and what the shamans actually saw. All I knew was that the more I searched, the more I didn't find.

Hours melted away as I endlessly hunted for something that didn't seem to exist on the internet. The only thing that came out of it was a cramped back and shoulders from hunching over my laptop for so long.

It was getting close to 3:30 pm when I realized I'd probably be showing McBride my journal. Like with Evelyn, I kind of already forgot what I wrote about McBride so I thought it'd be a good idea to check. Pulled out my journal and flipped to his page. Next to his sketch I had written, "The Violent but Loyal Jester." Beneath that I wrote, "Walking mayhem fueled by lust and bloodthirst. More beast than man. Doglike loyalty. Kind of funny."

I'm glad I did all these sketch pages in pencil. I erased all the notes and started from scratch. I changed his quick-trait to, "The Amusing Soldier." Beneath that I wrote, "Loyal and quick-witted. A tank you want in your army." There, that should play better.

My phone had been on vibrate and I didn't notice that Wynn had texted me. He said, "Translations are almost done. A lot to go over. Will meet you at Red's Tavern after I finish up here."

Packed up my laptop and journal then headed over to Red's. I thought about Wynn's email again. Was I getting pushed towards McBride right now? Is Evelyn a part of this? Was she influenced to give me her number and go to coffee with me? If so, can I bribe her phantom into influencing her to do some other stuff with me of the freaky and low-down dirty variety? Pimp phantoms. Stop it. Evelyn was the pimp. I'd be in her stable. Shut up little brain. Big brain is driving.

Big brain wanted to know if McBride was coming along for the ride or not. If so, why were we being brought together? Whose team were we all on as far as the phantom realm? Good? Evil? Do those concepts even exist in that realm? Shit, too many questions. Let's just see how this goes with McB.

Red's was only a couple of blocks away and I arrived right at 3:30 pm. The door was open so I walked in. The place was empty with only McBride behind the bar putting away some pint glasses. I walked over to the bar and took my usual stool. McBride acknowledged me but there was a hesitant look on his face and his energy was turned down to fuel-saving mode. I had never seen this version of McBride before.

"What's going on, McB? You alright?"

"Been thinking this shit ova' and don't know if I wanna get involved with whateva' shit you guys got going on."

"That's cool. I'm not really trying to recruit more people into this. This shit is really fucked up but seeing you said last night you wanted some answers, I thought I'd show up."

"I talked to my boy Rueben this morning. That junky kid from last night is dead. They think he mixed too much shit and OD'd."

Shit. What does that make me now? I've got death radar. Why can't I have hot-chicks-are-horny radar? Shit.

"The way you guys were jumpin' when that kid went to sleep is fuckin' with me."

"It's your call, McB. I can tell you everything if you want or we can forget about it."

McBride poured two pints and put one down in front of me and started to drink the other one. "Fuck it," he said. "Make with the answers. You guys some weirdo witches or sumthin? I figured the only way you could get a hot chick like Evelyn to hang out with you is because you joined some fucking cult or some shit."

"No cults. Nothing that stupid." I reached into my bag and pulled out my journal and dropped it on the counter. "Easiest place to start is by reading this. It's fucked up and sounds like a joke, but this shit is really happening to me."

"Poetry club, huh?" McBride picked up the journal and eyed the cover then looked back at me. "Alright then."

McBride grabbed his beer and walked over to a booth with my journal. He sat quietly for fifteen minutes, reading. I slowly sipped my beer and zoned out for a bit. What am I supposed to do with this death radar? Seriously, phantoms, what game are you playing? Why me? Why didn't you just poison Wynn instead of me and cut out the middle-man? As I was tossing thoughts around, the front door opened and Evelyn walked in. McBride gave her a quick glance then continued reading. She came over and sat down next to me.

"Hello, Joy."

"Hello, Phantom Freak. Did I miss anything?"

"Nothing much. McBride thought we might be witches or something. Oh yeah, and I apparently have death radar. That guy from last night died."

"Are you serious?"

"Sorry, didn't mean to be all jokey about it. The guy died and that's shitty. I'm just in a headspace right now really close to delirious. If I don't spin my situation as comical I'm going to snap."

"I don't blame you. If I were seeing what you are seeing I'd probably be locked in a closet right now making tiny cuts into my thighs."

I know that shouldn't have turned me on right there but it did.

"Any word from Wynn and the book?"

"Oh yeah. I forgot." I pulled out my phone and opened up the scan Wynn sent me and held it up for Evelyn. "Wynn sent me this scan from the book. He found your phantom."

She looked at it and I could see her face start to pale a bit.

"This is really happening."

"Or it's the most elaborate prank ever played on someone."

"It's just really hard to believe you know? Why would anyone want to believe this? I don't want to believe there is some creature I can't see floating above me, whispering to me, whatever that means. But you and this old book. I'm running out of excuses."

"I'd be crushed, but I really wouldn't blame you if you were to walk away from all of this and try to forget about it. This is uncharted fuckery. I have no idea what's coming next."

"You'd be crushed? More or less crushed than when you got ditched by that Loren girl?"

"I think you need to let me read your diary a bit so I can have some ex-boyfriend references to throw in your face whenever I want."

"So she was what you considered a girlfriend, huh? Someone you knew for an hour? Does that mean you go around telling people you and I are married?"

"Shit, you and me with what we've been through already? I tell people we're divorced but trying to work things out for the sake of our three kids."

McBride returned to his spot behind the bar and threw my journal down, then poured Evelyn a beer while refreshing mine and his.

"So what. This a fuckin' joke or sumthin?"

"I wish it were, McB."

McBride looked at Evelyn and asked, "And what about you girlie? You a part of the joke or what?"

"I met Serin a couple of days ago. Of course I thought this wasn't real when he told me. How could I? How could you? I get it. But over the last two days, everything that's going on is making me believe this is real. No jokes."

"You haven't heard all of it yet. What you just read in my journal is just the first part. What you don't know is that Wynn read my journal yesterday for the first time and recognized my sketches. His grandmother has this old book from Bangladesh that knows about what I'm seeing. He's actually coming here any minute with a translation of the book so we can try and figure out more. Here, check this out."

I showed McBride the scan on my phone Wynn sent me of Evelyn's phantom.

"This is out of the book. This is hundreds of years old. This is what I'm seeing right now hovering over Evelyn."

"And you see this kind of shit above me right now, too, huh?"

"Yours is different from hers but yes, you have one of these over you right now, too. I know, I don't want to believe it but I'm seeing it. And last night I saw the phantom over that guy in the red shirt start to blink on and off. Then all of a sudden it blew up and disappeared. That's why I reacted that way. Next thing you know he's dead."

This was new information to McBride and he stood there staring through me, working it out in his head.

"As I said, Wynn is coming here with what I hope to be some answers. I don't expect you to believe any of this but it is what it is and this is what we're involved in. When he gets here, we can go somewhere else if you want and we'll leave you out of this. You wanted to know. Now you know. It's your call if you want to be a part of this or not."

McBride focused in on me then over to Evelyn.

"He's not fucking with me is he, girlie?"

"From what I've seen, I have to say no. I think this is real."

"You got any friends that are as hot as you are?"

Evelyn blushed a bit then said, "I have a few friends who I think are very pretty."

McBride looked back over to me.

"Alright, I got your back on this. Shit sounds suspect as fuck but I don't see why you'd be fucking with me. Plus, if Evelyn here is going to be hanging out with you, maybe she can bring some of her hot friends around for ol' McBride."

And with that, we had our muscle. The Brain, the Muse, the Brute, and I guess I'd be the Voyeur. Although I think voyeur is used as a sexual term, like beating off while looking through somebody's window or some stupid shit like that. I don't know. Whatever. The Voyeur sounded cool to me.

We drank our beers and went over everything we knew with McBride so he was up to date. We went back and forth for twenty minutes or so until a couple of guys walked in and sat at the other end of the bar. McBride went over and got them drinks, then came back and refilled ours. At around 4:30 pm, Wynn showed up carrying a tablet and sat down with us.

"Aye, yo, what up there, Winny the Poon? You drinking?"

"Sure."

"Hi, Wynn."

"Hi, Evelyn. So did you two discuss things with him?"

"I'm right here, Winny. You can talk directly to your uncle."

"Okay, are you informed of what's going on?"

"Sure, I'm informed that you fuckas stumbled across some ancient Chinese secrets. Shit still sounds stupid as all hell to me but I'm on board. Especially since Evelyn here is going to hook me up with a bunch of her hot friends."

"In all honesty, McBride, my friends generally go for guys more like Wynn."

"Ah, girlie, you trying to hurt my feelings? What's wrong with me? Ol' Wynn here only likes them cartoon girls anyways. Real girls give him the fear, ain't that right, Winny?"

Wynn sighed then said, "Not to disregard the importance of your current topic of discussion, but I am holding a complete translation of a book that sheds light on what I believe could be the most significant discovery in human history."

"Of course. Just ignore the muse and the brute and show us what you got."

"Why you calling your girlie here a brute? That's not very nice."

Wynn turned on his tablet and opened the gallery then placed it on the bar. The tablet's case had a built in kickstand so it sat on the bar like a picture frame so we could all see it. Wynn pulled out his phone also and opened up a text document.

"What you see on the tablet is the first page of the book. Feel free to flip through them at your own pace. On my phone, I have the page by page translations. I've already read through some of it. Most of it is basic information unrelated to the phantoms. The first half of the book talks about the history of the province and the four townships. It explains the fishing and farming techniques as well as the other trades they practiced like weaving, metal working and carpentry.

"The second half of the book is more related to the people and the rituals. For example, they didn't have marriages but they did have something called The Twin-Light Ceremony for a couple who decides to live together and possibly have children. They also had something like a baptism for newborns but no kind of god was involved. It was more about the sun nourishing the child to grow and finding an honorable path.

"The last quarter of the book covers the phantom ritual and their interpretation of the phantom realm as well as all of their illustrations. Based on the wording of this section, I'm inclined to believe that the general populace wasn't aware of any of this. It was definitely written by a shaman who speaks of the townsfolk as being ignorant of their phantoms.

"Every twelve years, the four townships would come together for the Festival of the Black Moon. During this festival, different people from each township would present themselves as candidates to become the new leaders. The leader was the resolver of problems within each township. There was great honor in being one of the leaders. The shamans from each township would get together for the ritual, then would choose the new leaders.

"Their interpretation was that everyone was claimed by a phantom during childhood. These phantoms had a limited ability to be able to influence and manipulate us in different ways throughout our lives. They believed the phantom world was divided and what was happening on earth had direct consequences within their world. Humans were the game pieces and our world was their chess board. Their realm and motivations were unknowable to man. What the shamans did figure out was that the different types of phantoms correlated to specific human characteristics and behaviors."

"So these shamans were saying the same thing I've been saying, that our personalities are linked to what kind of phantom we have. They actually had chess in that isolated province, huh?"

"No, that was a liberal translation by my friend. The concept is intact though. To simplify it, the phantoms hold a certain amount of influence over us and are trying to position us for their own agendas."

"So how were these shamans able to see them? Did it explain any of that?"

"Yes. This is where it gets a bit bizarre. Let me show you this one particular page from the book."

Wynn flicked through a bunch of pages until he landed on an illustration. It was of a goat wearing what looked like an upside-down saddle with a funnel device hanging beneath it.

"Ah, what the fuck you got there, Winny, some fucking animal S and M type of shit?"

"This was part of the ritual. They believed the goat was the doorway to the phantom realm. The shamans would put this device on a goat then feed it something called *the dark roots*. And before you ask, the dark roots is a literal translation. My best guess is it's some sort of indigenous hallucinogenic plant like peyote. They'd feed it to the goat and wait. The goat would eventually urinate which this contraption would funnel into a bowl. The shamans would then drink the drug-laced urine."

"Oh, my fucking...."

Evelyn put her hand over my mouth before I could continue. I almost instinctively tried to make-out with the palm of her hand but caught myself. She looked at me and said, "Quiet."

"Thanks, Evelyn. I'd highly recommend disinfecting that hand of yours at first chance." *Shut up, Wynn.*

"So yes, they drank the urine which was said to let them temporarily glimpse the world of the phantoms. It said this phantom world was visible for two turns after the ritual then they would once again disappear. I'm assuming two turns means two days. During this time, they'd assess the men presenting themselves as possible leaders of the townships. The shamans would select the leaders based on whose phantom was most associated with honorable characteristics."

I swiped through the images of the phantoms on Wynn's tablet and was overwhelmed with a sense of relief and a sense of dread. I was relieved I wasn't insane. The dread I was feeling was from knowing that the shamans in the story no longer saw the phantoms once their piss drinks wore off. Why wasn't mine wearing off?

"What about the notes on the sketch pages?"

I flipped through the tablet images until I found Evelyn's.

"Here, next to Evelyn's. Do you have the translations for this?"

"Yes, I've got all the translations. These are basic characteristic traits and summaries just like your journal. Here, let me find the notes for that page on my phone."

"Hold on a second, Wynn. I'm not sure I want to know what it says about my phantom just yet. Why don't you do yours or McBride's first?"

"Yeah, you heard the girlie. What I got? The Cadillac chick-slayer phantom or what?"

"Serin?"

"What?"

"Would be a lot easier if you just flip through the tablet and find his phantom for us."

"Oh yeah. Sorry."

I looked up at McBride's phantom to refresh my memory then flipped through the pages on the tablet. The illustration of McBride's phantom was spot on and fairly easy to find. There was a number at the bottom of the scan that looked out of place.

"This is the one. What's with this number right here at the bottom?"

"After each scan was complete, I added a reference number for each page so I could match up the translation. Hold on—page thirty-six."

Wynn scrolled for a while on his phone looking for the translation for page thirty-six. McBride took a look at the tablet and pointed to the illustration.

"So you're saying this fucking thing right here is hanging out above me right now? What are those, some wings or sumthin?"

"That's what I'm saying. The illustrations in the book are accurate but they all are in black ink. What I'm seeing is in color. Yours has neon green skin which is almost glowing."

"Ok, I found the translation for the notes you see next to the illustration. Up at the top, the title translates to 'The Ox.' Below that it says, 'Aligned with disorder. Trustworthy to those who are close. Formidable and aggressive. Honorable.' That's the entire translation."

"Alright then. You clowns call me Ox McBride from now on. Who's next?"

"You go next, Wynn. I'm still not sure if I want to know what it says about mine," Evelyn said.

"Why's that? Have you been hiding your true self from us and you're really a perverted deviant?"

"No. It's just I've got reservations about being told by an ancient book what type of person I'm being manipulated into being."

"Ah, it don't matter, girlie. As long as you're hot, you can be a perverted whateva and I'll still like you."

"Thanks, McBride."

"I'm ready if you want to find my phantom on the tablet," Wynn said.

I took my first real look at Wynn's phantom. It was yellow. I'm not the racist. Blame the phantom. It had a strong resemblance to the stomach of a dragon. It was bulbous and covered with what looked to be fine scales. It had deep-set eyes on both sides of it, positioned like a whale's.

I flipped through the pages on the tablet and didn't find his phantom. I returned to the beginning and tried again and found it at the bottom of the second page of sketches. It shared a page with a different phantom so I must have glazed over it on the first pass.

"That's the one. And I'm not trying to be racist or anything but it is yellow, if you were curious."

Wynn took a look at his phantom. He noted the page number then scrolled through the translations on his phone until he landed at the correct entry.

"So what you got there, Winny? Good with numbers. Dishonorable with getting ladies or what?"

Wynn pretended to ignore McBride.

"At the top the title translates to 'the cartographer.' "

"Cartographer? What's that, some kind of mapmaker or sumthin? You making maps there, Winny? Maps to the fetish porn store or sumthin?"

Wynn looked up at McBride and for the first time cracked a smile at him. I couldn't get a read on what Wynn thought of McBride and just assumed he hated him. But I'm guessing Wynn had just never encountered someone like McBride and it took a while to acclimate to someone constantly making fun of you.

"The notes below the title say 'Methodical in pursuit of enlightenment. Timid, preferring isolation above interaction. Honest. Honorable.' "

"Ah, that's pretty good there, Winny. You sure you didn't make all that up to try to be as cool as the Ox ova' here?"

A group of three guys walked through the door and ordered some drinks with McBride, then took one of the back booths. McBride took them their drinks then came back over.

"Aye, yo, I was just thinking about some of the shit in your fruity diary. You said the pack of retards on campus and that geezer at the zoo didn't have phantoms right?"

"Right, not necessarily how you just said it, but yes."

"Shit's kind of obvious right? If these phantom fucks are playing us in a game or sumthin, then they probably ain't gonna choose some fucking broken pieces to play with right? You said them small kids at the zoo didn't have them either. Little fucking kids ain't got no value to them yet. Can't use the geezer cuz he's half dead in a wheelchair. Can't use the 'tards cuz their brains are twisted up."

"Those are valid points," Wynn said somewhat surprised.

"Fucking right they are. I know you guys probably think I'm a fucking monkey, but I got a 3.6 GPA last semester."

"You go to school?" Wynn asked a little too surprisingly.

"See there now, Winny. You're being your own worst enemy trying to judge books by their covers. No joke, I guarantee I'd fuck you up over a game of Jeopardy there, mapmaker."

Wynn's brain was short-circuiting. He had painted McBride into a box in his mind and McBride just prison-raped that box into oblivion. I didn't even know McBride went to school. We never talked about it before.

"Another thing, that pit bull and that mountain lion you said had phantoms. Makes sense, don't it, that some dick phantoms would recruit some vicious animals if they could? I mean a pit bull breaking off his leash and tearing up some kid is a hell of a tool. Same with the mountain lion. Phantom was probably using that cat to fuck shit up on that hiking trail. And maybe it takes them phantoms awhile to recognize their human or animal ain't usable no more. Maybe there's some kind of detachment process they gots to go through before they can dump one of their pieces. I bet if you go back to the zoo in another week that mountain lion ain't got a phantom no more."

Wynn was still staring at McBride, a bit awestruck. This stuff was obvious in retrospect but none of us had connected the dots yet. McBride was out-braining the cartographer.

"More valid points. Can I ask you what your major is in?" Wynn asked McBride.

"You can ask me, Winny. But I ain't got a major no more. I just picked up my BS in Marketing and am starting a Masters in International Business next semester."

"You...but...I mean you are doing this here at this campus or on one of those online universities?"

"There you go again, Winny. No, I don't waste my time on some dogshit online diploma. I graduated here. I'm getting my masters here. I will fuck you up on Jeopardy here, any day of the week."

"Sorry. I mean you just....it is just hard to...I uh..."

"Stop hurting yourself, mapmaker. What about you, girlie? You ready to have your phantom read or not? I mean, being hot is nine-tenths of being awesome. You don't need to care about all the other fucked characteristics you got."

"Thanks for the compliment, I think. I just am not as confident as I pretend to be. I mean this book, these translations, it's like looking yourself up in the dictionary and reading your own definition. What if my definition is…"

"You worry too much, girlie. So what, worst case scenario it says you're a piece of shit. Who cares? McBride still likes ya'."

"I hate to admit it, but he's right," I said. "Having McBride's approval is the cornerstone of existence."

"I know you think you're being funny there, chumpy, but my approval is like getting knighted by a king. Seriously, girlie, me liking you is all the validation you need in life."

"All right, all right," Evelyn said. "Let's get it over with."

I flipped through the pages on the tablet until I spotted Evelyn's getting-sexier-by-the-minute phantom. Wynn eyed the page number and scrolled through the translations on his phone.

"Ok, so the title there translates to 'the snare.' Below that, the notes say 'influential and magnetic when motivated. Agreeable to most. Compassionate. Honorable.' "

"Oh no, girlie, you really are a piece of shit."

"You relieved? I don't think it could have been much more complimentary. What are you hiding?"

"What?"

"Why would you worry about what it said unless you have some serious skeletons dancing around in your closet?"

"I don't know. I just don't like being judged by people or an ancient book."

"Aye, yo, I don't mean to be calling bullshit or nothing, but all them phantom translations are all rainbows and shit. You read through all of them yet there, Winny, or what? I mean, is everyone's phantom all honorable and shit? Ain't there any prick phantoms or are they all just playing a game of grab-ass with each other up there?"

"I didn't have time to read through the notes on the phantom illustration pages. I only got as far as the rituals, then came here. Let me skim through them."

Wynn browsed his phone. McBride went and served a couple of girls who walked in and took a booth. I looked at Evelyn and smiled.

"Pretty fucked up, huh snare?"

"It's a bit overwhelming but I'll take fucked up over boring any time. Not really fair, though, that we can't look up your phantom and know your title."

"I gave myself the title of the Voyeur if you want to use that."

"Why would you call yourself that? You a peeping tom?"

"Sort of, in a metaphysical way I guess. I don't think these phantoms are used to being looked at by one of us. I'm calling you *the Muse*, Wynn *the Brain* and McBride *the Brute*. It's my little superhero gang."

"Cute. We should have my artist friend sketch up a graphic novel about us."

"We need a few more adventures first, I think."

McBride walked back as Wynn looked up from his phone.

"I found plenty of these that are negative."

He leaned over and flipped through the tablet until he found a page he wanted.

"This one here is called 'the asp.' The notes read 'Dealer of falsehoods. Self-serving. Covetous. Dishonorable.' "

He leaned over again and flipped a couple more pages on the tablet.

"This one here is called 'the spear.' Below it reads 'Leanings towards violence. Narrow thinking. Without compassion. Dangerous. Dishonorable.' There's more if you want me to keep going."

"Can you email me the translations and upload the scans somewhere so I can download a copy when I get home?"

"Sure, I have a hosting account. I'll zip up the scans and upload them to the server and send you a link."

"All right, girlies. We got Serin ova' here who can see these things. We got us three that are supposed to all be honorable. We got a crusty book and a fruity diary. Oh, and he got death radar. So what now? What's our next move?"

We all kind of looked at each other, thinking over the question. What was the next move? Everything up until this point was discovery. What was the course of action now that we knew what we knew?

"Ah, ya' fucking killing me here. You guys ain't got shit, do ya'?"

"Look, McB, we didn't know any of this until just right now. All I knew was I got poisoned in Australia then started seeing shit. Just now we've got some perspective. This shit is nearly unprecedented. How are we supposed to know what to do with this? I mean, I'm sure we're all open to suggestions. What have you got? Let me guess, something involved with going back to the Lex?"

"I'm just saying, you brought me into this. You know who I am. I steamroll over shit. If these phantom fucks are playing us for chumps, we need to punch them in the fucking jaw or sumthin.'"

"Wynn sent me an email this morning which makes a lot of sense to me. Me being able to see these phantoms and Wynn knowing about and having access to this extremely rare book can't be a coincidence. We were influenced over time to come together. I'm not sure yet but I'd like to think you and Evelyn are part of the plan, too. There is something going on up there in their realm and they are making moves with us. I think shit might possibly unfold in front of us without us having to try too hard."

"So what then? Do nothing and just wait?"

"Unless one of you can think of something better. I've got to believe they wanted me to get poisoned by that flower so I could see them. I've got to also believe that Wynn was pushed into my life because I was supposed to see this book he had access to. All of this is speculation, of course, but I'm guessing they wanted me to see that guy die last night. I'm being prepped for something. I'm thinking because I'm surrounded by people with honorable phantoms, we're probably on the right side of things. So I'm kind of inclined to let them pull me to do what they want. I think if they went this far, whatever is going on must be important."

"So I guess it's up to your Uncle McBride ova' here to do the heavy lifting, as always. You can sit on your ass and wait for these fuckers to spell shit out for you, or you can make your own moves."

"Like what?"

"Get the fuck out of the city for the weekend. I say we all go to the craziest place there is. The place where people from all ova' the country and all ova' the world come and get dirty. Vegas."

"What are we supposed to do in Vegas that we can't do here?"

"It ain't about what we doing. It's about what your ass is seeing. Maybe this death radar shit you got is just one thing out of many you haven't figured out yet. Vegas is a fucking vortex of mayhem. What other place is there with millions of people from everywhere doing all kinds of different shit?"

Wynn looked awestruck again towards McBride and said, "It's actually a pretty solid idea."

"There you go again, Winny, sounding surprised and shit."

"I mean from simply a point of observational potential, Las Vegas has an incredibly diverse and dense population. I mean we could find places more local like a sports event or walking around downtown on the weekend but there is nothing around here comparable to the amount of variables available to us like in Las Vegas."

"There you go, Winny. You like that Pai Gow or what, buddy?"

"Look, you know I'm always down for a Vegas trip, regardless of the reason." I turned to Evelyn and said, "I wouldn't even ask you, but you are right here so it'd be rude of me not to."

"What, me going to Vegas with you guys?"

"Too much too soon kind of thing?"

"If it's the sleeping arrangements you worried about, girlie, you can bunk up with ol' McBride."

"When is this trip supposed to be happening?"

"I don't know. I'm basically free until next semester so I can go whenever. What about you, Wynn?"

"I have no obligations. I'm free."

"McBride?"

"I'm down for whateva'. Let's go tomorrow morning. I'll drive."

"Wynn?"

"I can go tomorrow morning if that's the consensus."

"I'm good with tomorrow, too. I guess it's tomorrow morning then. Evelyn?"

"Let me make a phone call."

Evelyn got up and walked outside to make her call.

"You two queers got the majors in plants and shit, right?"

"We're biology majors, if that's what you're asking. Covers a little more than just plants."

"Yeah, whateva'. Point I'm making is what do you think are the odds of us tracking down that black root shit from grandma Winny's home town? I mean, if we can get a hold of some of that, maybe we all could tune in to the fucked up show Serin here is watching."

Wynn stared at McBride for a moment. His wheels were spinning, then his eyes lit up.

"Proper scientific method. Serin ingested toxins from a stand-alone source. That's a dead end for us as the remains were obliterated and can't be reproduced. These shamans and their ritual, however, is possibly replicable. You mentioned the black root but the other variable in this ritual possibly could be the true catalyst and the drug might be just a helping agent in the process. Possibly replaceable by an alternate agent."

Wynn was talking more to himself than to us.

"Yo, queen of babble-on, what you saying? The black root ain't the key? You thinking the goat?"

"This is how I see it. If this black root tapped into the phantom realm by itself, then this would be common knowledge to all of Bangladesh. People do drugs but they don't feed them to livestock first. It's the part where the goat processes it that makes it do what it does. Who knows? Particular enzymes in the digestive system? It could be a host of things but to simplify it, there are two main variables in the ritual. There's the black root and there is the goat.

There are four possibilities here with only two variables. Both the black root and the goat are necessary. The black root is necessary and the animal can be replaced. The goat is necessary but the black root can be replaced. Or both the animal and the black root can be replaced and still produce the effect. Seeing we don't have access to the black root, we can't test the first two scenarios. Seeing our current goal is to replicate the effects, we have no reason to prove or disprove the final scenario with replacing the black root and the goat. That leaves us with the third scenario—the goat is necessary and the black root can be replaced. Possibly we can procure a more common drug like magic mushrooms and test out this scenario."

"That's the type of proactive shit we need to roll with, Winny. Great fucking idea. Yo' Serin, does that burnout Krueger sling 'shrooms or what?"

"Are you serious? Where are we going to get a goat? And even if we do, you really going to force-feed it drugs then drink its piss?"

"I've done worse there, gimpy. What the fuck you care? You ain't got to do it. I know a fucking goat we can use. Just need to get those 'shrooms."

"You know a goat? Are you shitting me right now?"

"What? My cousin lives east of here about twenty-five minutes. He's got like two acres at his place. Mad animals including some goats."

"And he'd let us drug one of his animals?"

"What he don't know don't matta'. He's gone for two weeks. He got some Mexican feeding the animals during the morning. Place is a ghost town after that."

"And you're on board with this, Wynn?"

"Four pairs of eyes that work are better than one pair. If we can tap into what you are seeing, then we as a group will be that much more efficient instead of needing you as a constant proxy. I'm on board."

"Yeah, so stop draggin ya feet. Call up that burnout Krueger and try to get some 'shrooms so we can make this happen. We can try it out tomorrow on the way to Vegas."

Evelyn walked back in and joined us.

"I called my boss. He's always in Vegas because he has a partial stake in another strip club out there. Anyway, I told him I was going tomorrow with a couple of friends and he got us a couple of rooms at The Flux comped. So rooms are covered if you guys still want to go tomorrow."

"Nice work, girlie. While you was out, me and Winny, with no help from your boy there, came up with a nice little plan."

"Oh yeah?"

"While you were on the phone, these two decided that a good way to start their day tomorrow would be to drink some goat piss."

"Actually, Evelyn, there is a mathematical probability that we can replicate the effects of the ritual and see what Serin is seeing. I think we might be able to substitute the black root with another type of drug. The chances it will work aren't definite but entirely possible and worth a trial run. McBride has access to a goat. We just need a substitute for the black root. We were considering magic mushrooms."

"So uh, too much too soon kind of thing drinking urine together?"

"Actually, Evelyn, we only need two of us to do this. If McBride and I do it, we'll be able to confirm it worked if both of us see the same exact thing, which we will relay to you and Serin separately. For example, if Serin does have a phantom and McBride and I both are able to see it, then we will point it out on the tablet independently as to have no influence on one another and to prove we aren't just hallucinating and are actually seeing a real phantom."

"Well, if this does work, then I'm going to want to experience it, too. Maybe we can save some of it and if it does work for you guys, then I'll drink some also."

"That will actually be good for the sake of experimentation. If it does happen to work, we should definitely find out if a stored sample can produce the same effect or if it loses its potency if it's not consumed immediately after expulsion. If it does work and also maintains its given effects after being stored, we could then possibly mass produce it for our later use."

"What time do you think would be safe to go to your cousin's house?"

"Ah, that Mexican is there like at the crack of dawn. We can get there wheneva'. Any time after 8:00 am should be good. And if he's still there, it don't matta'. He knows me."

"What about the magic mushrooms?"

"I can call Krueger but he's mostly pills and weed."

"I know someone," Evelyn said. "She's my hippy friend from yoga. She's all about Joshua Tree and Burning Man. I'll give her a call."

Evelyn walked back outside with her phone.

"I like that girlie of yours. She got mad resources."

"Well, I'm just glad I won't be drinking piss tomorrow morning. How are we going to collect the piss anyway? I'm thinking they don't sell those devices at the pet store."

"Shit, all we need is a milk carton and some string. Shit's not hard."

"I don't know how optimistic I am about this working or not, but say you two do start seeing what I'm seeing, you need to be warned that these things are straight out of a hellish freak show. So you'll be tripping on mushrooms and seeing real live creatures floating above every person you see. You guys think you can really handle that without shitting all over yourselves? It's a long ride to Vegas as it is without having to smell jean-shits for six hours."

"You just worry about yourself there, limpy. I ain't scared of shit."

Evelyn walked back in.

"She said no problem. I'm going to head over there right now and get them. A quarter ounce should be enough, right?"

"Who knows? Good enough for an experiment, I guess. Here, our experiment, our treat."

I pulled some money out and handed it to her. She pushed it back.

"Save your money. She's a friend and I highly doubt she'll even charge me. You guys can treat me for lunch tomorrow."

"Yeah, girlie, somewhere real nice. Any shitty restaurant in Barstow is our treat."

"I'll probably head home and pack after. So what time and from where are we leaving?"

"Why don't we just meet here? 8:00 am cool?"

"Sure. Be at my cousin's by 8:30 am and seeing these fucking phantoms by 9:30 am. We'll skip all the morning traffic that way."

"Okay, gentlemen. Give me a call if anything changes. If not, I'll see you all in the morning."

"Later, Evelyn."

She put her hand on my shoulder and squeezed it, then she headed out. I could tell that other parts of my body were now jealous of my shoulder. Grabbed my beer and drank it down. A couple of new people came in and sat at the bar. McBride went over to serve them.

"So what do you think, Wynn? You really believe all of this is happening?"

"It's a struggle. I'm conditioned to question everything. But all that we've been encountering has been lining up in one direction. It's a nearly unbelievable direction but I can't counter it at the moment. Words like 'destiny' make me physically ill. But really, you and I meeting? McBride having the idea of going to Las Vegas and having access to a goat?

224

Evelyn having connections for rooms in Las Vegas and magic mushrooms so easily after we decided we required them? It feels like we were placed on an imaginary train and we're all just along for the ride. I don't want to believe it. That's why, for me at least, to try this experiment trying to replicate the ritual is pivotal. I mean, the book is a strong piece of evidence almost impossible to ignore. But nothing compares to first-hand experience. If this works and I can see and confirm what you are seeing?"

Wynn started shaking his head, pondering over the possibility. He was right, the book was great and all but how can you really believe any of this until you see it for yourself? One person who says he saw a ghost is a dipshit. Four people all looking at the same ghost in real-time is a whole different fuckfest.

"I'm not saying you guys seeing what I'm seeing is a good thing, but I'd probably feel a lot less crazy if I had some company."

"I guess we'll see about that tomorrow, then."

"If anything, it'll be nice to watch you guys drink goat piss."

"Always the lowest hanging fruit for you, isn't it?"

"Keeps me happy."

McBride walked back over to us.

"You ladies want another?"

I slid my empty glass towards him.

"Yes, sir. I've got nothing to stay sober for."

"I think I'm going to go home," Wynn said. "I'll see if I can find anything out about the black root just in case tomorrow's experiment provides negative results."

"Aye, yo', I can call up my boy Darrell if you want, Winny. Give you some of his black root."

"Says a lot about the failures of the collegiate system, knowing you're a graduate."

"I told you, mapmaker, Jeopardy. I'll beat that ass."

"Until tomorrow."

"Later, Wynn."

Wynn grabbed his tablet and headed out.

"Just you and me, McBride. Last soldiers standing."

"I'm already pumped for Vegas, boy."

"We're going there for business, McB."

"Yeah, you say that now. Just wait 'til you got a couple drinks in you and your hot cousin. Naw, we'll have some fun, just you wait."

"You really going to drink goat piss tomorrow?"

"Shit, why not? I've drank tequila shots out the ass of a filthy Tijuana hooka' before. Can't be any worse than that."

"You're dirty, McB."

"Got that right, puss."

I ended up staying for about five more drinks, then realized with the lack of motor skills I was experiencing that I forgot to eat dinner and was starving. I saluted McBride then shuffled out the door into the crisp night air. Could have been my phantom whispering in my ear or just my own drunken decision but I got an idea of where to grab some food.

Chapter Thirty -Five
Dirty Pretty Temptress

Drunken decisions are drunken for a reason. They're not clear-headed decisions. If I were clear-headed, I'd have grabbed a sandwich and would have gone home and eaten by myself. But I wasn't clear-headed so I made my way over to Pizza Slim's to get some food. Really, I was going there to talk to Loren if she was working. Why? Ask the drunk me and I'm sure he'll have an answer. The sober me couldn't tell you.

I made my way to the front entrance of P-Slim's and peeked in. She was there behind the register taking orders. There was a line so I got in it. There was always a line. Maybe these were all guys she had at some point sunk her hooks into and were all here for some kind of closure. That was the genius business model of this place. I took a long hard stare at her phantom. It was a lot clearer than the last time I was here sketching it out. It was a full-on bastardized phantom version of an insect. I really wanted to see what the translation for her phantom had to say.

The line chugged along. Didn't have much of a game plan. Actually I had no game plan. What was my game plan? Shit, I'm next.

"What can I get you?"

"I'll take a Severus and two slices of the pesto if that's alright with you, Loren."

It just slipped out of my mouth as if this were a casual conversation between friends. She looked me square in the eyes and smiled.

"That'll be $14.38."

I swiped my debit card and she gave me my receipt. I started to walk away when she placed a metal stand on the counter with a laminated square of white paper on top of it with the number forty-two on it.

"Don't forget your number there, NAMBLA."

I looked up at her but she had already started helping the next guy in line. She remembered me, unless that was her pet name for all customers. I grabbed the number and found a table and waited for my food. Fifteen minutes later she brought the pizza and beer to my table herself, then sat down across from me.

"So how's it going, Loren?"

"Can't complain, NAMBLA. How are things with you?"

"Things are beyond explanation, I'd say. I was in here a couple of days ago and ordered from you."

"I know. Is this a stalker type of situation? I thought you were only into little boys."

"I'm not going to lie, it's always kind of been dancing in the back of my mind. That night. What happened to you? Why'd you ditch me?"

She sighed and almost looked a bit embarrassed.

"I'm sorry about that. I really am. I'm a bit flakey when it comes to certain drugs. I went home that night because I really wanted some whiskey. I was going to make us some drinks and bring them back in a couple of sports bottles I had. I made the drinks and as I was about to walk out the door and head back to the trail, it started to bother me that there were dishes in the sink. So I went back and washed them. Then I was compelled to dry them and put them away. Then I remembered that I forgot I had laundry to fold, which really bugged me so I did that. It continued to snowball as the mescaline kicked in harder.

On certain drugs, some latent OCD in me gets unleashed, I guess. I spent the rest of the night cleaning and doing chores and completely forgot about you until I woke up in the morning and saw the two sports bottles by the door. You showed up here the next day and I felt bad but figured the best thing to do was to pretend it never happened. Plus, I had a boyfriend at the time and didn't need to make things more complicated then they needed to be. I'm sincere, though, when I say I'm sorry. I'm not evil, just occasionally a flake."

"That explanation is about the most satisfying thing I've heard in forever. Thanks for telling me."

"I always felt bad, but socially awkward is what I do best, you know."

"Well, just to put you at ease, I'm not a stalker. If I come in here again it's because I'm hungry; so please refrain from spraying me with mace or stabbing me with one of your piercings."

"It's alright. Stalk me if you want if you ever take a break from cruising all those Boy Scout jamborees."

I just smiled and she smiled back. She got up and returned to work. I ate my pizza and drank my beer. Good job, drunken decisions. I felt cancer-free.

I'm pretty sure I could have asked her out for a drink or something right then. Why did I feel like I just cheated on Evelyn? Maybe I could bring Evelyn here for lunch and introduce her to Loren. Maybe they would hit it off. Maybe there'd be sparks. Maybe the three of us would drink a bunch of red wine and start flirting with one another. Maybe they'd fall for each other and ditch me. Ah, why do my fantasies have to go negative? They're my fantasies. Stay on track fantasies, for fuck's sake.

Finished up my food and headed for the door. I made eye contact with Loren one more time as I was walking out and threw her a little wave which she reciprocated. Slayer of women. I was floating. I floated the rest of the way home. Loren had her hooks in me again. But she had her hooks in the drunken me. The sober me belonged to Evelyn. Did I just cheat on Evelyn? No. We haven't even kissed yet. I kissed Loren. Am I cheating on Loren with Evelyn? Does sex need to be involved to consider it cheating? I don't know. I don't care. I'm drunk. I'm tired. I'm home. I'm on my couch.

I'm closing my eyes.

Chapter Thirty -Six
Road Tripping

7:20 am. I somehow managed to set my phone alarm before passing out last night. Crazy dreams.

Got up and powered through getting cleaned and packed. Out the door by 7:45 am with my backpack and a brisk stride. If I ignored the details, I'm about to go on a trip to Vegas with the lovely Evelyn. Too bad phantoms and McBrides are in the details.

Made it to Red's Tavern right at 8:00 am. Everyone was already outside eating bagels and drinking coffee. McBride pointed to the hood of his parked Jeep Cherokee which had an additional coffee and a bagel lying on top of a napkin.

"Morning, everyone. This is for me?"

"McBride was thoughtful enough to bring breakfast for everyone," Evelyn said.

That bastard just upstaged me.

"Thanks, McB."

"It's called being a team player there, boy. Nothing you'd know about with that dishonorable phantom riding ya' back."

An icy little monkey hand just played a piano-run down my spine. I could very well have a dishonorable phantom. I think I'm a good guy but shit. I bet Ariel thinks she's a smart girl and Angie thinks she's a trusting, level-headed girlfriend. I mean, the average person can never really see themselves for who they really are. Maybe my phantom is playing these three and using me to set them up for something. I don't know if I want their little goat piss experiment to work and find out my phantom is a shit-bird.

"So what's the word? We still going to the farm for a goat-cocktail?"

"We can roll wheneva'. You ladies need the bathroom first or what?"

"I'm fine," Evelyn said.

"Same here," Wynn said.

"So let's get this going then. In my ride the queen gets shotgun."

"Why thank you, McBride."

McBride walked around and opened the door for Evelyn. Bastard upstaged me again. Wynn and I hopped in the backseat. McBride jumped in and we headed out.

"So we're really doing this, huh?"

"Fuck yeah, we're doing this. I want to see these pricks for myself. Look in the back there. I made a piss-funnel for the goat. Sliced up a gallon jug and hooked up some fishing wire. Shit should work, right?"

Wynn and I looked over our shoulders into the back and saw McBride's contraption. Crude as it was, it looked like it'd be functional.

"Don't we need something to catch the urine in?"

"I got that covered, too, Winny don't you worry. Got a new thirty-two ounce sports bottle I snatched from the gym. Next stop, piss-city."

McBride drove on. The early hour mixed with the anxiety of our first errand of the day seemed to put the four of us in our own heads a bit. The ride was silent for most of the way.

I turned to Wynn and said, "I got your email here with the translations. What's the word on the scans?"

"I didn't think it was pressing seeing we were going on this trip and you'd have access to my tablet. I wanted to do some research last night and if I tried uploading the scans, it would have bogged down my internet."

"What were you researching?"

"I was exploring the option of figuring out and locating the black root in case today's experiment fails."

"Any luck?"

"There is something in the region I found, a tree called Kratom. It's not necessarily a hallucinogenic but the book never really specified the type of drug black root was and I was just speculating it'd be along the lines of a hallucinogen. This Kratom is part of the coffee tree family and is fairly common so if things don't work out today, I think we'd be able to find means of procuring some."

"Aye, yo, what you talking about Kratom for? Ain't that a part of the taint right below the nuts or sumthin?"

"Can I see the tablet for a minute?"

Wynn opened his backpack and removed his tablet. He fired it up and opened up the gallery, then handed it to me. I started flipping through the illustrations. Loren's phantom was still fresh in my memory and I was curious. A little risky to be doing this with Evelyn two feet away from me but I'd be good as long as nobody asked any questions.

"So what are you looking for?" Evelyn asked me.

Shit, why am I such a dumbass? Don't try to lie, she'll see right through it. How about a slight omission? I can get away with that right?

"Just looking up a phantom."

"You should look up that crazy girl Angie's. Betcha she got a fucked-up one."

Saved by McBride.

"Yep, might as well check out all the phantoms I had in my journal to see if the personalities I said they have line up with the book's translations."

233

My journal was in my backpack so I fished it out and flipped to Angie's page. I then flipped through the scans on Wynn's tablet but couldn't find a match. I flipped through them slowly a second time and still couldn't find a match.

"I don't see a match for Angie's phantom."

"I'm sure there's a lot of things not covered in my grandmother's book. I wouldn't think the populace of her province was either that huge or diverse. There's bound to be plenty the shamans didn't encounter or catalogue."

"How about your other girlfriend, Loren?" Evelyn asked me.

"What?"

"You heard me. I'm curious about her. Look her up."

"If you insist."

I felt guilty all of a sudden. I turned my journal to Loren's page. Not that I needed it as her phantom was still fresh in my mind from last night, but for appearance's sake. I went through the scans again and found a match for Loren's. I noted the page number, then opened up the translation email Wynn sent me on my phone.

"Read it out loud," Evelyn said.

"Okay. The title of her phantom is 'the wheel.' Below that the notes read 'Embracer and pursuer of change. Unwillingness to be governed. Strength in presence. Honorable.' "

"Sounds like a whore to me," Evelyn said jokingly.

"Don't talk about my wheel like that, you jealous snare."

McBride interrupted, "Aw shit, moment of truth there, Winny. We're here."

I hadn't been paying much attention to anything outside of the car on the ride there and had just noticed how rural it was out here. The houses were spread out, each with a large lot of land. Most were run down and the land was unkempt.

McBride pulled onto a long dirt driveway and up a slight hill. He parked in front of his cousin's place, which was an old one story ranch house with peeling paint and random junk scattered all around the perimeter. There was a chicken coop on the side of the house next to a failed garden.

We got out of the car and McBride grabbed his contraption and backpack out of the trunk, then led us past the chicken coop and around to the back. There was a bunch of mismatched plastic patio furniture under a weathered green plastic canopy. Past the canopy was an ancient woodshed that looked to be twenty percent wood particles held together by a weave of grime and termites.

Beyond the tool shed was a large chicken-wire pen about the same size the house was. Inside the pen were some trees, an old destroyed sectional couch, a water trough and three goats. McBride led us up to the chicken-wire pen and pointed at the goats.

"There you go. Which one you think wants to get high? That black and white fucker? He kind of looks like a junky, right?"

Evelyn reached in her sweatshirt pocket and pulled out a plastic bag with the mushrooms in it and handed them to Wynn. Wynn walked next to McBride and held out the mushrooms to him.

"I don't suppose you have a plan on how to get the goat to eat these?"

"Ain't you ever been around goats before? No plan needed. Little fuckers eat everything. Let's get this going. I'm thirsty."

McBride and Wynn walked into the holding pen. McBride pulled some thin rope out of his backpack and tied a loop around the goat's neck, then led it over to the fence and tied it up. Wynn then held the funnel contraption under the goat while McBride tied the fishing wire around the goat's back to hold it in place. It actually looked functional. McBride then put the mushrooms into his hand and put it in front of the goat. The goat didn't hesitate and vacuumed them up.

"Now we wait. What you figure? Twenty minutes to start kicking in? So after twenty minutes we'll get the sports bottle in position. If it pisses before that, it'll probably be bunk. What you think?"

"There was no reference about this in the book. The potency and type of drug could all be arbitrary as far as we know."

"So twenty minutes, then we'll try to do some piss-collecting. You think too much, mapmaker. Never get any shit done if you're sitting around trying to figure everything out all the time. Let your nuts do some decision making once in a while."

"Hey, you guys got this handled? Alright if we go sit down while you're waiting for the bartender to bring your drinks?"

"Me and Winny here got this. Throw us over a couple of those shitty chairs, though."

I walked to the patio furniture and picked up two plastic chairs, walked back and handed them over the fence to McBride. Evelyn and I then searched out the least dirty of the remaining furniture and settled on two more cheap plastic chairs under the green plastic canopy.

"You know what I just realized? I never got to ask you any questions. We just sort of bypassed the part where we talk like normal people."

"Well, tends to happen when you pull a girl into a world of phantoms with you and your sidekicks. Looks like we've got some time now to pretend to be normal. Let's take turns. One question at a time. You can go first."

"Okay. How many guys have you slept with? Just kidding. Please don't answer that. What's your family like?"

"Normal parents, still married. One older brother in the military. A few cousins here and there. They all live in the Seattle area. Nobody local. My turn. Same question."

"Parents are divorced. Only child. My Uncle Chester as you know lives out here. Technically, I have cousins but Chester never bothered to be a part of their lives so I never really knew them. Rest of my family is up in Portland. My turn. What are you studying in school?"

"I'm pursuing a degree in marketing. It's the third time I've switched majors. I kind of enjoy learning different things. I think I'm waiting until something really grabs me. So what do you plan on doing with a degree in biology?"

"No plan at all. How things are going, I'll probably be working at a carnival doing phantom readings or trapped in a government bunker somewhere getting dissected. What's your alcoholic beverage of choice?"

"Vodka for when I'm being social. Red wine for when I'm relaxing at home. Are you a dog person or a cat person or neither?"

"I grew up with cats. Never liked dogs. Dogs are like ugly drooling kids constantly in need of something. Cats are like chill adults. Totally cool with doing their own thing. Food, water and the occasional scratch behind the ears and they are all good. Too much effort and occasional child mutilations involved with dogs. Okay, next question is a bit more intrusive. Do you have a boyfriend?"

"What makes you think I like guys?"

Ouch, a sexy conundrum. On the one hand if she's into girls, I've got no shot. On the other hand, Evelyn with another girl sounds awesome.

"Um…"

"Joking. My mom instilled in me since I was twelve that as far as important decisions go, like falling in love, I wouldn't know shit until I was at least thirty. She said we all think we know something in our teens and early twenties but it is all smoke and mirrors. She drilled into me how guys in their early twenties were the worst kind of people and she'd disown me if I tried to get married before I was near or past my thirtieth birthday. She said I still wouldn't know shit when I was thirty but at least I'd have avoided my first shitty marriage altogether and could skip straight to my second shitty marriage minus any unwanted kids."

"Your mom sounds cool as shit."

"She is. She did kind of ruin the idea of dating for me, though. My longest relationship ever lasted about five weeks before I got bored and broke it off."

"So just casual sex and orgies for your twenties, huh?"

"And you? Sounds like we've only scratched the surface with the girls in your journal."

"I'll be the first to agree with your mom. I don't know shit and I'm the worst kind of people."

"Well, Wynn seems pretty sweet and smart. Maybe you can slip him my number for me."

"Alright, moving on. Next question. This one's important to me. There's a lot of things I can overlook but not this one. What kind of music do you listen to?"

We went back and forth. A real conversation based in this reality. There was nothing I heard that I didn't like. She was a cool chick, unbelievably attractive, sharp, hip and down for adventure. I felt kind of like a fraud but more of a benefactor of circumstance. Maybe it was being surrounded by scumbags all day at her work that made me worth hanging out with. Or maybe there were whispers in her ear she wasn't aware of. Regardless, I was happy.

Loren was pretty cool, too, though, I must admit. Seriously, there are guys out there who pull it off every once in a while. The right girls and the right finesse. There I go again. She's right in front of you and she is wonderful. Loren is pretty cool, too, though. Shut up! I looked at my phone. We'd been talking for thirty-five minutes and hadn't heard a peep from the piss-farmers.

"Hey, do you think we should see how the kids are doing?"

"I was about to suggest the same thing."

We got up and walked back over to the fence. McBride and Wynn were in the midst of conversation.

"What's going on boys? Anything?"

"Naw, this little fucker won't piss. He's definitely trippin' though. Check this shit out."

McBride put his hand in front of the goat's face and started wiggling his fingers. The goat started letting out strange little mewing sounds and stomping its feet. McBride removed his hand and the goat went back to being quiet and still.

"Shit's mad funny, right? Been sitting here with ol' Winny trying to figure out a way to make him piss."

"You come up with anything?"

"Naw, I was going to try to scare the piss out of it with an air horn I got in my trunk but the mapmaker here convinced me that was crossing the line. We don't fucking know. Dip its foot in warm water or sumthin?"

"Hey, hey!" Wynn blurted out while scrambling for the sports bottle by the goat's legs. The goat was pissing but it was pouring out of the funnel to the ground. Wynn grabbed the sports bottle and pushed the mouth up over the funnel. The bottle was clear plastic with measurements on the side so you knew how much liquid was inside. When the goat was done, the bottle had just over 16 ounces. Wynn screwed on the lid. McBride took off the contraption then untied the rope from around the goat's neck and gave it a couple of pats on its side.

"Good job, little fucker. Enjoy the rest of your high."

McBride grabbed the two plastic chairs that they were sitting on and walked out of the pen. He returned the chairs to their original spots, then turned to Wynn.

"How much we got?"

"Just over 16 ounces."

"What ya think? Five ounces each, then save the rest for girlie ova' here just in case the shit works?"

"All of this is speculative. How much we are supposed to take is an unknown variable."

"Hey, mapmaker, if I ask you a question and you don't have a helpful answer, then just say 'Okay' and roll with it. Five ounces each it is."

McBride didn't hesitate. He walked back over to the pen, snatched the bottle from Wynn, popped up the nozzle and started drinking. He stopped to see how much he had drank. He drank one more time until it was down to around 11 ounces, then handed it back to Wynn.

"It's easy if you just pretend it's shitty beer and not from a goat's dick. Cheers."

Wynn shook his head at McBride but also gave the faintest of smiles. He took a deep breath, then started to drink. It didn't go down as easily as with McBride. After the first swallow, Wynn stopped and had to compose himself. He then powered through it until there was just over five ounces left in the bottle. Evelyn produced a pack of gum from her sweatshirt pocket and held it out to Wynn and McBride. They both took a stick.

"Thanks, girlie."

"It's just as much for me as it is for you guys. Vegas is a long ride, especially with two guys in the car with piss-breath."

"Which one of you two wants to drive? Me and Winny just punched our tickets and could be seeing shit start to melt in less than thirty."

"By the way, Wynn, I forgot to ask. Have you ever done a hallucinogenic before?"

"No, but I read up on the effects so I'm prepared."

McBride started laughing.

"You're funny, kid."

"Seriously, Wynn, I don't know if or what the goat process does to the mushrooms or if it is still active in the piss, but if the hallucinogenic part stayed intact, there is nothing you've read that can prepare you for it. Especially if you start seeing phantoms on top of it."

"Don't freak him out, you guys. Don't worry, Wynn. If things get intense for you, just tell me and I'll help you through it. And just keep telling yourself it's only temporary."

"Thanks, Evelyn."

"Alright, who wants the keys?"

"I'll drive. McBride, won't you take shotgun and Evelyn you hang out with Wynn in the back, just in case?"

"Sounds good. Let's roll."

McBride threw his car keys at me way too hard and hit me in the chest. We piled in and headed back towards the interstate. Twenty minutes later we were on the 15 North en route to Vegas.

"I think I need you to pull over."

"What's a matta there, Winny, 'shroom-piss got you queasy?"

"Seriously, the shoulder is fine unless you want the car to smell like vomit."

I pulled over to the slow lane then came to a stop on the shoulder. Wynn quickly got out and scuttled ten paces behind the car then threw up. A river of goat-piss and bile came out of him in four violent heaves. He stood there for a minute and collected himself then made his way back to the car door.

"Sorry. Can I get another piece of gum before I get in?"

Evelyn handed him another stick of gum and Wynn chewed it for a full minute. McBride opened his glove compartment and pulled out a wet nap and handed it to Wynn, who opened it up, then wiped off his mouth and chin.

"Price of admission to the show Winny. I'm starting to feel it creep in, too."

Wynn got back in the car and rested his head against the window. When the slow lane had a break, I got up to speed and merged back on.

"Yep, the colors are turned up. Train has left the station. What up back there, Winny? Check your colors."

Wynn looked out the window and was fixated on the sky. Evelyn moved closer to Wynn and put her arm around his shoulder.

"This is....I....it's hard to...."

"Don't hurt yourself, Winny. First time is always a kick in the nuts. Put the mapmaker back in the closet and just try to enjoy it."

"McB, you see anything back there attached to any of us? The first thing I saw was a little gray piece of shit about the size of a fist. Then they started getting bigger and bigger."

"Naw, I don't see none of that. Might take a hot minute before that shit starts to show up. Who knows?"

We rolled on. Wynn was in a vegetative state and just stared out the window. McBride was surprisingly quiet also and was lost in his own head. I'd occasionally make eye contact with Evelyn in the rear-view mirror. It's been a hell of a courtship so far hasn't it, Joy?

I had some talk radio on the AM dial turned on at a low volume. I think the constant drone of voices was comforting to the both of them. A couple of hours passed and I pulled over at a rest stop right before the city limits of Barstow. There were only a couple of other cars there and it seemed like a safe place for a couple of guys tripping on piss-shrooms to stretch their legs. Everyone got out of the car.

"Hey! Aw shit, that little black and white fucker at my cousin's came through. It's working. I can see it."

"What, McB?"

"I've been in fucking zombieland in the car and was checked out that whole ride. Out here, I'm seeing it. All three of you got some gray shit flying over you. Holy shit. Winny, you seeing this, too?"

McBride walked over to me and started waving his hand through my blotch. Wynn turned off his autopilot and tried to return from inside his mind.

"I...I...Yes! I see it. It's there. It's actually there."

Wynn started to circle us and McBride started doing the same thing, trying to see our blotches at different angles. Wynn also made his way over to me and waved his hand through my blotch.

"How big are they?"

"What I'm seeing is about the size of your head. It's not exactly formed. More like a strange miniature cloud."

"Same ova' here."

"So if you guys are seeing them that big already, then it's definitely way more accelerated than it was with me. You'll probably be seeing what I'm seeing by the time we get to Vegas. What about you, Evelyn? It seems like it is working. You still considering going through with this?"

"Yes, I guess I will. I just want to eat lunch before I do it, though. I don't know about you two but I can never eat while on something like that."

"You ain't lying, girlie. Eating ain't on my agenda no time soon."

"So, can we swing through a drive-through or something? I'll eat in the car and make it quick."

"Sure. We need to get gas anyway."

Everyone used the restrooms, then we piled back in the car and drove another ten miles before hitting the heart of Barstow. I filled up the gas tank. The gas station had a little market and Evelyn grabbed a premade sandwich and some chips. We got back in the car and continued on. The boys were mostly silent again, lost in their own heads.

"How you feeling, Wynn?" Evelyn asked while finishing her food.

"I think I'm getting a handle on it. It was a bit overwhelming at first but it's no longer overpowering me or making me as anxious as it was. It's quite remarkable what it does to your perception."

"The fucking colors, Winny."

"Would you mind pulling over at the next off ramp? I think I'm ready to drink what's in the sports bottle but I want to be outside in case things go like they went for Wynn."

"Sure. Hope you got some gum left for yourself."

I pulled off on a desolate off-ramp and pulled to the side onto a big area of dirt. Evelyn got out and McBride handed her the sports bottle.

244

"If you need someone to hold your hair, girlie, just holler."

"Thanks, McBride, but I think I'll manage."

She pulled up on the sports bottle nozzle then held her nose with one hand while drinking with the other. She drank it all in one go. The bottle was empty but she continued holding her nose. She put the sports bottle on the ground, then fished out a stick of gum and put it in her mouth and started chewing. After about a minute of chewing, she slowly released her nose and cautiously took a couple of deep breaths, expecting her gag reflex to kick in at any time. But it didn't. The gum did its job and she got through it. She picked up the sports bottle, then returned to the car.

"Nice job, girlie. You're a soldier when it comes to drinking piss."

"Thanks, McBride. Such the charmer."

"You good to go?"

"Yes, I'm good. We can get back on the road if all of you are ready."

"Alright. Let me know if you need to pull over or anything."

"I will."

We got back on the road. Goat piss road trip to Vegas. How did I get here? What do they want from us? What phantom do I have? We powered on. All three of them were quiet. Another couple of hours passed by. They all were in different states of dazed and confused, lost in introspective jungles, not registering anything outside of their own thoughts.

It wasn't until I hit the Stateline that McBride came out of his own head and appeared to reawaken into consciousness. He looked at me, then out my driver side window where I was riding alongside an SUV that had a family of four inside.

"Them shits are getting bigger. They're spilling out the roof. That one in the front driving is purple. You seeing this, Winny?"

Wynn was still lost somewhere in his head. I looked over at the SUV and saw four fully formed phantoms. McBride was right, the driver's phantom was purple. McBride and Wynn were rapidly catching up to my own level of phantom vision. McBride reached back and shook Wynn's knee and Wynn snapped out of his daze and was back with us.

"What?"

"Look at that SUV out the window. You see any color?"

Wynn took a second to process what was just said to him. McBride helped him along by pointing out the window towards the SUV. Wynn seemed to finally understand, then looked out the window.

"They'... they're getting larger. The one in back closest to us looks red. The other three are still gray. Wait no, the driver's looks like it has purple in it."

"No shit, huh?"

"Why, what do you see?"

"I got the purple driver but nothing else."

"Serin, can you confirm either of the colors?"

"You both are right. I'm almost optimistic that this is working for real and not just the 'shrooms talking."

"Shit's wearing off already with me. Getting pissed out by a goat made them flimsy. I'll be back to normal in another thirty. What we're seeing is legit. Ain't that right, Winny?"

"I'm definitely feeling my faculties normalizing. I'm still a bit disconnected but nothing like I was back at the rest stop. What I'm seeing doesn't feel like a hallucination. I do propose, though, that if and when they are in full definition for us, that we apply something close to a double-blind study. Seeing none of us have seen Serin's phantom yet, when it's in focus, I'll see if I can identify it on my tablet and if so I'll show it to Evelyn. Then I'll flip to a random scan and you'll take your turn finding it on the tablet which you will also show to Evelyn. If Evelyn tells us we both picked the same phantom, then that should satisfy any doubts. "

"Whateva' you say, mapmaker."

I took a glance back at Evelyn who seemed oblivious to our conversation and lost behind her eyes.

"Hey, Evelyn? You still with us?"

Wynn leaned over and put a hand on her shoulder. She seemed to come out of hibernation when he touched her.

"Hi."

"Hey, girlie, you alright back there or what?"

"I'm uh, it's been a while."

"Stateline is coming up over this bend. I'm going to stop so we can stretch and hit the restrooms."

Another fifteen minutes and I pulled off at the Stateline exit. Normal road trips to Vegas always took a pit stop here to one of the shitty Stateline casinos. After five hours on the road, the fever for gambling would steadily rise and Stateline was always the hand-job of gambling. Not really satisfying but good enough. A quick twenty minute session at blackjack then power ahead the final forty-five minutes until Vegas. That was a normal trip. This was a little different as I was travelling with three people high on goat piss and starting to see phantoms. So I settled on a quiet gas station instead so as to not overwhelm my company with the onslaught of stimulus of a casino.

"Welcome to Nevada. Bathrooms around back."

I got out of the car and walked around to open Evelyn's door. She was glassy eyed. She got out of the car and looked up at me.

"I can see it."

"What's that?"

"There is something gray hovering over your back. Like a big cotton ball, sort of."

Evelyn walked next to me and waved her hand through my blotch.

"This is wonderfully frightening."

"Just you wait a couple of hours. The real freak show is waiting for you. Sorry, not the most comforting thing to say to someone hallucinating."

"It's alright. I feel safe with you guys, for some reason."

"Good. Just between you and me, you're my favorite sidekick."

She smiled and walked around me for a minute looking at my blotch from different angles.

"Although I'm almost horrified at this all being real, I'm glad I know you're not crazy now."

"I'm just glad I have some companions to this shit-show. Being alone with this madness wasn't fun."

"Walk a girl to the restroom?"

"Of course."

She slipped her arm through mine as we walked around the gas station towards the back. McBride and Wynn were already coming out of the men's bathroom.

"Ah, look at this. Romantic stroll to the gas station pissers, huh? I'm gonna go grab some beer. You ladies want anything?"

"Would you mind getting me a pack of cloves? I won't smoke them in the car. The smell has always been comforting for me when I'm like this," Evelyn said.

"Sure thing, girlie. I'm gonna bum half the pack from you anyways. What about you, Chauncey?"

"I'm good."

"You think you are but you're really a buster."

McBride walked towards the gas station market and Wynn went with him. Evelyn released my arm and stared glassily above me at my blotch.

"You alright?"

"It's just an extraordinary departure from where I was just a handful of days ago before you came into Angel's. I'm in Barstow with three random guys, hallucinating off goat-urine and taking my first steps into seeing things on another dimension. I'm on the fence to whether I should be excited or hysterical."

"I think hysterical will be the proper side of the fence for you in about an hour or two. But you have a pack of cloves coming so you should be ok. You also got us."

"And what do you think about us and this trip? Do you think you and Wynn were pushed together? Do you think us going on this trip is because of these phantoms or is this just us going to Vegas for no real reason?"

"It feels pretty certain, based on the circumstances, that Wynn and I were put on the same path. I'd like to think you were, too. I honestly don't know about this trip. That could have been all McBride and no phantom."

"I think I like the idea of this being a purposeful quest. I think I'll stick with that."

Evelyn walked up close and grabbed my hands. She stared me dead in my eyes and was inspecting them as if she was trying to find something. She then smiled and leaned in and we kissed. I must have got contact goat-piss high because I felt I was hallucinating. I felt a thousand disco balls start to spin in my chest. I think I heard some techno music playing. She pulled back and released my hands then smiled before going into the women's restroom.

Our first kiss. Magic at the filthy Stateline gas station restrooms. I'll take it. Did she do that or did her phantom make her do it?

I used the bathroom, then waited for Evelyn to come out. She slipped her arm back through mine and we walked back to McBride's car. McBride walked up with Wynn and handed Evelyn a pack of cloves.

"Thanks."

"No problem, girlie. What's the word? We ready to roll or what? I'm starting to get that itch for some cocktails and blackjack."

"I didn't know this was a vacation, McB. Thought we were on a phantom reconnaissance mission."

"Whateva', Agnes. If we're in Vegas, do like the Vegas do. Why can't we watch phantoms from the tables? My boy Winny here probably is a ringer with the counting cards and shit."

"We'll see how much card counting and partying you'll be wanting to do once the phantoms are in high definition for you. But sure, let's get going."

We got back in the car and back on the 15 North. Another thirty-five minutes and the Strip was in view off in the distance. The final stretch. Once you see it, you always think it is only one or two exits away. Desert illusion. It still took another thirty-five minutes to make our way to the parking lot of The Flux through the Vegas traffic.

The Flux was off the Strip a couple of long blocks. It was more of a boutique hotel and a fraction of the size of the themed mega-hotels on the actual Strip. The Flux was more of a hipster destination than a regular tourist hangout. Their parking garage was only five stories and rarely was filled to capacity. We found a spot on the second floor and got out of the car and grabbed our bags out of the back. The heat was borderline suffocating, even in the cover of the parking lot. I instantly felt sweat starting to form on my lower back.

"Aw shit, Winny, you seeing this?"

McBride was looking above me. Wynn followed the gaze of McBride.

"They're here. I mean, it's in focus."

Wynn looked over at McBride's, then at Evelyn's. McBride looked over at Wynn's and then Evelyn's. Evelyn wasn't seeing what they were seeing yet but she seemed to notice a difference in her own perception.

"Holy fuck, these things."

"McBride, don't say anything else."

"What's that?"

"Scientific method, remember? We need to both try to identify Serin's phantom independently on my tablet and show Evelyn to see if we truly are seeing what we're seeing."

"Alright there, Winny. How about we do that shit in the room, though, with the AC cranked? God damn sauna out here."

"Yes, let's move this inside. Vegas casinos don't exactly ignore groups of stoned people loitering in their parking lots. Evelyn, what do you think about checking in? Are you in any kind of mindset to be dealing with reception right now or should we find someplace to lounge for a while?"

"If any of you can light one of these cloves for me, I should be okay."

McBride unzipped the small pouch of his backpack and produced a lighter and lit it up. Evelyn pulled a clove from the pack and leaned in and lit it, taking a small drag.

"Okay."

We made our way to reception and I walked up to the counter with Evelyn while McBride and Wynn hung back. Just as promised, the rooms were taken care of courtesy of

Evelyn's boss and they even threw in a stack of free tickets and coupons to different attractions around Vegas. We made our way through the casino and up to the eighth floor to our rooms, which were adjoining. We opened up the doors that connected our rooms and settled in. McBride cracked open the beers he bought back at the Stateline and handed them out. Everyone accepted.

"Alright then. What say we get Winny's little science project out of the way so we can go have some fun?"

Wynn pulled his tablet out of his bag and flipped through the scans while occasionally looking up at my phantom for reference. I kind of hoped, like Angie's, that mine wouldn't be in there either. Something about being defined by the type of inter-dimensional parasite you had floating above your back was a bit intimidating. Wynn took two passes through the scans then seemed to find the right one. He looked up over me, then back at the tablet. He then walked over to Evelyn and showed her the scan and page number.

"That's it. Yours is in here as far as what I'm seeing. Let's see if McBride will pick the same one."

Wynn swiped the screen back to the beginning of the scans then handed the tablet over to McBride. McBride flipped through the scans and seemed to find it rather quickly. He then showed it to Evelyn.

"So what's the verdict?"

"You both picked the same one."

"There you go, Winny. Science homework is done. Time to go out and play."

"Serin, you want to see it?"

"Might as well."

Wynn handed me the tablet and I looked at the illustration of the phantom that held influence over my life. It had the otherworldly feel of a creature they'd find at the deepest and darkest depths of the ocean. I got a bad vibe from the illustration. I didn't recall ever seeing this type of phantom before on anyone else.

"You ready for the translation?"

"Not really. But I guess not reading the translation isn't really an option."

Wynn searched his phone for the translation for the page with my phantom. As he searched, I grew a bit tense. I wanted to be able to dismiss what I was about to hear as just an opinion, but this was different. This was a catalogued behavior of people with the same phantom. I wasn't escaping this judgment I was about to hear. Wynn found what he was looking for on his phone.

"Ok, the top part translates to 'the dual.' "

The dual? That sounds, well that sounds ambiguous but still foreboding. I tensed up even more.

"So the following parts translate to 'A traveler of light and dark. Not accustomed to conflict. Uninvolved awareness. Undefined allegiance. Neither honorable nor dishonorable.' "

They all stared at me, not accusatory but puzzled. What does that mean? I'm neutral or I've got a bi-polar phantom.

"I knew you was fucked-up with your busted phantom."

"Neither honorable nor dishonorable. Well, at least you can say you're unique," Evelyn said.

"I don't trust em'. Let's ditch this no-honor-having chump and go have some fun."

"Got anything to add, Wynn?"

"It's interesting. I'd think it just means they never got a definitive read on the other people who had this particular phantom. I wouldn't mark it off as something negative. I'd just say it's an inconclusive observation."

"Thanks, Wynn. That actually makes me feel better. And I am rolling with you three, all honorable. Kind of puts me on the same team, right?"

"Fuck no, you're not on our team. No honor, no jersey. You need some new friends. You need to go to Canada or sumthin and find some other boring, undefined chumps to hang with?"

"Thanks, McB."

"You're welcome, sweetness."

"So what's next, Ox?"

"What you mean, Sally?"

"I mean, it seems like you or your phantom have been kind of running the show. It was you who got us to the Lex where I saw that guy's phantom explode. It was your idea to come to Vegas. It was you who got us the goat. If this is really a thing, I'd say you are the bloodhound sniffing out the trail. So maybe you can try to tune in and hear the whispers or something to see what our next move is?"

"Alright, no-honor guy. I'm gonna finish this beer, then grab a quick shower. I'll see if the fucker floating above me shoots me a fax or sumthin."

McBride picked up his backpack and beer and locked himself in the bathroom.

"I think I'm going to freshen up, too. It's probably just paranoia because of the drugs but I feel the goat-urine coming out of my pores," Evelyn said.

"That's the sexiest thing I've ever heard."

"Be quiet, no-honor guy."

Evelyn walked through the adjoining doorway to our room and disappeared.

"Just you and me, Wynn. We've come a long way since our flight to Australia."

I held my beer up and Wynn clinked cans with me.

"You do know the significance of this whole situation, right?"

"What, the situation where we are seeing demons from a different dimension that have direct influence on the human race? Where do you see any significance in that?"

"Don't be a jackass. This trip to Vegas was spur of the moment and not thought out because we still hadn't verified whether these phantoms were real or not. Now that we have verification, we need to seriously weigh the different paths that are before us."

"What, about what we're doing in Vegas?"

"This trip could be meaningful or superfluous. We don't know yet if anything will become of it. I'm more concerned with what comes after. What do we do with this knowledge? On one hand, I feel an obligation to the scientific community to enlighten them to what we now can prove. On the other hand, I can only believe that this knowledge given to the general public would lead to the destruction of society."

"That bad, huh?"

"Think about it. Humans are wired to fear and dislike anything different from what they are. Racism is a relic of the infancy of the human brain that we never evolved out of. You look different from me, therefore I fear and dislike you.

"Now imagine down the road when they synthesize and mass produce the catalyst into a sports drink so everyone who wants to see the phantoms can easily do so. Imagine a new frontier of metaphysical racism where people with dishonorable phantoms are ostracized and pushed away. They'll have no other course of action but to push back. I see it as an inevitable downward spiral that will end in another civil war or an all-out genocide."

"I see it, too. This becoming common knowledge would no doubt turn shitty. What about the government?"

"Not a viable option for us unless we find a foolproof way of protecting ourselves. I mean, the potential of knowing someone's phantom on just the frontier of espionage alone is worth more than all of our lives. We'd have to create fully detailed packages of everything and set them up for timed shipment to all the major media outlets before we'd even be able to approach the government, just so we'd have some leverage. But then what do we gain by approaching the government anyway?"

"I don't know—token jobs that we don't show up to but get paid for. Tax exemption. Some of that government weed they grow in the laboratory."

"So, just like the flowers you discovered in the Daintree, your only motivation is financial?"

"It's not me, it's my no-honor phantom. It likes easy money. I say we at least put it on the table of discussion with the others. For now, though, let's just get through Vegas and see if anything comes out of it. If not, all four of us will figure something out. McBride probably already posted a viral video about everything anyways."

"It's baffling that guy is going for a masters. Makes me question the validity of the entire academic institution."

"Don't mistake his brutishness for stupidity. Two different things. Some creatures are just wired for chaos."

Wynn and I finished our beers. McBride finished up with his shower. Evelyn walked back in wearing new clothes and brushing her wet hair. As soon as she entered the room, she stopped in her tracks, wide-eyed.

"What's a matta', girlie?"

"I can see them. They're no longer blurry."

"Welcome to the freak show. Feel free to scream if you feel the need."

"They are amazing."

Evelyn walked around the room looking at them from different angles.

"What do you say, girlie, which one of us got the best-looking demon?"

"If I had to choose, I'd say Wynn's is the least horrifying."

"Aw, why you always trying to hurt my feelings?"

"McB, did you come up with any ideas or what?"

"Yeah, I was getting to that. This is real fucked up but what isn't these days? I'm in there in the shower and out of nowhere a stupid idea pops in my head. And I'm in there trying to figure out if this was my idea or did this dickhead floating above me really just shoot me a fax."

"Only one way to find out. What you got?"

McBride walked over to the nightstand and grabbed the pile of coupons and free tickets we got when we checked in.

"These. All these stupid coupons and shit. I thought, or this fucker above me told me to think, that these are our next move."

"What, are we going for a helicopter ride over the Hoover dam?"

"Naw, all these tickets and coupons have a front and back side. I'm going to toss this pile in the air. The one's that land front-side up we keep. The others we remove. I'll keep on doing this until we're down to one front-side up. Whatever thing it is, we do."

"Sounds about the right amount of insane to me. Anybody got any better ideas? Wynn?"

"My curiosity outweighs any reservations I have. I'll go along for the ride."

"Evelyn?"

"I might just hang back and go to the spa. No, of course. Even if nothing happens, it's still kind of a fun idea."

"Right, until the last coupon standing is for a free lunch after a two-hour presentation about Vegas timeshares."

"Well, if that really is a coupon then maybe I will go to the spa instead."

"Or maybe it will be a coupon to the spa and our heads will explode. McB, the floor is yours. Let's ride the coupon trolley to crazy town."

McBride shuffled up the stack and threw them up to the ceiling. There were about twenty-five different sized, double-sided, laminated coupons that hit the ceiling and fluttered to the floor. Laws of probability would say around half would land face-up and the other half face-down. The laws of probability just got bitch-slapped by the realm of phantoms. It took us a minute before it settled in. It wasn't necessarily obvious with all of them lying on the floor. Most of them had info on both sides and it took a second to determine which side was the front and which side was the back. But after removing the obvious ones first, then the less obvious ones next, it slowly set in that this was phantom fuckery.

"Do you know what this means? It means they not only have influence over what's in our head, but they can manipulate objects in our physical world."

There was an iciness in the room as a ghost had just literally reached out its tentacles and made it so only one of the coupons was face up. McBride bent down and picked the coupon up and held it up to us.

"Two chumps for the price of one. Fuck it. Always kind of wanted to go on that stupid thing.

Chapter Thirty -Seven
The Djinn

EnSpire was the latest hot-shit Vegas hotel. Money from the Middle East and architects out of Dubai combined to create this latest of mega-hotels. It was one of the tallest structures in the US and dwarfed everything else on the Strip. The place was dumb. I say that because two beers at their bar ran $32. Their cheapest blackjack table was a $75 minimum. $450 a night for their shittiest room on a weekday. It was dumb because I couldn't afford it.

The building itself was a wonder of architecture and a monument to excess. It had powerful yet elegant angles that stretched up to the sky. At the top of the hotel, close to a quarter mile from the ground, was an outdoor observation deck. They charged $28 per person just for the elevator ride alone to the top.

The floor below the observation deck had a shamelessly expensive restaurant which of course offered their patrons the best view in all of Vegas. There were a few cheaper options for food on the actual observation deck along the lines of $14 hot dogs and other fast but stupidly overpriced items. The whole top two floors were a money trap. They had different souvenir booths and small attractions like a rock climbing wall and a professional photo booth.

The main attraction on the observation deck was *The Djinn,* a small suspension rollercoaster ride that dangled its riders out past the edges of the observation deck and looked straight down fifteen hundred feet towards the Strip. That only cost $35 per person.

We piled into a taxi and made our way over to EnSpire. It was amazing how a less-than-five-mile trip could take thirty minutes in Vegas traffic. There was some kind of time vortex when in a Vegas taxi and the meter was running. We finally got dropped off at the main entrance and made our way in. It was a spectacle of extravagance. Gold and pillars and lights and fountains and music and chandeliers. It was a straight dick-slap to the senses. Evelyn locked arms with me as she still seemed a bit high and fearful of getting swallowed up by the radiating excess of this place. McBride and Wynn were back to normal.

"Aye, yo, I got to make a quick pit stop before we head up. Follow me."

McBride started walking onto the gaming floor and we followed until he found what he was looking for, a roulette table. He dug into his pocket and produced a fold of cash and peeled off four hundred-dollar bills. He then placed the cash down on the red area on the roulette table.

"Money plays, bitches."

"What are you doing?"

"Tradition, son. Every time I roll to Vegas I throw down some loot on red. If I win, which I usually do, that means it's gonna be a good trip."

"And if you lose?"

"Well, that's the kind of trip where I end up smacking a couple chumps around."

"Great. Come on red."

"No worries. I figure the fucking nightmare monkey on my back wants to keep me happy."

The roulette dealer spun the ball and then after a moment waved his hand over the table signifying no more bets. The ball slowed and started popping in and out of the numbered slots. It finally settled in the slot for eighteen which happened to be red. McBride didn't even flinch, as if it were all preordained. The dealer put the marker on the table then swept all the losing bets off the playing area, leaving just McBride's bet where it was. He then placed down four black chips by McBride's bet, then removed the marker from the table. McBride scooped up his money and chips, then we followed him over to the cage where he exchanged his chips for cash.

"One more pit stop. Drinks and the stupid elevator are on your Uncle McBride."

We made our way over to the nearest bar and McBride insisted on a round of shots on top of a round of cocktails for everyone. We then walked over to the tower elevators and McBride bought us four wristbands that gave us access to the observation deck. After a fifteen-minute wait in line, we entered the extra-large elevator and started our ascent. The elevator was a good thirty-second rocket ship ride that let us out on the penultimate floor.

Once we walked out of the elevator we could instantly feel the vibrations of the rollercoaster and hear the muffled screams coming from the floor above. We walked by the expensive restaurant which was packed with tourists. We made our way around and walked up the staircase which led to the observation deck. Once at the top of the stairs, the view caused my legs to feel rubbery. I immediately wanted to catch the next elevator down. It hit Evelyn the same way, as her grip on my arm tightened.

The observation deck was encircled by a fifteen-foot wall of glass. Granted, there were seating areas, concessions, people and other attractions up there but for those of us who didn't enjoy heights, the whole atmosphere was unnerving. It felt like the whole area was an infinity pool, but there was no water and only a horrific fall into the lower stratosphere waiting for us at all the edges.

By the way Evelyn was gripping my arm, I didn't think there was any chance she'd be getting on that rollercoaster, which was perfect for me because I didn't want to go on that fucking thing either. McBride continued leading the way as if he'd been here a thousand times before. Even though we had just drank a round of shots and were still finishing up our cocktails, McBride went straight for the rooftop bar and ordered another round.

"Here you go, people."

"Thanks, McB. Now what? Got any plan of action besides gambling and drinking?"

"This fucker," he pointed up above him, "wanted us here. I say we post up over on those benches by the ride and drink our drinks and see what happens."

"As good a plan as any."

We all walked over to some benches that were adjacent to the entrance of The Djinn. There were about a hundred and fifty people in line waiting for Vegas's most thrilling attraction. Well, third most thrilling if you were counting the drugs and hookers on Fremont Street.

The Djinn was horrifying to look at. With feet dangling, the riders were taken up a hundred-foot ramp above the observation deck. Once they reached the top of the ramp, the track veered down and then off the side of the building. The passengers flew face first straight towards the Strip fifteen hundred feet below them. At the bottom of the drop, the track swoops them back up into a corkscrew that twists thirty feet directly over the middle of the observation deck. Once the corkscrew completes, it then drops back down on the other side of the building into a loop where they are momentarily upside down with nothing but the night between them and the roof of the parking garage a thousand feet below. Once out of the loop, the passengers coast around the outside edge of the roof before returning to the loading station. No gracias, says the pussy with the hot girl on his arm.

"We're not going on that thing, are we?" Evelyn asked.

"What, girlie, you don't like fun or sumthin?"

"I can't imagine the grand plan of the phantom world right now was to get us to ride a rollercoaster. I'm guessing we're just supposed to be up here to see somebody or something."

"You sound kind of suspect there, buddy. Maybe you got a point but it sounds a bit like you got your skirt on about going on this ride."

"I've got my skirt on for nothing, McB. You buy the ticket, I'll go on it." Bluff.

"Alright, Daisy, my treat." *Damn.* "What about you, Winny?"

"Shouldn't we be concentrating and observing and not concerning ourselves with amusement rides? Are you already over the fact that we are seeing into this new realm of entities? Look around you. Everybody here has a creature floating above them, including you. We should be focused on our surroundings and trying to understand what we are here for."

"So, Winny got his skirt on with all that nervous rambling. When we see what we're here for we'll see what we're here for. Me riding that coaster ain't getting in the way of nothing. So why don't you sit tight, Winny, with girlie over here and scout out the bench area. Me and this clown are going for a ride. Holler if you see anything."

"I guess I'm going on a ride. Any chance you want to switch places, Wynn?"

"No, I'm not really interested in that right now. I'll sit here with Evelyn, if that's ok with her."

"That's more than alright with me. See you guys when you get back."

Evelyn linked arms with Wynn on the bench. McBride led us to the ticket booth and used the coupon from the hotel room to get us two passes to ride The Djinn. We got in line. How'd I get here again? The ride carried around thirty passengers at a time and the ride itself only lasted thirty-five seconds so the line moved along a little too quickly for my liking.

"You look a little nervous there, Janice. Will holding my hand make you feel safer or sumthin?"

"I don't know what you're jabbering about. This ride is lame compared to some of the ones at Six Flags."

"Tough guy, huh? Ain't buying it, though. Them rides ain't at fifteen hundred feet and I think you're soft when it comes to heights."

"You win. I don't like heights. Good for you. I'm still in line, right?"

"What's a matta', snippy? Afraid ol' Winny is moving in on your hot cousin while we're in line? How'd you pull that off, anyway? She doesn't seem blind or retarded."

"I'm not going to lie. Between this phantom shit and exposing her to your dumbass, I have no idea what she's still hanging around for. I'm not complaining though."

"Best not be. After all the fours and fives you've been dog-pounding."

"Right, I'm super jealous of those tatted-up meth freaks you hook up with at the Lex."

"Don't knock it til you try it, little lady. Those strung-out chicks got no boundaries."

"You're a sick fuck, you know that, right?"

"At least I'm rolling with some honor, you no-honor-having chump."

The line had been moving and we were getting close. The ride had just returned to the loading zone and the passengers were getting off, making way for the next thirty or so people in line. There was one guy behind the control podium who worked the buttons. There were two other workers who went row by row getting people in and out of the ride and making sure everyone's harnesses were locked into place. The new passengers started boarding and were getting settled into their seats. That's when our reason for being up there revealed itself.

"McB, look! Are you seeing this?"

I pointed over to the loading zone.

"Holy fuck. Is that what you saw at the Lex before that kid dropped?"

"Yes. I think they're all about to die."

Every person getting strapped into The Djinn had a flickering phantom. It was a mesmerizing scene, that many phantoms flashing at once. Wynn and Evelyn had noticed it and ran over to us in line.

"Is that it? We need to do something?"

McBride didn't hesitate and bull-rushed his way to the front of the line. Evelyn and Wynn ducked under the rope that separated the public from the people in line and we three followed McBride. McBride started hollering at the kid behind the control podium.

"Aye, yo, kid! Get these people off the ride. Something is fucked up."

"Excuse me, sir?"

"Get these people off the ride. Some shit's about to go down."

The kid pushed a call button on the podium and a voice crackled through a small speaker. The kid said into the speaker, "There is some guy up here yelling. Send someone over."

"Just get the people off the ride, kid."

"Sir, could you just wait a moment. Security is on their way and you can speak with them."

"Fine. Just don't start that fucking ride."

All the people now strapped onto the ride had heard McBride. Most were visibly concerned and mumbling. Within thirty seconds there were four security guards up at the front of the line with us.

"What's going on?"

"You need to pull these people from the ride. There's something wrong with it."

"Sir, we're going to need you to calm down a bit and explain yourself."

"There's something going on with that coaster. Those people are about to get fucked up if you don't get them off."

"What makes you say that, sir?"

McBride grabbed Wynn and pulled him forward.

"This kid is an engineer. He just saw a piece of the ride fall off. Ain't that right?"

"Uh..yes. We were over at the window watching the last ride and clearly saw a piece of the hinge assembly fall out. The structural integrity has been compromised. You need to get these people off the ride."

"Look, guys, I don't know what this is about but there is an instrument panel on that podium. There are hundreds of sensors over every part of this ride. If there is any point of failure, that podium lights up and we shut down the ride. The podium is not lighting up is it? So I'm going to have to assume you are mistaken in what you think you may have seen."

"Look, chief, systems fail, even in this overpriced piece of shit hotel. My boy here saw what he saw." McBride then yelled out so everyone could hear him. "Aye, yo, all you people on that ride, that shit is about to break. Tell them you want to get off or you're going to get fucked up."

"You know causing a commotion in a casino isn't the smartest of ideas. You four need to step out of line right now and come with us."

"You dumb fucker. Why the fuck would we be making this shit up?"

With that, the phones emerged from people's pockets and started recording McBride, hoping for something worthy of a few likes on social media, the modern day currency of self-worth.

"That's enough, sir. Get out of line now and follow these gentlemen to the elevator or you will be forcibly removed."

"Hold on, McBride."

Evelyn grabbed McBride's arm and approached the security guard and stared deep into his eyes.

"Sir, I apologize but this isn't a joke. There is something wrong with the ride. I know I can't convince you of this and completely understand your position. But may I make a proposal?"

The security guard seemed to soften immediately with Evelyn talking to him.

"I'm listening."

The Snare was using her powers. The security guard was almost hypnotized by her and her words.

"Get these people off the ride and do a test run with nobody on it. If nothing happens, we'll be happy to be wrong and will buy tickets for each empty seat."

"That's thirty-four seats, Miss. That would be just over a thousand dollars. This isn't something I could let you and your friends walk away from. I'd lose my job, you understand."

McBride pulled out a wad of money from his pocket and held it up.

"We got your fucking money, guy."

The security guard looked over to McBride and it seemed the spell had been broken and he was back to being annoyed. Evelyn quickly pushed McBride's arm down and caught the gaze of the security guard again.

"We'll pay, sir. Just, please, get these people off."

The security guard seemed to get lost in Evelyn's eyes for a moment, then refocused. He turned to the kid behind the podium.

"Get these people off. Let's do a test run so we can defuse the situation."

The kid behind the podium nodded and hit a button which released the harnesses that locked the people into the ride.

"Sorry, folks, we're going to have to ask you to disembark. Please exit to your right. You may stand over near the exit walkway until the test run is completed then you'll be allowed to take your seats again."

McBride slapped his hand on my chest the same instant Evelyn grabbed my arm tight. The passenger's phantoms all stopped flickering.

"We did it."

"Right, but that means this thing really is about to crash or fly off the rails or something."

We started looking around us trying to see if there were any new flickering phantoms as the track of the rollercoaster passed directly over the observation deck and the people on it. What if this thing snapped during the corkscrew and crushed everyone up here that was underneath it? After doing a visual sweep, there was nothing flickering on the observation deck to be seen.

"What if this thing falls off the rails and down to the Strip? It's going to kill anyone down there."

"Aw shit. What can we do? No way would they clear the Strip for our dumbasses."

"What? We just let it happen?"

"We've done all we can. Maybe it's something like a harness failure and everyone would have slipped out on the loop or something."

Just then the ride workers finished closing all the empty harnesses and all the people were clear up against the exit pathway. The kid behind the podium looked at the security guard and the security guard nodded. The kid pushed the button and the sound of hydraulics hissed as the coaster released and latched into the chain mechanism that moved it up the incline towards its first drop. We knew something was coming. With each click up the incline we tensed a little bit more. People had continued recording us and the ghost ride of The Djinn, hoping for a complete story one way or the other.

"There's nothing more we can do? McBride, any last minute whispers?"

"I ain't got shit. We did what we needed to do. Whatever happens, happens."

"Wynn?"

"What more can we do but spectate?"

The Djinn reached the apex of the hill. There was a quiet amongst the crowd as everyone was aware we thought something was wrong with the ride and, regardless of our believability, even the slightest promise of something about to go wrong was fascinating to the crowd of people. There was one final click, then a second of silence as the coaster glided over the crown and began its descent. There was something abnormal about an empty rollercoaster. It flew down the first drop, then swung into the corkscrew that crossed over the observation deck.

What if the weight of the passengers were the original cause of the problem? Without the passengers, that's around six thousand pounds less weight it's carrying now. What if it runs just fine empty but the weight of the next set of passengers causes the problem? All this was flashing through my head when a shotgun blast went off and everyone ducked and gasped. But it wasn't a shotgun, it was a locking joint of the ride exploding on the last turn of the corkscrew. Pieces started disintegrating and raining down around the handful of people that were beneath it.

The ride then began its second descent over the side of the building and into the loop. It was happening. The coaster continued down and made it to the forty-five degree angle of the loop when an even louder shotgun blast sounded and the thirty-four empty seats disengaged from the track and flew off into the night. Most people were cowering from the noise. McBride pushed his way through to the wall and we followed him. We caught the plummeting coaster at the tail end of its flight. Its final destination wasn't well lit but the explosion of concrete and dust was unmistakable even at this height as it smashed into the roof of the parking garage. People started to come around and were pushing their way over to where we were against the wall of glass.

McBride turned to us and said, "Let's get the fuck out of here."

He took off down the staircase as the entire lower floor of people were making their way up the stairs to see what was happening. We followed McBride closely and made our way to the elevator. Nobody was around, as the workers had also left their posts to follow the commotion on the top floor. We passed under the ropes that made up the line to the elevator and McBride started tapping the button. The doors opened right up and we piled in. It was an express elevator and only had an up and down button on the inside panel. McBride hit the down button and the doors closed.

"Holy Shit, McB, good going getting us out of there."

"When this elevator stops, just follow me. We're going to high-step it to the nearest exit and get the fuck out of this joint."

"Right. It's all commotion up there right now but that security guard is going to eventually wonder how we knew something was going to happen and try to hunt us down."

"If we get stopped, everyone stick to the same story. Winny and girlie here saw a piece of that coaster fall off and we were just trying to do the right thing. That's it. Don't add details. Keep it simple."

"You really think they're going to be looking for us?"

"Maybe. We'll know in about fifteen seconds when these doors open. My guess is no but might as well cover our shit."

The descent was rapid. It was bullet train to hell for the first thousand feet then gradually eased in speed over the final few floors. It came to a stop and the doors opened. There was plenty of activity as the elevator workers and security guards were diverting everyone out of the immediate area. Word had reached. No more rides to the top. Nobody gave us a second look as McBride strode out of the elevator and merged into the crowd. We followed closely.

Security personnel were moving briskly from all directions heading towards the tower elevator area. We kept our heads down until we were through the double doors and out on the sidewalk in front of the building. Although the idea of a rollercoaster plummeting a thousand feet and smashing into the roof of a parking garage may sound like an earth-shattering event, it appeared to go unnoticed at the front of the casino. The building was huge and the parking garage roof was ten stories up and on the opposite side. From out here, drowned out in the cacophony of sounds emanating from the Strip, it probably sounded no more severe than a trash bin being dumped into a garbage truck. This would not have been the case if the failure happened on this side of the building.

McBride casually walked into the taxi line behind two other groups of people. Within two minutes we were in our own taxi headed back to The Flux. None of us spoke until we were back in our rooms.

"So that was fun. I wonder what the real point was," I said.

"What do you mean?" Evelyn asked.

"I mean, people die every day. I can't imagine their phantom game would throw much weight on a rollercoaster accident unless there was something more to it."

"I completely agree. A lot of this has been troubling me and that is definitely one factor of it."

"What you got there, mapmaker? Worms doing some dancing in that peanut head of yours? What they saying?"

"My best guess is that someone important was going to die on that ride. Someone important to their game, whatever that may be. But what's really bothering me is how they knew. How did they know this accident was going to happen and, if I'm right, and we saved someone important, how did they know that person was on course to die on that amusement ride at that exact time? Do they have some predictive powers? Do they have access to different timelines and are working backwards? If they do have access to

272

different timelines, then why were the people's phantoms blinking if their outcome was already predetermined to be saved by us? Are they the gatekeepers to a multiverse? It's all a jumbled mess of possibilities."

"Ah, you're thinking too much again, mapmaker. You think you're gonna figure these fuckers out? You need to relax before you stroke out or sumthin. Have a beer."

"McB, you do know there were about a dozen people shooting video of you beefing with that security guard. Once this story goes public, those videos of you and us are going to go viral. They will hunt us down eventually."

"What they got? Simple. We was up there having drinks and about to go on the coaster when Winny and girlie saw something break off and came to warn us. That's it. Stick to that and what else they got? You ever been up there before?"

"No."

"None of us have, right? They got mad cameras all over that joint. What they gonna say, we snuck past all their security and sabotaged that coaster? They ain't got shit. If anything we'll get comped some rooms for being heroes or sumthin. I ain't worried."

"Fine. So what now? Are we going to continue to run errands for these things? I mean, it feels like we did something good but for all we know we just saved the antichrist from dying."

"You're the only one around here with no honor. I don't know what team you're on but us three are champs."

"All of this was quickly decided and spontaneous. My suggestion, if we go forward with this, would be for extensive field study. Observation and documentation. Compile as much information as we can for as long as we can still see what we are seeing."

"Of course, the mapmaker wants to spend all day writing notes and shit. What about you, girlie? You got a say in all of this."

"I think all four us together makes us balanced. I think if we stick together on this stuff we'll make good choices."

"What's our next move then?"

"We got two nights here comped. We might as well stay and do some observing like Wynn suggested. Maybe head over to Fremont Street tomorrow and just people watch."

"I'm down. What you say there you two?"

"I'm good."

"Me, too."

"Alright then, kids. What say we take the rest of the night off and head downstairs for some drinking and gambling? They got that club on the second floor supposed to get jumping around eleven. Your boy Serin over here can show you that no honor equals no rhythm. This guy's dancing is chick repellent."

"McB here can show you how to throw your own feces when around other gorillas."

"Whateva', salty. Won't you change that shirt or sumthin?"

"I actually am going to take a quick shower. Standing next to McBride in line for The Djinn gave me contact stench."

"Keep at it, princess."

Chapter Thirty -Eight
Bye

I walked through the adjoining door to our room and unzipped my bag to grab some new clothes. I was emptying the pockets of my jeans when I noticed four missed calls and a missed message, all from my mom. I called up my voicemail and listened. Fuck. I called my mom and spoke with her for ten minutes then packed up my shit. Fuck. I walked back into the other room where the three of them had on the local news which was on scene at EnSpire with aerial shots of the fallen rollercoaster on the roof of the parking garage.

"That was quick."

"I just got off the phone with my mom. My Uncle Chester just wrapped his car around a tree, more than likely drunk off his ass as usual. He's in intensive care. My mom was his emergency contact. She's flying into town and I need to get back to pick her up and deal with my uncle."

"How bad is it?"

"My mom spoke with the hospital and he's stable but pretty fucked up. Broken bones and a smashed-up face. Just lucky he hit a tree and not something real."

"This for real, Herby Herb, or you just trying to get out of going to the dance club and getting exposed?"

"Shit's for real. I've got to grab a taxi and get to the airport and fly back on the next flight."

"You want some company?" Evelyn asked.

"If that company is you, I do. But I like you too much to drag you into this nonsense. No, you guys enjoy yourselves as much as you can without me. I'm going to be tied up for as long as my mom is in town so I'll catch up with all of you when you get back. There's a flight that leaves in ninety minutes I'm going to try to catch, so I've got to go."

"Beat it then, clown. Tell your mom hi from McBride."

"Shut up, McB."

"Alright, Serin. Sorry about your uncle. I'll give you a call when we get back."

"Cool, Wynn. Don't let McBride catch you in the shower. You can take the gorilla out of the prison but not the prison out of the gorilla."

"Ya betta' beat it, Alice, before I throw you in the shower."

"I'll walk you to the taxi," Evelyn said as she got up from her chair.

"Later, guys."

"Later, Herb."

Evelyn and I made our way down the hall and down the elevator to the lobby. She walked me outside and grabbed both of my hands and stared at me.

"Sorry about your uncle. Sorry you have to leave."

"It is what it is. Whatever you do, just don't come back in two days saying you think you're in love with McBride and want to give your relationship a chance."

She smiled and said, "Wynn is more my type."

"Well, if you guys see anything of interest or you get bored or something, feel free to give me a call."

"I will."

She leaned in and we kissed. I felt like I was on the final ride of The Djinn, flying off the track into the abyss. She was The Lure and she had me enveloped in a web of electricity.

Right then I wanted to wish my family out of existence and stay there with her. It was her power and she was using it on me right at that moment, whether she was aware of it or not. But the setup was too well crafted. There wasn't a chance of me staying. How could I? Oh, I've decided my mangled uncle and hysterical mom aren't enough reason to abandon a trip to Vegas. Wasn't going to happen. We broke off the kiss and I swelled with sadness. Stupid Chester, although it was more than just bad decision making. You were being whispered to. Have another drink, Chester. You can drive home, Chester.

"See you in a couple of days. I hope your uncle is alright."

"Thanks. Maybe when you get back we can try to do something normal together? You know, something without goat piss and McBride."

"You didn't win me over with dinner and a movie, you know. You might want to consider keeping things strange to keep my interest."

"Drinks and a cockfight?"

"Now you're talking. See you in a couple days, Herby Herb."

"See you in a couple days, McEvelyn."

She grinned and walked away as I got in line for a taxi. Thirty minutes later I was at the ticket counter paying way too much for a one-way flight home. Fucking Chester.

I had time for a couple of beers at the airport bar while waiting for my flight. The TV was on with no volume. It was on a national news network that had just picked up the story about The Djinn. *Disaster avoided in Las Vegas* was the tagline on the screen. There was a reporter standing in front of EnSpire talking about the incident. In the top-right of the screen was a smaller box showing aerial coverage of the crash site on top of the parking structure. The bartender was placing down my second beer when the news coverage shifted to full-screen. Someone had already sold their phone video.

The video was shitty quality but there was no mistaking that I was looking at us. I was looking at a shaky side-view of myself and McBride having it out with the security guard at the entrance to The Djinn. There were brightened circles around our group that were added to the video to highlight us. The good news was that there wasn't any negative tagline to the video like *terrorists at large*. Even if we were tracked down, our story would hold.

The plane showed up on time and I took a window seat near the back. It was a full flight. Different circumstances all the time but flights home from Vegas always held a certain level of depression. Some lost too much gambling and now needed to figure out how they're going to cover rent. Some drank too much, did something to jeopardize their marriage, and were flying home guilty. Others may have simply left Vegas early and were leaving behind something wonderful, even if temporarily. Possibly permanently.

We took off and I was already itching for an in-flight drink. The desert air seemed to always be choppy coming in and leaving Vegas. Ten minutes in, the turbulence was aggressive and to my added depression, in-flight services would be cancelled for safety reasons unless the turbulence subsided. It didn't. Turbulence never bothered me aside when it kept me from having a drink. Other people on the flight weren't so comfortable. There were murmurs and the occasional gasps when the drops and rattles got violent. I actually tried to close my eyes and lean against the window to try to sleep but got a nice smack against the glass when the plane took a big bounce. The captain announced we were going to ascend again and try to get above the rough air.

I pulled out my phone which I forgot to turn to airplane mode. Evelyn had shot me a text. It read, "We just saw ourselves on the news. McBride thinks it's awesome. They are using the word 'saviors' so I think we'll be okay. Talk to you tomorrow." Nothing cornier than emojis. She didn't use any. She was perfect. I looked up from my phone and went numb.

Every phantom of every passenger on the plane was flickering. I went from fear to panic to acceptance in about three seconds. I knew I was fucked. I quickly went back to my phone and started typing. "Evelyn, everyone's phantoms on the plane have got the strobe effect. Something bad is about to happen. I'm devastated it's ending like this but at least you are still fresh in my mind. You are the...."

There was a blinding flash as the wing on the other side from me exploded and ripped a hole through the middle of the plane. My phone flew to the ground and tumbled behind my seat as the plane thrust down into a nose dive. The masks dropped from the ceiling but they wouldn't be needed. The plane was in freefall and there would be no pulling out of it. I was set up. Fucking Chester. The screams were piercing and hopeless.

A young guy unbuckled himself and flew to the back of the plane right past me. Over all the commotion, I could distinctively hear the snap of his neck as his head smashed into an empty seat three rows behind me. I closed my eyes and tried to summon Evelyn's face but it wouldn't come. My brain was short-circuiting with stimulus overload.

When I was a kid on a plane ride, I always thought if this scenario ever happened, I'd crawl into the overhead luggage bin and survive in there from the crash, somehow padded by the luggage. My other great idea as a kid was to get to the emergency exit door and jump out right before the plane crashed, somehow defying the laws of physics and rolling to safety. For a second, I almost considered the overhead luggage bin idea.

By the end of our descent, I swear I could feel something like a magnetic push right before the tip of the plane met the earth, as if the ground were bracing itself. In an instant, the plane crumpled and exploded. Metal and flames ripped through my body.

That shit hurt.

Chapter One
Hell-oh

You'd think I'd be happy to still be in some state of existence after dying in a plane crash. Not really. Not quite sure what happy means right now. I can still see my death frame by frame. There's no sadness or fear linked to it. It just sits in my mind as a benign sequence of images.

The plane managed to hit nose first and the force of the sound of initial impact was enough to make my eardrums rip apart and spray blood. Foot by foot, the rest of the plane met the earth, crumpling in a pile of exploded parts and fire. When it was my turn, an armrest from the row in front of me smashed through my ribcage and separated me from most of my heart and lungs. At the same moment, the intense fire from the fuel engulfed everything. There was a split second where the skin on my face and hands instantly blistered while my clothes ignited and infused with the skin beneath it. The final impact was a complete obliteration of my body as my bones were pulverized and my flesh compressed to where my blistered skin exploded from the pressure.

A handful of hours earlier, I was just a guy kissing a girl out in front of a Vegas hotel. There at the end I was reduced to scattered chunks of blackened flesh undistinguishable in an orgy of melted plastic, metal and fire. Sounds like it'd leave quite the emotional scar but in all honesty I'm pretty apathetic towards everything right now.

I can see Evelyn if I concentrate, but seeing her face in my mind is just another benign image. I'm well aware that I was

281

pretty much in love with her but those feelings aren't accessible here in this place. I feel sterile, wiped of humanity, which isn't surprising considering what I can see of my new self. When I look down and side to side, all I can really view of my new body is fiery red plastic-like skin with thick networks of veins and tendons. I can't see any appendages and if I were to guess, I'd say I looked like a wrinkled red pear tilted on its side.

I do feel something behind me. I don't have the angle to see what it is but there are definitely some things coming out of my back. Even though I can feel them, I haven't figured out how to move them yet. As I've been roaming around, I haven't found any kind of liquid or reflective surface so I have no clue what my face looks like now, if I still have what would be considered a face.

If I were to try to apply the concept of time, I'd say I've been awake in this new form for an hour. I have no idea if time is still a thing. This is a physical reality though. I'm not a ghost or anything, I don't think.

When I first arrived, I was disoriented as all hell. I couldn't focus. Everything was like looking through a cheap kaleidoscope. I eventually realized that I'd never tried vision through three eyes before and that was the issue. After some trial and error, I managed to shut my middle eye and this new world came into focus. I don't know yet, possibly seeing things with all three eyes has some sort of advantage here. I'll probably give it another try but not right now. I feel completely separated from my humanity so none of this is fearful or worrisome. It just is what it is.

The landscape is interesting and boring at the same time. The ground is somewhat like sand but a closer look reveals an infinite ocean of diamond-like miniature rocks. There is a sky with two distinct light sources. So I'm either in a binary star system or this entire place is a virtual reality and I'm looking at a manufactured sky.

The land is pretty desolate and flat. Far off in the distance there is something dark. It might be a structure of some sort or a mountain. I'm too far away to make out any details but from this distance I'm thinking whatever it is it must be pretty immense.

I keep trying to use my arms and hands but there are no arms and hands to use. For that matter there are no legs either, although when I try to walk I end up gliding forward somehow. It feels like being on an elliptical machine. The faster I swing my imaginary legs the quicker my propulsion.

I tried making noises with my mouth but there no longer is a mouth. If I pretend I'm taking a strenuous shit, I can manage vibrations, kind of like the slow purr from a thousand-pound cat. When I do it, the diamond-like miniature rocks below start to form a pattern of concentric circles around me. I'm pretty positive now that I had backed the wrong horse back in my old life. Zeus is nowhere to be found out here and this is definitely not looking like Mount Olympus.

I haven't felt anything since being here. No pain, no hunger, no urge to take a piss, no real emotions. I don't think I'm breathing or at least I'm not pretending to breathe like I'm pretending to walk. Maybe I have gills or breathing isn't a thing here either.

The only thing remotely prominent in me is an almost instinctual desire to move towards that thing I can see off in the distance. I have this inherent locator clip and that thing is the homing beacon pulling me towards it. For some reason I feel that it's a place where I'll be able to possibly find a link back to my old world. I don't know why I'd know or think that but it feels like it was information that was just pre-loaded into this new package I'm inhabiting. I'm pretty confident that there are answers not too far ahead.

I'm also pretty sure I am a shit-bird phantom now.

About the Author

M.J. Waters was born in Oakland, California where he had some unique Bay Area experiences growing up. He was at the A's game where Ricky Henderson broke the stolen base record. He was at a Hayward bowling alley and Too $hort happened to be bowling on the lane next to him. He was in his backyard reading Tom Sawyer for school on October 17th, 1989 when shifting tectonic plates made the self-important humans feel really small and insignificant. He was also around to see the blaze and aftermath of the 1991 Oakland firestorm that made neighborhoods vanish.

M.J. Waters moved to San Diego when he was twenty years old and would begin to stretch out a collegiate career to thresholds previously thought unachievable. He ended up with a degree in Philosophy which was somewhat inspired by Patrick Swayze's character in Roadhouse. He spent half a year travelling Mexico in his early twenties, driving from San Diego to Merida in the Yucatan Peninsula where he ran amuck and got into adventures of a deviant nature.

Years later, M.J. returned to Mexico for his friend's wedding where at the resort he was staying he would meet his eventual wife. Poor, poor girl. If only you had gone to Hawaii instead of Cancun for vacation you'd be free of all this grief and suffering. After dating for a while they tried out and went on a game show called The Amazing Race where they ended up winning the Million Dollar prize. Or possibly they failed to correctly accomplish an agonizingly insipid common task and were eliminated on the 5th leg and have been emotionally scarred ever since. Or maybe they went on the Price is Right. Who knows?

They eventually got married in Florence, Italy and after the wedding had an incredible trip to Siena and Rome. Or maybe they got married in Florence, California and had the reception at the Chuck E. Cheese on South Alameda St.

M.J. and his wife manufactured two daughters along the way. These two daughters were born with really pretty faces and give M.J. a shadowing anxiety for whence they become teens.

M.J. might eventually write another book as he awaits the reception of The Phantom Paradigm with a personal goal of selling twelve books.

If M.J. Waters, through social media and word of mouth can generate a total of twelve or more books sold, M.J. will be able to afford a cheap bottle of wine to celebrate with and then will start writing again.

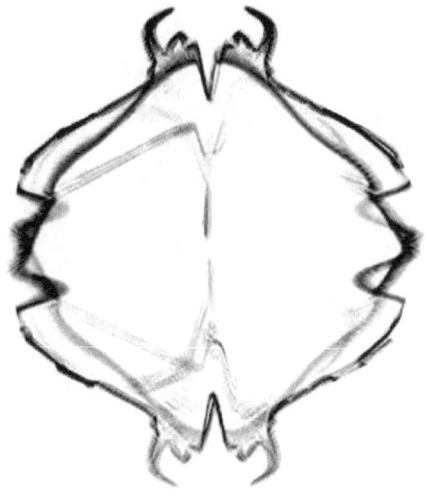